THE BAD BOY

THE LAMBRIANUS

GILLIAN GODDEN

Boldwood

Thank you to Avril and Julie C

First published in Great Britain in 2023 by Boldwood Books Ltd.

Copyright © Gillian Godden, 2023

Cover Design by Colin Thomas

Cover Photography: Colin Thomas

A CIP catalogue record for this book is available from the British Library.

Paperback ISBN 978-1-80280-136-1

Large Print ISBN 978-1-80280-137-8

Hardback ISBN 978-1-80280-135-4

Ebook ISBN 978-1-80280-139-2

Kindle ISBN 978-1-80280-138-5

Audio CD ISBN 978-1-80280-130-9

MP3 CD ISBN 978-1-80280-131-6

Digital audio download ISBN 978-1-80280-132-3

Boldwood Books Ltd
23 Bowerdean Street
London SW6 3TN
www.boldwoodbooks.com

1

MIXED EMOTIONS

'Where the hell is he, Knuckles? He knows what time he's supposed to be here.' Quickly glancing at her watch, Scarlet muttered under her breath to the man stood beside her and cast him a sideways glance. The casual shrugging of his shoulders didn't help her mood and anger burned inside her. 'He knows what time the ceremony is, I told him myself. I'll wring his bloody neck!'

'It's only 8.50 a.m. He's got ten minutes yet,' Knuckles whispered.

'Okay, you might have got a smart watch for Christmas, but that doesn't make you smart or able to tell the time!' Scarlet snapped. Standing in the church full of people, she furtively looked around for any sign of Adam, her younger brother and business partner. Adjusting her large dark glasses, she looked at the coffin at the front surrounded by flowers and photos. 'I hope there's room in there for him, and you too if you keep looking at that bloody watch.'

'Alexa,' Knuckles whispered. 'She tells me everything.' He nodded, tapping the screen of his watch.

Angry at Adam's absence at the funeral, and Knuckles' off-hand comments about his new-found digital world, Scarlet felt her face flush. 'Well, I hope she's told you I'm pissed off!' she snapped again, trying hard not to raise her voice for others nearby to hear her conversation. She looked around at people she knew and smiled graciously to show that nothing appeared to be wrong. The pew she was in had started to fill up, but she'd left her large handbag beside her on the seat so Adam could sit next to her.

'Toilet break,' said Knuckles, and he started to sidle past her.

'What... now? Why didn't you go before we got here? There are no toilets in here; it's a bloody church.'

'Outside. I'll look.'

'Oh, go and piss up a tree or something, it wouldn't be the first time. God, what a day. Adam doesn't turn up and you're doing a disappearing act. Don't be long,' she called after him.

The sombre surroundings gave her the creeps as everyone greeted her before they took their seats for the funeral. She had been to far too many funerals in the past; lastly, but not least, her own parents'.

Mournful music softly filled the church as the vicar walked towards the family at the front and spoke to them soothingly. Scarlet looked at the coffin and then towards the mourners who were desperately trying to fight back the tears and felt a lump rise in her own throat. Casting her eyes around the church, she found it hard to recognise anyone. Everyone looked exactly the same dressed in their black clothing, including herself. Today she wore a black two-piece skirt suit, with only her pearl earrings and necklace as accessories. Her blonde hair was in a chignon, instead of flowing down her back towards her waist. It wasn't a fashion parade, after all.

. Her mind wandered to her own family as she remembered the sadness of past funerals. Her beloved father, Tony Lambrianu, had been accidently shot in his own nightclub by some drunk arguing with his girlfriend while pointing a gun at her. Scarlet's mother,

Francesca, had been standing nearby and when the gun had swung in her direction, her father had jumped in front of her to save her, getting himself shot in the process. That had been one of the saddest days in Scarlet's entire life. She'd loved her father, worshipped him even, and missed him every day. Although her mother had died years later of an aneurism and stroke, they all knew Francesca had truly died years before from a broken heart. It was as though she had waited until Adam had turned eighteen, and was not a child any more, before finally reuniting once more with her beloved Tony. Scarlet wondered what it must feel like to be loved that much. Her own marriage had been a farce.

Tony Lambrianu and his brother Jake had run gangland London with their friend and business associate, Ralph Gold. With Ralph's connections with Don Carlos, the head of the mafia in Italy, they had ruled the world. When Tony had died, it had become Scarlet's place to keep his memory alive and run the family business. Katie, Scarlet's twin sister, had married a member of Don Carlos's firm, Chris, and since Don Carlos's unfortunate death, Chris had become the new Don. Together, Chris and Katie lived in Italy on the family's vineyard which continued to thrive under Chris and Katie's watchful eyes. She missed her sister, but they saw each other often. Sometimes it was quicker to fly to Italy than it was to travel up the M25, she mused.

Scarlet now ran the family business with her younger brother, Adam. Eighteen years younger than her, he had started by mopping floors and working the bar in their nightclub. He had moaned about it, but she had insisted that, like their father, he knew everything about the business before he took it over. Now in his late twenties, Scarlet had to admit that Adam was a good businessman, but she felt he was reckless sometimes.

Julie Gold, otherwise known as Aunty Julie and who had been a close friend to both of her parents, was still very much alive although she never admitted her age and no one could guess it because she'd had so much Botox and plastic surgery that Scarlet thought she looked younger than herself sometimes. There was no way Julie Gold was going to age gracefully. The thought of Julie brought a smile to Scarlet's face and almost made her laugh. She had never changed and was still full of one-line quips to make you squirm and laugh. When Scarlet had complained about Adam's reckless, womanising ways, Julie had just laughed and said she had known the 'original' playboy, Tony, and what did she expect his son to be like? It was in the genes.

Glancing at her watch again, Scarlet pursed her lips. Each time the church door opened, she expected Adam to breeze in with that smile that could charm the knickers off a nun. He had his father's sapphire blue eyes, the same as her own, but he had their mother's auburn hair, which made Adam stand out even more.

Breaking into her thoughts, Knuckles returned to his seat beside her.

'Where the hell have you been? You've been gone ages and you're all hot and sweaty. On the other hand, don't tell me. I don't want to know.'

He shrugged. 'Was rushing.'

'Why, are you incontinent or something? I hope you've washed your hands. Adam still hasn't turned up. Thank God the ceremony has been delayed a while because people are still coming in,' she snapped.

Knuckles, as usual, remained expressionless at Scarlet's rant. He had started off as a leg breaker and a street soldier for her father until she had requested for him to drive her. He quickly became her full-time driver and body guard, constantly at her side.

Knuckles was nearly seven-foot tall, and almost as wide. There wasn't an ounce of fat on him and he worked out two or three times a day. He had lost his hand in some fight or another and had it replaced by a prosthetic hand, which years ago had been rough and ready, but these days was almost bionic and people often struggled to tell the difference until they felt his powerful vice-like grip. He rarely spoke or showed emotion, and although he took everything in, he never gave an opinion. In the earlier days, Julie Gold had called him 'Shrek' because of his looks and height.

But when Scarlet had been at a very low ebb and depressed after her divorce from her disastrous marriage, she had found solace within those big strong arms. Fondly now, she thought of her own children, her twins, who had been the product of that liaison. And to her surprise, Knuckles was an excellent father, much more so than she could have imagined. He had also been an excellent father to Adam when he had been orphaned. Knuckles had taken Adam under his wing and looked after him like a younger brother.

The vicar started to speak, and her heart sank. Turning to take one last look at the closed church doors, she let out a deep sigh and faced the front.

* * *

'You got any change mister?' The homeless vagrant sat on London Bridge with his back to the wall and shook his polystyrene cup, stained with dregs of tea and filled with just a few measly coins, towards people quickening their pace and ignoring him as though he were invisible. His grey, shabby overcoat was wrapped firmly around him, covering the layers of clothing he wore underneath to keep out the cold. His knitted soiled hat, pulled way down and covering his eyebrows, failed to hide the lank, grey hair at the sides of his head that matched his grey beard. Again, he waved his cup in the air at the busy office workers rushing past with their briefcases. Coughing loudly and holding up his fist to his mouth, he spat phlegm on the pavement to clear his throat. His tired eyes watched the disgust of passersby as they muttered expletives and widened the gap between themselves and him.

He stretched out his legs and spied a man hurrying towards him engrossed in a conversation on his mobile phone. He was the typical city worker, dressed in a dark suit and tie and flowing over-coat. The homeless man had seen him before, and knew he would throw some spare change at him out of annoyance or guilt maybe. The man always seemed to be in a rush to get to work and he always had his mobile phone glued to his ear. The vagrant watched him intently. This was his victim.

Blindly rushing with the crowds, elbow to elbow, on this busy morning over London Bridge, the young office worker tripped over the homeless man's legs. Embarrassed, he lay sprawled on the floor face down, wincing in pain.

'Sorry mister, do you need a hand?' The vagrant began to ease himself up on to his knees to help, and proffered his soiled woollen-gloved hand to help him up.

'I'm fine, you prick. Why on earth are you sitting here on a busy Monday morning sticking out your legs? I'd sue you if I thought you had anything,' the man spat out.

'Sorry son, no offence. I just wanted a cup of coffee or some-thing. I haven't eaten since yesterday. I hope your mobile phone is okay.'

Instantly the suited man raised his head and looked around the pavement. No one had stopped to offer assistance; if anything, he had almost been trampled underfoot along with shouts for him to 'get out of the way'. Scrambling forward, he spotted his mobile as it was kicked by a passerby. His heart sank, already suspecting the screen would be broken. Reaching across people stumbling over him, he grabbed his mobile and almost kissed it. But looking at it closely, he could already see he was right. It had been stood on and kicked about and he realised he was going to have to spend the rest of the day sorting it out.

The vagrant, who had now stood up behind the man on his knees checking his phone, pushed the suited man's briefcase and kicked it hard through the crowd to the other end of the pavement. He then carried on assisting the suited man. 'Sorry mister, let me help you up. How's your phone?'

'It's bloody broken, what do you think? You people are a public nuisance. Why don't you just stand on a corner and sell *The Big Issue* or something?' Irritated and annoyed, the suited man tried switching his mobile on, praying to God it would burst into life.

'Can't afford it, mister. You have to buy them to sell them.' The homeless man reached out his arm to help the suited man up, and saw the man grimace at the soiled woollen glove. But he accepted his help, nonetheless, brushing the dust and dirt from the pavement.

The vagrant glanced behind him and saw the briefcase now almost hidden in the crowd. 'You okay otherwise, mister?' Looking around, he pointed across the pavement. 'Is that your briefcase?'

Forgetting that when he'd fallen, he'd been holding his laptop case, the suited man looked around and his heart sank again. He could already feel his knees burning from where he'd possibly scraped them on the pavement during his fall. His hand was bleeding and his ego had taken a thrashing. What a horrible day this had started out as, and it had begun to rain, which made everyone walk even faster.

'Fuck! My briefcase. It has my laptop in it.' Panicking, the man pushed his way through the crowd and picked up his briefcase from the edge of the pavement. 'Oh Christ, look at my bag.' The man almost felt like crying. Just going by the dusty battered case, he knew it was broken. Shoving his mobile into the inside pocket of his coat, he adjusted his tie and started to walk forward. 'I'm not even going to look inside it, my nerves can't stand it. This is *your* fault! You stupid tramp,' he shouted while rolling up his coat collar to shield him from the rain.

'Hey mister, you got any spare change for that drink?' The vagrant held out his hand and waited. 'It's not my fault you office lot are always rushing around not looking where you're going. Go on, mister, I have tried to help you.'

The suited man let out a deep sigh. 'Do you realise the trouble you've caused me? You sit there, trip me up, break my bloody phone, possibly my laptop and now you ask me for money.' Without thinking, the suited man swung his leg back and kicked the homeless man, making him wince in pain.

'Hey mister, it's not me who's the liability here. If you weren't so busy talking on your phone while walking, you would have seen me, then you wouldn't have fallen over me. What about my injuries?' he whined. 'That's assault. Even us homeless have rights,' he said, rubbing his leg.

Red faced and flustered, the suited man reached into his pocket and looked at the meagre change in his hand. 'Here, take it. Take the bloody lot. Anyway, we'll probably be meeting again if my boss realises how late I am and sacks me. Now just piss off.' He threw his change into the air. It made a chinking sound as it fell down on the pavement, and he rushed off and joined the jostling crowds walking towards the tube station.

The vagrant waited and watched while the suited man disappeared into the crowds, then he began picking up his soiled carrier bags and walked in the opposite direction along the pavement, leaving the loose change scattered on the floor. Looking past the crowds, he saw the council road maintenance van at the kerbside with its hazard lights flashing. He hurried to it and climbed into the back. As it drove off, the man quickly stripped himself of his clothing and fake grey beard.

'Fuck, the glue on this beard hurts; it's nearly pulling my chin off.' Reaching into his bag, Adam took out a packet of wet wipes and washed his face. Once he'd finished, the driver of the van pulled over and let him out on a quiet street wearing just his boxer shorts. The driver smiled, then, doing a three-point turn, drove away in the opposite direction.

Running down the road, Adam saw his beloved motorbike. Draped over it was his helmet and his leather trousers and jacket. Looking at his watch, he cursed himself. Today had taken longer than he had expected, and he knew Scarlet would be boiling mad. Donning his black helmet, he smiled to himself, jumped on his motorbike and roared away.

Arriving at the cemetery, he took a sigh of relief. Everyone was coming out of the church and following the coffin to its plot before it was lowered into the ground for everyone to bid their last good-byes. He was late, but not that late.

Hearing the roar of the engine, members of the congregation turned and looked at the black motorbike almost skidding to a stop. Scarlet lowered her dark glasses as she looked at her younger brother. 'If he'd driven any closer to this plot he'd have fallen into that hole,' she snapped.

'He's here,' whispered Knuckles, shrugging.

'Yes, and what a bloody entrance!'

The vicar stopped speaking and waited as Adam walked towards them and stood beside Scarlet and Knuckles. 'Sorry every-one. London traffic.' Taking off his helmet, he shook his head, letting his wavy auburn hair fall back into place and smiling charm-ingly at the crowd.

'Take that bloody biker jacket off and show some respect,' Scarlet spat, while trying not to cause a fuss.

Casting her a sideways glance, he whispered, 'I can't, I've got nothing underneath it. Now, be quiet, the vicar's waiting and it's freezing.'

'Off!' she demanded through gritted teeth, clearly not believing him for one minute.

Grinning, Adam nodded. 'Fair enough.' Flashing a row of perfect teeth towards the waiting crowd, especially the ladies, Adam slowly unzipped his black biker jacket before taking it off, showing only a tight, black vest underneath. Adam flexed his muscly arms for added measure. Knuckles undid his black tie and handed it to him.

Mischievously, Adam put the tie around his bare suntanned neck and stood there. People started to smile back and stifle their laughter behind their hands, while Scarlet flashed an angry glance at him. 'Fucking clown,' she snapped.

Adam looked up at the crowd and held out his hands apologetically. 'My apologies everyone, please carry on and let us lay this beautiful, strong woman to rest. I know she would forgive my attire; that is the kind of woman she was,' he said while wiping away an invisible tear for good measure. Instantly, he could see his boyish charm had won them over, and if anything, they scowled at Scarlet who had made such a fuss, making her blush slightly.

Once the funeral ceremony had resumed, they all stood paying their respects and shaking hands while agreeing to meet at the wake. After everyone had moved on, Adam, who was slightly shivering by now, picked up his jacket and put it back on. 'I'll meet you at the wake Scarlet. Promise.' Cheekily, he kissed her on the cheek and walked away. Revving up his motorbike, he shook his flyaway hair before donning his helmet and riding off in a cloud of smoke, while waving at everyone.

Scarlet got back into her waiting car with Knuckles, who was driving. 'He's such a vain prat. Just wait until we're alone. Doesn't he realise Jean was one of the matriarchs of the East End? Everyone knew her and respected her. She was ninety-six years old and did a lot of work for Papa in her own way. He would have been mortified at Adam showing disrespect like that. He couldn't be bothered to turn up on time, and he couldn't be bothered to wear the right clothes. Shame on him!'

All the way from the cemetery to the East End pub for the wake, Scarlet muttered and complained about Adam's behaviour while Knuckles carried on driving in silence. He knew better than to answer. Scarlet was just letting off steam and it was better she did it in the back of the car and had cooled down a bit before she vented her anger at Adam.

Along his route, Adam had popped into a shop and picked up a white shirt to wear. When Scarlet saw him dressed more respect-fully, she gave him a nod of approval. Adam made his way to the bar and started chatting to everyone, lifting the solemn mood and making people laugh. Everyone liked him and fell under his spell. In their own way, he and Scarlet were comical without realising it. Scarlet always disapproved of Adam's mischievous ways but melted at his flattery and charm and couldn't stay angry at him for long, while Adam always seemed to be on the wrong end of her temper. Between them they made a good match.

Scarlet leaned closer to Knuckles and whispered, 'Knuckles, two drinks and we're done. I have a lot of work to do, and I can't hang around all day listening to stories from times gone past, because that's all they're going to do now once they've started drink-ing. You're going to ring my mobile in half an hour with an emer-gency – got it?' Scarlet instructed. 'I'll put it on loud speaker so they can hear. After all, nobody has ever heard you speak, have they?'

'What emergency?' Frowning, Knuckles looked at her seriously and waited for an answer.

'Does it matter? Just say it's urgent business,' she snapped. 'For Christ's sake, is this my lot in life to be surrounded by idiots? Talking of idiots, where's Adam?'

'He's over there, carefully listening to stories from times gone past to make the family feel better.'

Scarlet glared at Knuckles with her piercing blue eyes while detecting the sarcasm in his voice. Although she had to admit, he was right. Adam was doing exactly what she didn't want to do, paying attention and comforting the many families and friends of the recently deceased Jean. Scarlet excused herself and went to the ladies, and as she did so, Adam sidled up to Knuckles.

'Well, how long has she given you before you make the call?'

'Half an hour.'

Grinning to himself, Adam walked away to rejoin the others. After twenty minutes, he looked at his watch. Looking across at Scarlet, he saw her do her usual thing of standing near a crowd of people who would hear her mobile and the fake call that would reveal she was needed elsewhere. She'd done it many times before to get herself out of a situation. He grinned at the fact that Scarlet didn't realise they all knew this ploy.

Taking out his mobile, he dialled her number and watched her answer her mobile in fake surprise, turning on the loud speaker. A deep Scottish accent she didn't know greeted her. 'Miss Scarlet, your knickers are on fire. You should come home immediately.' Adam laughed and ended the call, musing to himself that he may as well be hung for a sheep as well as a lamb.

Blushing, Scarlet turned towards Knuckles and noticed he wasn't holding his mobile, then she glared across at Adam and knew exactly what he had done. 'Sorry darlings, it seems I have to leave you all. Goodness knows what that call was about, but it seemed urgent,' she lied while waving over to Adam. 'We have to leave Adam; it seems something has cropped up.'

'Really?' His feigned surprise annoyed her more. 'Surely you don't want to rush off this quickly? Show some respect, Scarlet.' He threw Scarlet's own words back at her while giving her a cheeky wink. Scarlet couldn't help but smile.

'Check mate Adam,' she laughed. 'Sorry, everyone I have to leave, apparently my knickers are on fire. Jimmy!' she shouted to the barman. 'Send the bill for the wake to me and for Christ's sake break out some champagne and give Jean a good sendoff.' Everyone cheered and gave her a round of applause and Jimmy gave her the thumbs up. Linking her arm through Adam's, Scarlet walked towards the door with Knuckles hot on their heels.

2

BITS AND PIECES

Once back at the club, Adam walked into the office. He knew he'd get there before Scarlet. Her Rolls Royce, fighting its way through London's busy traffic, wasn't as quick as his motorbike. He looked around him to check the room was empty before shutting the door and taking out his mobile. 'Is it done?' he asked.

'Yes, Mavis is taking it to the police station. Sorted.'

'I'll be in touch.' Ending the call, Adam could hear the sound of Scarlet's heels walking down the hallway and opened the door to her and Knuckles. 'Before you start on me, let me take a shower and get dressed first, eh?'

'It's a shame you didn't get dressed earlier. Where were you? Oh God, don't tell me, hastily leaving another bimbo's bedroom! Well, as it happens, I want a shower myself to get rid of the stench of death.' Undoing the clasp of her chignon, she let her hair fall down her back and ran her hands through it. Sitting in one of the high-backed leather chairs at the large desk in the office, she kicked off her shoes and put her feet up on the desk. Then she opened one of the drawers and took out a whisky bottle and two glasses. Pouring the whisky, she held out a glass to Adam.

'I'm shattered. Those things drain me. I'd offer you a drink, Knuckles, but you're driving. There's some coke in the fridge if you want one?' Knuckles shook his head. 'Okay let's both go and have a shower after this and then you can tell me what or who was so important that you were so late, and maybe we can get some business done.'

'You look done in, Scat. What time did you get to bed last night? Or this morning?' Adam corrected himself. He knew Scarlet was a workaholic, and last night had been some councillor or MP's party at the club, with Scarlet playing hostess.

'About 4 a.m., but it was worth it. All those wonderful members of parliament and their influential friends. Always keep your enemies close, Adam. They would turn on us at the drop of a hat if things went tits up, but for now we're friends which means planning permissions granted and the right introductions to the right people who just might be needed one day. Anyway, Julie was there and you know she loves to party.'

'Oh my God, no wonder it was late.' Adam laughed. 'Anyway, why wasn't Julie at the funeral? If anyone knew Jean, she did. Didn't she used to spy for Ralph?'

Raising one eyebrow, Scarlet gave Adam a knowing look. 'It's not spying, it's keeping your ear to the ground. There is a difference. Everyone knows Julie doesn't get up before midday and then it takes two hours for her Botox to set.' Scarlet wagged a warning finger at Adam. 'Don't tell her I said that. She'll have my guts for garters!'

Adam couldn't stop laughing. Although it was true; everyone still lived in fear of Julie Gold's sharp tongue. 'Did she bring her entourage of young men with her and hold court?'

'Yes, did you expect anything else? All six of them waiting on her hand and foot in their tuxedos. Nice looking young men. She has taste, I'll give her that.'

'Yeah, and she pays a fortune for it.'

'She has a fortune, Adam. And if surrounding herself with twenty-year-old male escorts pleases her, then so be it. She misses Uncle Ralph more than she admits and has never remarried. The only man she is actually friends with, apart from you that is, is Mark, Ralph's old driver. I did wonder about those two once, but it's not my business. Come on, let's get showered and then you can tell me what you've been up to, because I know it's not a woman. The only thing that puts that glint into your pretty blue eyes is business.'

Adam grinned. 'And your pretty blue eyes look tired, Scarlet. Take a nap, and we'll talk later. Now go and do as you're told.'

* * *

Mavis stood at the desk in the police station. 'Excuse me, officer. Is this the place for lost property?' she asked.

The desk sergeant looked up from his form filling. 'Not really, miss, but if you have something, you can hand it in here.' Puzzled, he looked her up and down. It was a rarity for someone deep in the heart of London to hand in lost property. But, he mused to himself, stranger things had happened.

'I found this bag, looks expensive. Me and my friend was going over London Bridge, and it looks a bit battered, like it's been run over. But when I looked inside it, it's one of those laptop things. I'm not up to scratch on those things but my grandson has one. I wondered if anyone had reported it missing?'

Nearly yawning at the old woman's drawn-out explanation, the desk sergeant tried to be polite. It was indeed a laptop case and as he looked inside he saw there was indeed a laptop inside. Investigating further, he could see it was smashed and no good to anyone, but the woman had meant well.

'I'll check to see if one has been reported missing, otherwise let me take your details and if it's not collected you can claim it. Finders keepers.' He smiled. 'Although, I might say, these days it's not the done thing to open strange bags lying around. You need to be more careful. But thank you; let's hope it gets to its rightful owner.'

'Oh, I see what you mean. Bombs and stuff. You see it on the news all the time. I won't want it, so never mind about contacting me, but in my day, you did the right thing and that was hand things in to the police station. Be it an old bag or a million pounds.' She smiled and gave a wave as she walked out of the station.

The desk sergeant was flabbergasted. No one around here would hand in a million pounds. Come to think of it, they wouldn't hand in a ten-pound note! Labelling the bag, he looked at his screen and true enough, he saw that someone had reported it missing. Picking up the telephone, he dialled the number.

'Is that Mr Williams?' Once the speaker on the other end confirmed his name, he carried on. 'This is Desk Sergeant Watts. You reported your laptop missing this morning and said you had picked up the wrong bag. Is that right?' he enquired.

The voice on the other end seemed nervous. 'Yes, officer. I had fallen over some tramp and when I stood up, I picked up a laptop case, thinking it was mine. It looked like mine, although a bit battered, but inside wasn't my laptop. It looks like a kid's iPad or something. Broken, of course.'

'One has just been handed in, sir. A lady says she found it on London Bridge and has brought it here. I've looked inside and the laptop seems broken, but do you want to come and see if it's yours?'

'Absolutely! Can I come now? What police station are you at?'

The desk sergeant moved the phone away from his ear as questions were fired at him. The man was jubilant, and the sergeant could hear the excitement and relief in his voice. He informed the caller which police station he was at and quickly ended the call. Raising one eyebrow and putting the phone down, the sergeant felt he had done his good deed for the day.

'Kim! Kim!' Jamie Williams almost danced to his colleague's desk in the office and whispered in her ear. 'That was the police. Can you believe it? Someone has handed in my laptop. I'm going there now. Thank God.' Holding his hands up in prayer, he looked at his friend with relief.

'You're a lucky so and so if it is yours. What have you been doing all morning?'

'Trying to get some files together in case mine was lost forever. I was shitting myself. I was going to be sacked for sure. There's so much customer data on that laptop, it's untrue. I seriously wouldn't have wanted to hold my hands up to that.'

Kim could see the relief in his face. 'What condition is it in, have they said?'

'Broken apparently, but that doesn't matter. As long as the hard drive is intact, I can access all of my files. Not a word Kimmy, not a word.'

'Next time, you might take a leaf out of all our books and not take your laptop home with you. You can't take data protected information from the office and you know that. If that is your laptop, and I hope it is for your sake, you're one lucky bugger. Go on, I'll cover for you. Oh,' she shouted after him as he walked away to leave, 'and don't call me Kimmy!'

Jamie almost fell out of the taxi as it approached the police station and quickly paid the black cab driver with his card. 'Blimey mate, I've never seen someone so pleased to see a cop shop,' the cabbie shouted after him and laughed.

Jamie gave his name and presumed it was the same officer he

had spoken to minutes before. After a few moments the desk sergeant appeared with his battered bag. 'It looks exactly like the one you have, sir. Can you identify it as yours?' the sergeant commented.

'Yes, of course. Mine has got a Batman logo on the bottom. It's a sticker, I'm a fan,' he explained. His rambling bored the sergeant. He'd worked a long shift and all of this for a piece of broken metal didn't seem worth it. Turning the broken laptop over, he could see it did indeed have a Batman logo on it, just as described. 'Well, it looks like it's yours, so I just need you to sign a few things. What about that iPad that was in the case you picked up?'

'Oh, that was useless. I've brought it with me, but it's broken. Probably worse than mine, but my laptop might have saved data on it.'

The desk sergeant could see that Mr Williams was eager and excited over the laptop and realised that whatever was on it was extremely important to him. Jamie signed all the paperwork and hugged the case to his chest. He couldn't believe his luck and felt like punching the air. He swore to himself that he would never take it out of the office again – until next time.

He'd had a few late nights lately and had not been concentrating at work, especially since he'd split up with his long-time girlfriend and had to move out. That was why he'd taken his laptop home, so that he could catch up. If his boss ever found out, he would lose his job and his reputation. His life was a mess and so was his work.

Everyone had a laptop and a main computer in case they had to move around the office to different meetings. The main computer didn't contain all of his clients; the ones stored on his laptop were the clients he looked after most with the most generous of commissions. There was no way he was going to share their details with senior brokers so that they could steal all his hard work. Now all he had to do was access the hard drive with all of the information he needed to carry on.

* * *

Sitting at his desk in his large leather chair felt good. Scarlet had insisted he had their father's chair as he was the only biological son of Tony Lambrianu. There was his older stepbrother Bobby, who Francesca had had from a previous relationship, prior to marrying his father. Bobby was a doctor and a very good one and was twenty-two years older than himself. They were close and met up regularly, but, as a doctor he was always busy and lately they had both let things slide on the visiting department.

So here Adam sat, in the office of his father's nightclub and in his chair. Sometimes he doubted he was good enough to take over the family business. Was he up to his father's standard? Tony Lambrianu had been a legend. This club, Lambrianu's, had been his first ever club and the one he was most proud of and where his father's heart had always been. With its lavish pink neon lights, lighting up his name outside for all to see, his father had made his mark and apparently, he had worked night and day with Jake to establish this place.

Adam tried hard to remember his father, but he had only been nine years old when he'd died and Adam's memories were hazy. He'd been a very handsome man, and a ladies' man, by all accounts, until he'd met their mother. His sharp suits, showman ways and his hot-headed Italian temper were part of his enigmatic personality. But Adam knew his memories were different to Scarlet's and he remembered a kind, caring man who had never missed one of Adam's school plays, who had tried his best to pick him up from school when he could, and who had spoken to him every night on the phone before Adam went to bed. Scarlet and Katie had adored him as their father too, but they'd also got to see him as a brilliant businessman – a part of Tony that Adam had never been privy to. Adam had never been to the club as a child and so it didn't hold the same sentimental value that it did for Scarlet and Katie.

Some days he felt haunted by the huge portrait of their father that hung in the foyer of the club, as though the great man himself was watching over him, making him feel inadequate at times.

Hearing a knock at the door, Adam straightened his tie and awoke from his reverie. 'Come in.'

'There you are, Adam. Your laptop is all fixed and updated.' Sitting the laptop on his desk before him, Adam smiled at his tech wizard Bruce and they both burst out laughing. 'There are a few others with the same data, Adam. Everyone is in place just waiting for your say-so.'

'I haven't spoken to Scarlet yet, Bruce. As my business partner, she needs to know about this. She will disapprove, of course – that is her way – but she needs to be informed. Who have we got as watchers?'

'Well, first we have Norman. He's a bit simple but he's a good guy. Although he has a prison record as long as your arm. Mostly petty theft and a failed cannabis farm, and then there's the matter of him still being out of prison on licence because he murdered his wife. But he's in his seventies now and got nothing to do but sit indoors and look out of the window. And the good news is, he doesn't even know what he's looking at. All he knows is to watch that computer on that page and let me know if the prices go up or down. The guy can hardly read let alone make out those figures. And no one ever goes into his house because he's a little lax on hygiene.'

'He seems ideal. How did you find him?'

'Those dealers from Liverpool I told you about. They used to work with us until they all got banged up at His Majesty's hotels. They all put his name forward and I went and spoke to him. He smells a bit, but when I told him his friends had said he could help me, he listened. Didn't know what the hell I was talking about, which is good for us, but agreed as long as we oiled his palms. He doesn't want money, though. He wants goods.'

Puzzled, Adam looked up at Bruce. 'Goods? What kind of goods?'

'Shopping, fags, and he needs a new television because his is knackered. He would also like someone to help clear his garden because the council have complained about the mess and the height of the grass.'

'You're fucking kidding me. Is that it?' Adam couldn't believe his ears. No one did that kind of work for a bit of shopping.

Bruce shook his head. 'I also think if we do drop him a few quid now and again, he will be eternally grateful. Told you he wasn't the full ticket, although maybe he's not so stupid when you think about it.'

Adam couldn't believe his ears. Most people asked for thousands of pounds, but apparently not this Norman man. 'Well, I liked working with the Liverpudlians. They were good, honest thieves and dealers. If they recommend him, that's good enough for me. What about the others?'

'Even better, Adam. There's a nurse not far from Norman. Poor cow hasn't got a penny to scratch her arse with. She wants to buy her council house, 'cos the mortgage is cheaper than the rent and as she's getting on a bit she'd like a bit of security. Her house has three bedrooms and sooner or later the council are going to ask her to downsize to a one-bedroom flat. She has no family to speak of, except a daughter who never visits. If she had a bit of a deposit stuffed under her mattress – she's a couple of thousand short at the moment – then the bank would let her have the mortgage. She knows her way around a keyboard and she has more to lose than us. A disgraced nurse going to jail? She'd never get another job. She would lose her home and have a ten-foot by ten-foot cell to share.'

Adam had his misgivings about the nurse, but was prepared to listen.

'The other two are much the same. Some woman who's had a mini stroke and has only been given domiciliary carers twice a day from the council. She would like someone there on a more permanent basis, like a live-in carer. And there are a lot of illegal immigrants out there with nowhere to live prepared to do it. They get an address and she gets a carer. I know it sounds bleak Adam, but all they have to do is watch a computer and do what we tell them and we answer all their prayers. And then of course there's your friendly accountant who knows more about money laundering than we do.'

Katie and her husband, Chris, were both accountants by trade and kept a close eye on the business's books. 'Let's leave our accountant out of this for now.'

Bruce nodded, knowing the conversation was coming to a close. 'Of course. By the way, how did it go this morning? Was Scarlet angry because you were running late? I have to say Adam, today worked like a charm. It was a genius stroke to have that bloke followed for weeks, and then for you to hook up with his girlfriend – she certainly gave you a lot of pillow talk. Thanks to her we knew he took his laptop home and exactly what was on it. I presume you've given her the brush-off now?'

Shaking his head, Adam smiled. 'I haven't given her the brush-off yet, actually. She had valuable information to share and very loose lips telling me about her partner making millions in cryptocurrency. But I've made it clear that I'm not into relationships, just a good time and a bit of fun. It's up to her if she wants to carry on seeing me as I've made my feelings clear. She's not the kind of woman for me – she has far too much to say.'

'Well, thankfully, that dick of yours impressed her enough. I agree she let her mouth run away with her, but that's her problem... and his. He's obviously let her see him squirrelling away on his laptop about his clients and what he does at the stock exchange. Anyway, what about old Pete, the retired bingo caller? Do you think he could be a watcher for us?'

Adam shook his head. 'Pete likes life on the inside too much. He has more friends inside prison than he has on the outside. No sooner does he come out than he pinches a packet of biscuits to get himself arrested again. He attracts too much attention... although there is someone with time on their hands who I would trust with my life. What about Knuckles?' Adam looked up at his friend Bruce and saw the frown appear on his brow.

'You ask him if you want to but leave me out of it. He's one scary monster and makes King Kong look like a midget. He never smiles and stares right through you like an undertaker measuring you up. And you'll have to see what Scarlet says.'

'See what Scarlet says about what?' Refreshed and wearing a pink cashmere dress with matching shoes, Scarlet glided into the room with her hair down, showing off just a little of her diamond earrings.

Shocked at her sudden presence, Adam and Bruce stared at each other for a moment and then back at Scarlet, who had now pulled out her chair and sat waiting for an explanation. 'Let's have it.' Picking up her gold cigarette holder and putting a cigarette in it, she lit it and blew the smoke into the air.

'Money laundering Scarlet, that's what. Official money laundering,' said Adam.

'We launder enough money, Adam. Too much sometimes, so what makes your idea any better?' Frowning, she waited.

Clearing his throat, Adam stared directly at her. 'Don't treat me like a fool Scarlet. Yeah, I'm the younger brother, but I have the same scheming blood in my veins as you! I've done my homework; I have the data and now all I have to do is move things around a little. It's crypto money. Digital wallets... just numbers on bits of paper to most people, unless you know what you're doing. And I do.'

'What are you on about Adam? Cryptocurrency? I've seen and heard about it, but it's useless. People want cash in their pockets not bits of papers with numbers and figures. How are you going to launder money with it?' Scarlet laughed at Adam's attempt at being the businessman, although truth be told, she wasn't quite up to scratch with cryptocurrencies and didn't want to show it. She took another drag of her cigarette.

'That's because you're a dinosaur Scarlet,' Adam snapped. 'How many people down the supermarket do you see paying in cash? They all use plastic and that's just numbers on a screen. It's all plastic and digital now, Scarlet. This is the twenty-first century and we have to move with the times. That's where I was this morning. I've acquired what I need to begin with. I'll start small and there will be no suspicions because I've been playing the market for a couple of months already now.'

Scarlet glared at Adam and then at Bruce. 'You can fuck off now Bruce; you're not needed here. I wish to speak to my brother alone.'

Turning to look at Scarlet, Bruce blushed slightly. He could see the way her sapphire blue eyes were darkening, which meant she was nearly at boiling point. It was definitely time to leave. Turning towards Adam, he nodded and left.

Standing up, Scarlet shut the door and walked over to her brother. For a moment they both paused and looked at each other defiantly. With one swing of her hand, Scarlet slapped him across the face, making Adam jerk backwards.

Rubbing his cheek, he sat up again. 'Don't ever call me a

dinosaur in front of your prick friends again! Do you hear me?' she shouted angrily.

Realising his mistake and rubbing the burning sensation on his cheek, he nodded. Her harsh slap had almost made his eyes water, but he was determined not to show it.

'Now pour me a drink and explain this idea of yours sensibly, without insulting me,' she snapped and sat down. Her own hand felt hot and was stinging. She hadn't meant to hit him so hard, but sometimes her temper got the better of her.

Once Adam had poured them both a drink, the mood seemed to lift slightly, and he welcomed the warm whisky down his throat. 'Someone mentioned cryptocurrency to me, and then one of our business suppliers mentioned it, too. In different countries it's used a lot, and we're way behind here in the UK. But our drug suppliers have mentioned it in passing a couple of times which is why I looked into it. A lot of cash is hard to dispose of in some countries without suspicion and so they transfer it to Bitcoin. Or rather, whoever owes them money sells it to them on the market at a drop-down price. Inflation goes up and down and people want to sell so as not to lose money. You can also cash your shares in for real cash. That way it looks legal and above board. Dare I say it Scarlet, our drug suppliers use it a lot. It saves them burying it in their back gardens.'

Puzzled but intrigued, Scarlet took a sip of her whisky and leaned forward. 'But is that all it's used for? It seems like a worthless investment if so.'

'No, it's not. It's growing and becoming more common. A lot of people take it as currency now. You can buy a Rolex, limousines and although Amazon don't take it directly, they can put you on to the supplier that does. Come on Scat, all we're doing is cutting out the middle man and buying direct. There is a commission to pay, but there is a price to pay on all the money you spend isn't there?'

'So, if we pay a commission Adam, how do we make money?' Scarlet asked. Mentally, she knew this digital world wasn't her hottest topic, and mused to herself that maybe to the younger generations she was a dinosaur.

'We don't use our own money. We don't sell our own shares.' Adam winked and grinned at her. He could see he had captured Scarlet's interest and the idea of not spending her own money pleased her. 'Fernando, our friendly supplier, mentioned that we should use Bitcoin, because it's easier to get rid of and lighter to carry.' Adam laughed. 'Anyway, when he said that I did my research. I bought a few shares, nothing major, just a thousand pounds to try it and watched the market go up and down. The same with any stocks and shares. People buy and sell when the time is right.'

'Yeah, I got that bit, but how do we not use our money? Tell me the important part. The interesting part.' Scarlet wanted Adam to get to the point. The money-making point.

'Patience Scat. After all, it is a virtue.' He grinned. 'Stockbrokers... they have clients and act on their behalf. Well,' he scoffed, 'the rich and famous do, not Joe Bloggs dabbling for a few quid. But the rich have realised it's a good way to launder their own money. Stockbrokers act for them and buy and sell when the time is right. But to be able to do that, and here's the interesting bit Scarlet.' Flashing a smile, he paused. 'The stockbrokers have to keep a lot of data about their clients. Who they are, what shares they have, their passwords or QR codes, which are effectively pin numbers for their digital wallets... I know, I know,' Adam laughed, 'let's not get technical; you're only interested in the crunch.'

Pursing her lips impatiently, Scarlet waited. She couldn't quite get her head around it and would need to do some research of her own.

'I know of a stockbroker and his girlfriend who explained all of this to me when I expressed an interest. Probably hoping I'd use him. He's good, but sloppy. Recently, life has got in the way of his professionalism and he hasn't been performing on all cylinders. I've had him watched over the last few months. He does the same thing every day, even goes to the same Costa Coffee shop. You know Scat, he has a bloody boring life.'

'Yeah, and your story is just as bloody long winded. Get to the point Adam. You've been stalking a stockbroker for months who likes a coffee, so what?'

A little disgruntled by Scarlet's lack of enthusiasm, Adam felt it was time to come clean. 'He takes his laptop out of the office. Nothing unusual in that, but it does contain a lot of client details and a decent hacker can obtain those files. And it just so happens I know a good hacker. That's why I was late today. I dressed up as a homeless person and went begging on London Bridge. I knew this stockbroker – his name is Jamie by the way – would be there at that time. I begged for money and tripped him up while he was rushing to work. As usual, no one paid attention as they are too busy getting on with their own lives. I wanted his case containing his laptop. I'd bought a similar bag to his and Bruce filled it with some broken iPad of his nephew's, and during this stockbroker's distress we swapped bags. The stockbroker wouldn't realise until he got to his office, and by then it would be too late. I had his laptop containing all the data of his clients. Including all their shares to sell or buy.'

'Is that why you had no clothes on under your jacket for the funeral? You were dressed up as some old vagrant, and that's why you were late...?' Scarlet asked.

Adam nodded. 'Yes, that's why I didn't have any clothes at the funeral. I didn't expect you to order me to strip though!' Sitting back in his chair with his arms around the back of his head, he grinned. 'The ladies enjoyed it though, and it took the seriousness out of the day,' he laughed.

Scarlet sat back in her own chair and gave a half smile. 'So what happens now?'

Adam smiled. 'No real crime has happened as yet. We've done nothing. But, when we start emptying those accounts, it will be the crime of the century.'

'And did you have any help stealing the laptop?'

Raising one eyebrow smugly, Adam replied, 'I had a driver come and pick me up and drop me off by my motorbike.'

Scarlet frowned. 'Who?'

Adam smiled. 'Ask Knuckles. Do you really think I would trust anyone else?'

Confused, Scarlet looked at Adam, her eyebrows furrowed. 'But Knuckles was with me at the cemetery. I think I would notice if there was two of him...'

Suddenly the stark truth dawned on Scarlet. Knuckles had disappeared to use the loo and had been gone a long time. She remembered how he had come back hot and sweaty. Shocked, she inhaled on her cigarette. For once she was speechless. 'How long has this been planned?'

'A while, and don't worry, because we both have alibis just in case. Knuckles was with you and I'm always late.' Adam shrugged. 'As you're always reminding me, I'm not a morning person, especially after being at the club all night,' he stressed.

Standing up, Scarlet walked to the door and opened it. 'Knuckles! Get the fuck in here. Now!' She knew, as always, that he would be close by. After a few minutes, she heard his footsteps and saw him. 'Inside my office!' She indicated with her thumb.

Scarlet was angry. Her face was flushed, and she couldn't make her mind up who to hit first. 'You lied to me. You said you were going to the toilet and all the time you were on some heist nicking laptop cases with him!'

Standing there expressionless and ignoring Scarlet's outburst, he answered, 'Did take a piss. Didn't lie about Adam. You never asked.'

'How the fuck can I ask, when I didn't know? Adam I can understand, because he's a reckless, thoughtless, fly-by-the-seat-of-his-pants idiot, but you are just an idiot. What is your excuse?' Stressed and angry, Scarlet couldn't help raising her voice at them both. She felt like the headmistress before two naughty schoolboys.

Knuckles looked around the room for inspiration, which didn't come. 'Don't have one. Just helping.'

'Well, you haven't bloody helped. And what's more, you did all that while I was mourning at a funeral.' Breathing heavily, she sat down.

Knuckles looked up at the ceiling and then back at Scarlet. 'You weren't mourning. You didn't like Jean. You said the only reason you went to the funeral was to make sure she had really died.'

'What the fuck! How dare you. I think I like you better when you don't speak. Jean was a good woman,' she defended herself.

Adam nearly burst out laughing. He knew Knuckles had cornered her. 'He's right though, Scarlet. You said she was an interfering old cow, and you were glad to see the back of her.' Adam looked towards Knuckles and grinned. They both knew Scarlet was getting nowhere fast.

'So, what now?' she asked, ignoring their comments. She had to admit it was true and she had been caught out.

'Now, my lovely sister, the work begins. When the laptop was picked up, the data was downloaded straight away. You know Bruce can get into anything. You might call him a nerd, but he knows his stuff. He picked up the briefcase with the laptop and now he's brought me this one. Over time, we have acquired watchers, who are people who have nothing else to do all day but sit and watch the computer to see if the price of the digital money goes up or down. Actually, we were wondering if Knuckles would be a watcher. He sits in the car a lot of the time waiting for you. He has time on his hands...' Adam tailed off.

Frowning, Knuckles looked at the laptop on Adam's desk. 'Do I get one of them?' Knuckles asked. Nodding, Adam could see he had interested the giant.

'Oi, Knuckles works for me. Just me.' Turning towards Knuckles, Scarlet dug him hard with her elbow.

Totally ignoring Scarlet, having got used to her outbursts over the years, Knuckles looked at Adam. 'I'd like a red one.'

With her hands on her hips, Scarlet paced up and down while smoking her cigarette. 'Will somebody listen to me? I am here, you know. Scarlet Lambrianu! Adam, Knuckles works for me and I need him at my side. He hasn't got time to piss about looking at computers all day. Knuckles, you can shove your red laptop up your arse 'cos you're not getting one.'

Adam stood up; he knew it was all a bit much for Scarlet to take in without blowing a fuse. Putting his arm around her waist, he kissed her cheek. 'Sorry Scat. It was all my fault. Nothing to do with Knuckles. He did warn me you wouldn't be happy.' Adam cast a warning glance at Knuckles not to say anything, because they both knew Knuckles hadn't warned him about anything. 'We haven't done anything illegal yet Scarlet, not much anyway, and if you don't approve, we will let all that lovely money stay where it is. You're the head of this partnership and I trust your judgement.'

'My God Adam, you must want this badly if you're prepared to flatter me like that. Okay, I give in, but I give you one month to show a profit. Personally, I would like Katie and Chris to look this over first...'

'I agree, and we will tell them when we have something to say. One month you say?'

'Okay, yeah, one month only.' Scarlet turned towards Knuckles. 'Now, I have a club to sort out and you, Adam, need to get that shower you were going to have earlier. You're starting to go off!'

As Scarlet walked down the corridor towards the club, she couldn't help smiling. It sounded like a good plan and maybe, just maybe, there could be some money to be earned. But she decided not to say anything to the others just yet. If it made money she would tell them, but if it fell on its arse, she would brush it under the carpet and no one would be any wiser.

3

CHANCE ENCOUNTERS

The darkness of the club and its flashing lights made Adam think he was seeing things. He couldn't be sure what he'd seen but he had a fair idea. Leaning over, Adam whispered into the young woman's ear, 'You do realise, if the management see you doing that, you will be escorted off the premises?' Adam couldn't help smiling. What he had just witnessed was a rarity in his nightclub, and he couldn't believe the cheek of it! He wanted to laugh out loud but didn't. Lambrianu nightclub was exclusive and only for the rich and famous who never cared what they spent. But standing at the bar with Bruce, he had noticed a group of young women sat at a table and one of them was furtively passing around a bottle of water. Concentrating on the scene before him, it wasn't long before he realised that the bottle full of clear liquid was definitely gin or vodka. He decided to go over and make his presence known – a friendly warning from himself was better than a scene from Scarlet.

The woman blushed slightly as she half turned to him and smiled. 'Are you going to say anything?' She grinned and looked over at her friends. Although they were all dressed in the best clubbing outfits, Adam noticed there wasn't a designer label amongst them. There were about ten of them and they all seemed to be of mixed ages, which he found unusual. Twenty-year-old women didn't usually go clubbing with forty-year-old women unless they were family. As they sat in the horseshoe booth with its pink velvet seats in the dimness of the club, he saw there were glasses on the table, even a couple of bottles of wine. As far as he was concerned, the mystery got deeper, making him more curious.

Turning fully to meet his eyes, the woman paused. 'Do you want some? Then you can't tell, can you? I presume you work here – are you a waiter or a bouncer?'

Adam let out an enormous laugh. Looking down at himself, he laughed again. He was wearing a tuxedo and a bow tie. Yeah, probably to some people he did look like a waiter!

'I'm not a waiter.' Throwing his head back, he laughed, showing off his perfect set of white teeth. His sapphire blue eyes flashed and glinted. 'But I do work here.' The table of girls had stopped laughing and now they were staring at him. Puzzled, he looked around at them all. 'Is something wrong?'

'You are one hot bloke!' laughed one of the older women at the table. 'Look at them, their jaws have dropped.'

'Well, thank you ladies.' Quickly changing the subject, he grinned. 'Are you on a hen night or something?'

'No.' The older woman spoke up again. Obviously, Adam mused to himself, she was immune to his charm. 'It's the work's Christmas party.' Picking up her glass, she took a sip.

Confused, Adam looked around at the table. 'Christmas party? It's January. Didn't anyone tell you Santa has been and gone?' Oozing with charm, he pointed to a spare space on the seat. 'May I?'

Giggling to each other, they all moved up to give him space. 'We've never been to Lambrianu's before, but earlier on this year they were advertising big discounts for January group bookings, so we thought we'd wait. Our bosses paid for the meal and a couple of bottles of wine, but now we're on our own and as gorgeous as it is, the bar prices are through the roof! Are you sure you don't want a drop of this in your glass? We've bought some lemonade and were just topping it up with our own booze,' said the woman who he'd caught with the water bottle.

Vaguely, Adam remembered Scarlet organising the discounts. January anywhere was a quiet month after the mayhem of Christmas, so she had offered a discount and a set menu to group bookings only, guaranteeing their custom. She had taken all of the money in advance with a no-return policy fee. These ladies had obviously wanted to wait and come here. He looked around at the place he took for granted. The club was part of his everyday life and he never saw it through other people's eyes. They had postponed their work's Christmas party to come to here and were very excited at the thought. Inwardly he smiled; he didn't want to look like he was mocking them.

Looking up, he saw one of the doormen approaching the table and looked up.

'Mr—'

'Adam!' Adam butted in quickly before he could finish calling him Mr Lambrianu. He winked. 'Is there a problem? Is my break over?' he asked nonchalantly, while glaring at the doorman to follow his lead.

'Yeah Adam, your break's nearly up and it's time to get back to work.' He nodded and walked away.

'Well, girls,' Adam said, 'it seems our time is over.' Looking over at the woman who had initially caught his eye, he leaned closer to her ear so she could hear him above the music. 'Be careful taking out your booze... err...' Stopping short, he realised he hadn't caught any of their names.

'Jennifer. My name's Jennifer, Adam.' She smiled. 'And I will. We're going soon anyway; our cab is ordered for 11.30 because it's cheaper before midnight and there are a lot of drop-offs along the way.' She pulled her ear away from his mouth and looked around at her friends, then back at Adam. 'You smell lovely.' The words had left her mouth before she had realised what she was saying. Embarrassed, she looked at her friends, who laughed and teased her. 'Go on Jen, take another sniff,' they laughed, elbowing and nudging each other. 'Does he smell good enough to eat?' All the worse for drink, they laughed and joked. Jennifer looked up at him apologetically. 'Sorry, I didn't mean to embarrass you in front of this lot.'

'I'm not embarrassed, I'm flattered. Anyway, where do you all work?' Adam shouted to them all above the music, trying to save Jennifer from more embarrassment. They shouted the name of a well-known supermarket.

'Surely you're all supposed to be open around the clock.' He laughed. 'Let's hope I don't need a bottle of milk when I leave here.' His warm laughter floated around the table, putting them at their ease and making them all giggle and laugh. Taking a mental note, Adam stood up. 'Nice meeting you all. I'd better get back,' he lied and walked away as they waved and said their farewells. His first port of call was to make his way to the bar. 'Melissa,' he called to the barmaid, 'do me a favour. Send two bottles of champagne to that table over there. Get the DJ to announce they are the winners of the draw they entered when they made their booking.'

Melissa nodded. 'Sure thing, Mr Lambrianu.' She knelt down to pick up two silver champagne buckets and started filling them with ice.

Adam walked back into the shadows at the far end of the bar where he and Scarlet often observed the club without being noticed.

As he picked up his drink and took a sip he heard a roar of excitement, loud enough to drown out the music. He knew instantly that his champagne had been delivered and then he heard the DJ announce that the supermarket girls were the winners of the prize draw. Their excitement was electric and Adam felt good about himself. With a small gesture, he had made their evening complete and they would talk about it for weeks.

'What fucking draw is that? Has that got anything to do with you Adam?' Scarlet sat on her high-backed silver stool. Wearing a white and silver tasselled dress, showing off her suntan and blonde hair, she picked up her champagne glass and took a sip while waiting for an answer.

'Market research and promotions Scarlet. All good business. They work at the local supermarket and supermarkets have lots and lots of customers.' He grinned. 'Guess what they are going to tell them all? They are going to say they had a great night out at Lambrianu's nightclub and that they got free champagne. Word of mouth is better than advertising Scarlet.'

Disgruntled, Scarlet took another sip of her drink. 'Just don't go giving the good stuff away to all and sundry. I thought you were just trying to impress some more of your bimbos.' Scarlet strained her neck to see past the crowd to the girl's table. 'Although I see some are past their sell-by dates.'

'You know Scarlet, when you sit up in your chair like that and crane your neck, you look like a meerkat,' he laughed. 'They are having a good time. And it was you who offered the discounts for January, which is why they're here.'

'January is a shit month and some money is better than none. At least it pays the electric bill. I had to do something,' she snapped. 'One of us has to do the thinking.'

'Yeah, and you really need the money, don't you?' Dripping with sarcasm, Adam picked up his drink and walked away towards the office.

* * *

'Well, well, well. A young man in his twenties hiding away and drinking alone? It was unheard of in my day.' The loud cackle of laughter made Adam look up. Julie Gold in all her finery stood in the doorway holding her usual glass of champagne. A wry grin crossed Adam's face. She had got older like the rest of them, but inside she was still the same old Julie and nothing was ever going to change that. Dressed in a white trouser suit, cream top and a leopard print scarf flowing around her neck, she grinned through those bright red lips that he had seen from the day he was born.

'Hi Julie, it's nice to see you.' Adam sat back in his chair, ran his hands through his dark mane of wavy hair, and sighed. Pushing the whisky bottle towards Julie, he put his hand out and offered her a seat.

Walking towards him, she grinned. 'Well, when people say it's nice to see me, it usually means they're in trouble or want something. Which one are you?'

'Neither Julie, it's just good to see you.' Taking a glass out of the bottom drawer of his desk, he poured her a drink.

'That uppity shrew Scarlet been giving you a hard time, has she? Pay no attention Adam, she always was a spoilt brat with attitude. Personally, I think she needs a good slap to bring her down to earth, but we won't go there. I've always got your back, you know that, don't you?' Julie's voice softened as she reached over and put her hand on his.

'I've just had a few ideas Aunty Julie, but I'm sick of always having to seek approval. Never mind.' Adam smiled and shook his head. 'I'm just having one of those days.'

'What ideas?' Intrigued, Julie sat forward. She liked new ideas, especially if money was involved. Wagging her finger at him, she grinned. 'And don't call me Aunty Julie, it makes me sound old coming from a grown man like you. Now tell me, what ideas?'

Taking a huge gulp of his whisky, Adam shook his head. 'Oh, it's nothing and it wouldn't interest you. It's all about some internet scam, but Scarlet says I only have a month to prove myself and then she wants to involve Katie and Chris. I've taken all the risks Julie, so why do I have to run everything past the family first? All they will do is dismiss it.' Adam threw his hands in the air. He felt deflated.

'My goodness we are feeling sorry for ourselves, aren't we? Where are your balls, Adam? And as for the internet, you under-estimate me. I know my way around a keyboard and a few websites. Google and Amazon shopping have become my best friends since the pandemic. Run it past an old woman who has seen it all and done most of it. And get a grip Adam, you're a grown man!' Julie filled her glass with more whisky and sat back. She could see Adam had a lot on his mind. Sometimes she felt he was a troubled soul, and it was her duty to his parents' memory to help him.

Letting out a deep sigh, Adam stood up and closed the door and sat down again. 'Well, here goes Julie, but let me finish before you dismiss it.'

Julie nodded her head in agreement and said nothing. She listened as Adam poured out his story of his Bitcoin plan and how he had stolen the laptop containing all the data. His story seemed to go on forever and at last he picked up his drink and waited. 'That's it, Julie. All of it. So go on, tell me it's stupid.'

'Personally Adam,' she said, 'I prefer Dash as a cryptocurrency. It's more up to date, although Bitcoin is more commonly known. Dash is also recognised by retailers. It even has plans to compete with PayPal. Everyone is looking at Bitcoin and overlooking the others. Personally, I like anything that's silent but deadly, a bit like my Ralph.' Smugly, Julie took a sip of her own drink and winked. 'Do you really think I'm just a coffin dodger that doesn't keep her finger firmly on the pulse Adam?'

Adam's eyes widened. 'How the hell do you know all that? You never cease to amaze me Julie.' Adam couldn't contain his laughter. 'Come on, how do you know about it?'

'Covid pandemic Adam; what else was there to do while everything was closed? I admit, I didn't know a lot about the internet, but if you surround yourself with enough young men who have to stay in the house with you, they can teach you all sorts... apart from the obvious that is.' She winked playfully. 'I enrolled in courses online. I sat in bed, eased my back, had my box of liquors and I learnt. I made use of those times we were locked away and kept those little grey cells working, and I saved money on Botox. If I wore a mask it covered all those bits of the face that droop.' She grinned, her eyes twinkling, excited at sharing her achievements with someone who understood. Putting her finger to her lips, she smiled. 'Top secret Adam,' she warned, 'but I even helped with the Samaritans' help lines, listening to isolated people who were missing their families and afraid of the future. Now that is strictly between us. I don't want people thinking I'm going soft in my old age,' she cackled.

Looking at Julie, Adam felt better. Her jovial flippancy had lightened his mood. Although he was flabbergasted and shocked, Adam listened. 'Well, you really have taken the wind out of my sails, Julie. I don't know what to say. You're full of surprises.'

'Even at my golden age Adam, I would hate to be predictable. I even joined the Open University and I am more educated now than I ever was in my teens and early twenties. Christ, I could even get a proper job, God forbid!' She grinned. Blowing her long, red fingernails, she rubbed them on her jacket in a cocky manner.

Adam sat there stunned. He didn't know what to say to Julie's revelation. 'I'm sorry I underestimated you Julie, it was rude of me to think you wouldn't understand.'

'Oh, shut up Adam. You're always apologising like your mother used to. I prefer it when your father's side of your nature pops up. He would have done all of this. Your dad and Jake were future thinkers, just like you are. Scarlet's just pissed off because she never thought of it first. You're the next generation of Lambrianu, Adam; she's the fucking dinosaur!'

'Thank you, Julie! Christ, you've made me feel better. So, without digressing, what do you think of my idea?'

'I think it's great, and you have already done the tricky bit – you've stolen the data. My suggestion would be not to clear all of the accounts, just take a bit from each of them; that way people will presume stocks are down and accept their losses. Ralph and myself dabbled in stocks and shares all the time and you have to accept that's the name of the game. Sometimes you win, sometimes you don't. Who is your partner in all of this?' Frowning, Julie waited with bated breath. She hoped it wasn't Scarlet, but she knew Adam was loyal.

'Bruce. You've met him; he's been in on this with me from the beginning and computers are his lifetime skill. We organised this together.'

Julie tapped her fingers on her chin and rolled her eyes to the ceiling. 'Is he the one with Asperger's or Autism?'

'He has Asperger's, Julie, but it's nothing to be ashamed of!' Adam protested, immediately defending his friend.

Julie glared at him. 'I never said it was, I was just trying to recall him. I don't like labels Adam; people treat you differently. He has his odd ways, but don't we all.'

'I didn't mean to offend, it's just that people do think he's odd, but he's my best friend and I hate it when people call him weird. He likes routine and he doesn't like social gatherings, which is a shame, because I run a nightclub!' Adam laughed.

'I had a sister once.' Julie's mind wandered off into the distant past. 'She had all kinds of mental health issues not helped by her heroin addiction. That's why Josh has the issues he does. But they have never held him back and art was his way of expressing himself. As you know, he's a graphic designer for an advertising company now.'

'Josh has done amazingly. We used to be good friends, but now he lives in America, we see less of him. It must be hard for you.'

'Not really Adam.' Julie smiled. 'Have you never heard of Zoom? We speak all the time.'

Adam burst out laughing. 'Fuck, Julie Gold, you are amazing and I'm a prick. You know everything!'

Julie was infectious and always brought a light note to a worrying situation. She never took anything seriously. 'Well, Adam. You have had your moan and told me about your ideas. Let me also look into them and I would like a meeting with you and Bruce tomorrow morning to discuss it further. As for Scarlet, for the time being let it be swept under the carpet. Be your own man Adam and make your own millions, just like your father did.' Julie's eyes glistened with excitement and a great big grin crossed her mouth. 'There's perfume and pussy out there Adam and you're sat in here with an old crock like me. Get out there and flaunt it. I am going home, my car's outside. Tomorrow at 11 a.m. come to my house, away from big ears.' Blowing him a kiss, Julie got up and walked out, leaving Adam in awe of this legend that was his Aunty Julie.

Gulping back the last of his drink, Adam stood up to leave the office. He felt much better now, and realised he should have gone with his gut instinct and not told Scarlet. Walking into the thriving nightclub full of people enjoying themselves, he looked over to the table were Jennifer and the supermarket girls had been sat, but sadly the table was empty. Looking at his watch, he saw that it was after midnight and of course they had gone home. Julie's comments immediately popped into his head, and he smiled. Perfume and pussy indeed! What was she like!

4

A NEW VENTURE

Bleary-eyed, Adam heard a knocking on the door of his apartment. Looking at the digital clock beside his bed, he saw that it was only 6 a.m. Rubbing his face, he turned and saw the woman's figure beside him and sighed. His head throbbed and he remembered drinking far too much last night and partying far too hard. Sitting on the side of the bed, he pulled on his boxer shorts and walked towards the door. 'Okay, okay I'm coming.' Answering it, he saw it was Scarlet.

'Adam, are you alone?'

'No, I'm an alpha male in my twenties, why would I be alone?'

Tutting disapprovingly, Scarlet pushed her way past him. 'Katie is coming today; I'm going to meet her at the airport, and I wondered if you'd like to come with me?' Scarlet walked over to the kettle and switched it on. 'Strong coffee, that's what you need. Who were the women you were with last night? It looked like Battersea had lost some of its dogs,' Scarlet laughed as Adam sat down at the kitchen table.

'No idea. Some models, I think. One of them is through there though, so keep it down.'

'You're an alley cat Adam,' Scarlet laughed. 'Seriously, I'm picking up Katie and her tribe in a couple of hours, so are you coming? It's been a while since we've seen her and personally, I miss her.'

'I miss her too, Scarlet. She is my sister.' With the fog clearing in his mind, Adam remembered his visit with Julie. 'But I can't this morning, I have somewhere I need to be. I'll come to yours later. I presume that's where she's staying?'

A disappointed look washed over Scarlet's face. She'd wanted a family reunion but it wasn't to be. 'What's so important that you can't meet your sister off an aeroplane?'

'She'll understand Scarlet. I'll see you later.' Avoiding the question, Adam stood his ground and refused.

'Well, she isn't staying with me, she's staying at the house. My apartment isn't big enough for all of them.'

Instantly, Adam's ears picked up. 'She's staying at Mum and Dad's house?'

'Well, it is the family home Adam, even though you rarely visit. I have cleaners in there regularly and it's free for any family member to use. Bobby goes there quite a bit with his wife when he wants to get away from it all. We should all start arranging family dinners there on Sundays again. Life has just got in the way.'

Scarlet ran her hands through Adam's tousled hair and ruffled it. 'You need a haircut.'

'Why? My hair is my fortune, like Samson,' he laughed. 'Sorry about today, Scarlet, but I have a few things planned. I also need to pop by the betting shops and pick up what's owed. Everyone has been betting online recently and the owners don't think they need protection any more. We need to show them how wrong they are. I'm going to pay a friendly visit, unless you want to?'

'No, you go. I will see to Katie and we'll meet later at the house. Do you need back-up?'

Adam raised his eyebrows in a bored fashion. 'No Scarlet, I don't need back-up. It's just a friendly chat and if that doesn't work, I'll blow the place up!'

Scarlet burst out laughing. 'The old ways are always the best, Adam.'

'I thought I heard voices.' A young woman sauntered into the kitchen with a satin sheet wrapped around her and yawned. 'Do I smell coffee?'

'Yeah, help yourself,' said Adam.

'I'll make one and take it back to bed. Christ, I didn't realise it was so early?' Looking at the clock in the kitchen, the young woman winced. Pouring the water into her coffee, she picked up her mug to walk away, then turned. 'Are you Scarlet Lambrianu?' she asked.

'You know I am dear, so don't ask. I won't ask your name, because it will be a new name tomorrow. Now go and get dressed lovey, we're talking,' Scarlet snapped. The young woman took her coffee and strutted away. 'For God's sake Adam, you should have a revolving door on that bedroom. You know all those wannabe starlets want a story to tell. Find someone normal. Trust me, I've been there and done that.'

'Well, there are no journalists in here Scarlet, and I don't think she's hidden a camera anywhere. I would definitely know,' he laughed.

Standing up, Scarlet gave him a quick clip around the back of the head. 'Cheeky bugger. I will see you for dinner. Be careful now.'

Watching her leave, Adam felt guilty about not telling her about his meeting with Julie. When Scarlet was quite herself, like this morning, she was fun and good company. Other times she could be the very devil herself.

Walking back to the bedroom, he grinned. 'Cheryl, why are you up and dressed? Don't you want a shower first?'

'I thought about it, but your shitty sister has put me off the idea.

I can have one at home and incidentally, my name is Sherry!' she snapped.

'What's in a name darling? We could save water and take one together.' He grinned mischievously, while watching the smile spread across her face.

'You have a lot to offer a girl, I suppose.'

'You'd better believe it!' Sweeping her up in his arms, Adam walked towards the bathroom, mentally noting that he had a little time to kill before his meeting with Julie.

* * *

'Bruce, you have to come; you can show Julie the data we've accumulated. She knows her way around the internet. Believe me, I'm as shocked as you are. Come on, I know she can be a little intimidating, but she's on our side... trust me.'

'Adam, she scares the shit out of me. She's like Al Capone in a dress.'

Adam had cajoled and done his best to get Bruce into the car with him to attend Julie's meeting. He knew Bruce wasn't comfortable with people, but he also knew that once Bruce got into his stride with his laptop, he would overcome his shyness and forget about Julie. He could see that Bruce was nervous and just parking up at Julie's driveway was intimidating. Adam smiled at the statue of Ralph Gold Julie had organised in front of the house. It was very life-like, and it made Julie feel better. In December, she'd even put a Father Christmas hat on him. Adam knew her sense of fun was also her way of hiding her feelings. If she needed to know that Ralph was still there and looking over the household as he always had been, then so be it. Julie rarely showed her feelings but this was her pledge of love without saying the words.

'Come on Bruce mate, chin up.' Adam got to the door when

almost immediately, one of Julie's male helpers opened it. The young man, no older than himself, was dressed in skintight black trousers and a white vest displaying his muscles and tan. 'I'm here to see Julie,' said Adam, not knowing what else to say and hoping this man didn't think he and Bruce were applying for a job!

'I'm Lewis,' the young man said. 'She's in the recording room, Mr Lambrianu. The red light is on so we can't go inside yet. Can I get you something to drink while you wait?' asked Lewis.

Adam looked at Bruce and shrugged his shoulders. 'I didn't know she had a recording room. What has she got, a band or something?' Adam laughed. 'Just coffee thanks Lewis.' Adam held out his hand to shake Lewis's, which was met by a big smile and a handshake to boot.

'Maybe we should leave?' whispered Bruce.

Adam could see Bruce was feeling anxious about the meeting and this delay wasn't helping. 'No, we're here now and if nothing else, I want to know what she's recording.' They both sat on the sofa in the drawing room and no sooner had Lewis brought the tray of coffee in, than Julie appeared.

'Sorry about that, boys.' Looking at the tray of coffee on the table, she smiled. 'I see Lewis has been looking after you.' She grinned.

Adam stood up. 'Okay Julie, recording room? Come on, before we start, you have roused my curiosity. What recording room?' Adam spread his hands, waiting for an explanation.

'Oh that. Well, I was going to tell you anyway because it's only fair if we're going to be partners in crime that I should share.' Julie swept her long fingernails through her ash blonde hair and beckoned for them to follow.

'Oh my God, do you think it's a dungeon where she keeps all these blokes? I've seen *Fifty Shades of Grey* Adam,' whispered Bruce.

'I'm not deaf, Bruce,' Julie shouted, 'and if I had a red pain room, I wouldn't take a spotty oik like you into it. Now come along. It's cards on the table time and I am going to educate you with some Gold magic.' She laughed and swept along the corridor wearing a leopard print kaftan trimmed with black fur.

'Jacqueline!' Adam shouted. 'What are you doing here? Shouldn't you be at the club?' Adam recognised the young pretty woman as one of the strippers that worked at the club.

Embarrassed, she picked up her holdall. 'I'm just leaving Mr Lambrianu.' Nodding to Julie, she almost ran out of the door. Bewildered, Adam looked at Julie.

Julie opened a huge oak door and waved. 'Ta-dah!'

Adam and Bruce walked in pensively. Adam could almost see the sweat appearing on Bruce's brow. Inside they could see recording cameras on tripods, light fittings and a backdrop of white. Adam cleared his throat and moistened his lips with his tongue. 'Are you filming, Julie?'

'Yes. I told you I have taken the initiative as far as the internet is concerned. Everyone is doing it and so I cashed in on it and kept your poor jobless strippers in work. What were they supposed to do when you closed the club because of Covid? So, they do their routines here and I film them and upload them onto a website. The men watching have to pay subscriptions and we all make a wage. Good idea, isn't it?' Julie giggled.

Gobsmacked, Adam looked at Bruce who stood there stunned. 'The boys do a routine for the ladies, too. I thought it was a bit of fun at first, but Christ, there's money in it. The girls get paid for doing the same thing they do at the club and I can use the footage again and again.' Julie flung her hands in the air and shrugged. 'Everyone's happy and their bills are paid. I wish I'd thought of it sooner,' she cackled.

'You're making porn movies?' Adam asked. Julie had seen a chance to make money. As always, her mind was firmly on business.

'Not porn, striptease. Exactly the same as the club. I also have chat lines, come see.' Pleased that she could share her accomplishments, Julie walked them further down the hallway and putting her finger to her lips to silence them, she opened a door. Inside were four or five women of assorted ages talking dirty into soundproof phone booths. Stunned, Adam and Bruce stood there and took in the scene before them. This was not exotic. One woman, possibly in her fifties, was sat there in her hair curlers quoting passages from porn magazines. Adam wanted to burst out laughing. He had never seen anything so funny in his life. One woman was doing a crossword while she spoke. Their total look of disinterest in what they were saying was laughable. Carefully, Julie shut the door. 'I've been busy, haven't I?' She beamed.

'Busy? You're a fucking whirlwind Julie; you're like the Tasmanian devil,' Adam laughed. He thought he'd been prepared for anything today, but definitely not this. This was hilarious. He looked at Bruce, whose jaw was firmly on the ground, and they both burst out laughing. Adam was glad of this, because it had immediately broken the ice and made Bruce feel more comfortable.

'Come on boys, it's time we talked business. Our business, not mine.' Julie steered them back into the drawing room, and Adam noticed that Lewis or someone had refilled the coffee pot. 'Shall I be mother?' Julie laughed. Pouring them all a drink, she sat back. 'So, Bruce, what have you done so far?'

Bruce shook his head, not knowing what to say, and looked to Adam for support.

'Don't look at him, look at me. Well, by all accounts you have done an awful lot. You've downloaded all the data and have information on everyone's accounts. Do you have access to these accounts? Can you withdraw from their digital wallets?' Once Julie saw Bruce nod his head, she smiled. 'How many are on the list?'

'About forty. There's quite a lot of money in those accounts.

That broker had rich clients from all over the world. It's not just your average Joe we're talking about,' said Bruce.

'Good. What we're going to do next is register our own broker business.' Holding her hands up, she stopped them both. 'The fewer lies you tell, the closer to the truth it is. We're not brokers, we're business people who employ brokers. So, we register properly, the same way I have for my stripper website. It's all above board, boys. No come back.'

'But,' interrupted Bruce, 'if we employ brokers, they'll know what we're doing, won't they?'

'No, Bruce, they won't. Because we're going to drip feed from their accounts. We're not going to be greedy. Greed causes suspicion. We take a little bit out of each one and put it into different accounts. Anyway, are you telling me you don't know any dodgy brokers, because I certainly do. All the rich and famous are stashing money away from the tax man. It's a fact of life. For now we will start small but we need a front. A smoke screen if you like. One of my many social media personalities will go online and buy some e-stock that you're going to sell at a drop-down price. You're going to sell only to me, no one else. Lewis!' Julie shouted. Once Lewis had popped his head around the door, Julie told him to fetch her two laptops. 'Right, Bruce, go online and sell from one of those client's accounts. How much is in that one?' Looking at Bruce's screen, Julie noted a lot of the clients were from Saudi Arabia or America. Her long red fingernail scratched the screen as she said, 'Try that one.'

Adam and Julie waited while Bruce tapped into the account easily. 'There is around three million in this one; how much do you want me to take?'

'Half a million for now. We have forty to choose from so let's not get greedy. I'm going online now while you advertise your sale.'

As instructed, Bruce transferred the half a million out of the client's digital wallet, paying a 50,000-pound commission. Instantly,

Julie went online and bought the shares. 'Fuck sonny boy, it's like eBay.' Julie laughed. 'Actually, in the good old days, travellers' cheques were like that. Bloody cheek that when you cashed them in you had to pay commission. Sorry, digressing. Right, now take 50,000 out of one of the other accounts and put it into my pseudonym – that way it costs me nothing, but it shows I buy and sell, which is what we're going to do next.' Bruce did as he was told, using one of Julie's different accounts.

'Firstly, Julie.' Clearing his throat, Bruce carried on. He felt stronger now, on firmer ground as this was his subject. 'To sell it we need to go to an exchange and click sell. Then we choose how much we want to sell. Exchanges take a fee but you can sell to a buyer direct. As long as you both agree, you can convert it into cash and straight into your bank account. I have all the QR passcodes for the digital wallets. To be honest, this broker was really sloppy,' Bruce scoffed. 'There are ATM machines where we can withdraw immediate cash, for a fee. They charge you to get your own money. Like you say, just like travellers' cheques, but you have no surety of finding another ATM so you have to go with it. It's not traceable as long as you have your Bitcoin address or the pin number to your digital wallet, which we of course have.'

Julie's face flushed with excitement. 'Right, let's go and try one of these cash machines. Let me slip into something first and then we'll head off. Sort out a code Bruce and an account. Let's see how much cash we can get.' Excitedly, Julie left the room while Bruce and Adam looked through the many accounts they had access to and chose one.

Julie's chauffeur drove up and down the West End until they found the cash machine, and then Julie almost pushed Bruce and Adam out of the car. Hovering between them, Julie watched as Bruce worked his magic and simply put the amount he wanted and then the code. The machine asked him if he wanted to pay the fee and once he had filled in all of the information, Julie's eyes stared at the money as it came out. She almost jumped up and down with excitement. 'Quick boys, in the car. Fuck, this is a twenty-first century bank robbery without the guns. I love it. I fucking love it,' she shouted in the back of the car and burst out laughing.

'We're going to need different bank accounts Julie,' Adam reminded her.

'No, we need offshore bank accounts. Do you really think I have all of my money stashed away in England with these interest rates...? Bollocks! We're going back to mine to get everything sorted.'

Adam shook his head. 'I can't Julie, I'm demanding money from some of the betting shops on our turf. They're underpaying because they don't think they need as much protection and it's my job to show them that they do.'

'God, I miss gangland. You could smell the fear and get off on it.' As an afterthought, Julie looked at Bruce. 'Do you have a proper job Bruce?'

'Yes, I teach computer science at the local university.' He blushed, almost embarrassed by his achievements. 'It's nothing major, but it pays the bills.' He shrugged.

'Well, you work for yourself now. In fact, you work for ABG Holdings. Keep that three grand you've just withdrawn as a retainer, you've earnt it. But keep your job at the university, it's a good cover. You haven't won the lottery so don't go throwing money around yet. Patience is a virtue, so they tell me.' Julie grinned.

Puzzled, Adam looked at Julie. 'ABG Holdings?'

'Yes, I just thought it up. Adam, Bruce and Gold Holdings,' answered Julie. 'Always keep it legal and pay tax, that's what Ralph used to say. Anyway, if we become a coinage market, we can take commission off people as well. Win or lose we get our commission.'

'For Christ's sake Julie, you're like a runaway train once you have the bit between your teeth.'

Julie smiled. 'Let's start transferring. Is that okay with you Bruce? You two get 25 per cent each and I get fifty. Those watchers are going to be using my equipment. Are you sure they are okay and understand that they inform us the moment shares drop and need selling?'

Adam was swept away with her enthusiasm. 'We've checked them and put everything into place.'

'Good boys. I'm beginning to like you both more and more. But seriously, this is all about trust. I provide everything you need, including the offshore accounts in your names. Believe me, you might think I am a greedy bitch taking 50 per cent, but 25 per cent is a fucking lot of what I have seen in those accounts. Plus, if we're ever caught for fraud I would take all of the blame. You both did my bidding without knowing – you can grass me up or whatever. How many years in prison do you think they are going to give an old bird like me in God's corridor. Do we have a deal?'

Adam strongly disagreed with what Julie was saying. 'No Julie, we don't grass each other up. Anyway, it won't happen.'

Julie waved her hand in the air, dismissing Adam's principles. 'Well, if it doesn't, there isn't a problem, but that is the deal on the table.'

Sighing, Adam looked at Bruce. 'What do you say Bruce?'

Bruce nodded. 'Deal, Julie.' Adam agreed.

'Good, Gold and Lambrianu together again. Sounds good, doesn't it?' As an afterthought, not to leave Bruce out, she asked him his surname.

'It's Saint-Carr. My name is Bruce Saint-Carr, Mrs Gold,' he said politely. 'My mum's name is Saint and my father is Carr. They double-barrelled it.'

Julie paled and looked at Bruce. 'Oh my God, someone has just walked over my grave. I've got goosebumps at the back of my neck,' she said and shivered slightly.

Adam put his arm around her shoulders. 'Are you okay Julie? What's wrong?'

'Your uncle Jake, Adam, do you remember him? His name was Sinclair. He was your dad's partner and brother, even if not biologically. Have you heard Bruce's name when he says it quickly? It sounds like Sinclair.'

Puzzled, Adam told Bruce to repeat it. As Bruce's words sank into his brain, it dawned on him that Julie was right. Bruce was totally ignorant of all this and sat there watching them reminisce about their mutual friend.

'Well, Mr Bruce Sinclair, we're going to change your name properly; that way we are assured this scam is going to work. Gold, Lambrianu and Sinclair: what a fucking team!' She nodded and shook their hands. 'I also want to find out more about this broker you robbed. How is he this sloppy yet he has top-class clients...?' Julie rolled her eyes to the car roof and mused to herself, 'If his boss ever found out he'd fucked up and let his laptop get into the wrong hands, he would never work again. Christ, lads, he would be lucky to get a job as a road sweeper! That would be gross misconduct taking data like that offsite without authorisation or insurance. In fact, with a little pushing, I think we might have just found our broker. Mmm, blackmail always makes me feel good.' Julie laughed and nudged them both in the ribs.

Shocked, Adam looked at Bruce, and then at Julie. 'You want us to give him a job?'

'We'll see. Let me do the homework on that one and get back to you. He's fucked though, isn't he? Sooner or later clients are going to start complaining to his boss about their lack of funds and transactions they've never made. And it will look like he's been fiddling the books. Embezzlement even.'

'Christ Aunty Julie, you must have led a colourful life with Uncle Ralph! How do you know all of this?' Adam grinned.

'You'd better believe it, and cut that "aunty" shit. You only know half the story.' She smiled. For a fleeting moment she thought about Ralph and how much he would have enjoyed this new money-making scheme and it saddened her. Dismissing the thought, she looked at Bruce. 'Right, can you get started on the accounts while Adam here is off demanding payments?' When Bruce nodded, Julie added, 'You two are going to be millionaires in your own right. Let's do this, boys!'

Adam looked at Julie and grinned. 'I'm not short of a few quid already, Julie,' he remarked.

'I said in your own right Adam! Not that silver spoon you were born with,' Julie snapped. 'Well, let's not argue about it now, I'm too happy.'

'Talking about being happy.' Adam felt it was apt to change the subject. 'Katie is flying in today. She's staying at the house. I'm meeting Scarlet and her tonight for dinner. Are you going to come?'

'Not tonight, Adam. Me and Bruce are going to be busy. I will see her tomorrow maybe. Is she coming alone or are the kids and Chris coming too?'

'Not sure. Scarlet never mentioned Chris.'

'Good. Then I will probably arrange to see her tomorrow.'

Adam felt it strange that Julie had suddenly seemed to have turned against Chris. She was almost snubbing him, which was dangerous for anyone, especially as he was now the mafia godfather who ruled Italy. He didn't want to push it but it seemed as though there was definitely some unfinished business between Julie and Chris.

5

UNFINISHED BUSINESS

After a hectic morning with Julie and Bruce, Adam felt in high spirits. But he had other business to attend to. Julie and Bruce had dropped him off at the club in the West End so that he could pick up his beloved motorbike. Riding around the back of the betting shops, Adam smiled to himself. Just as he had hoped, the staff were out the back entrance near the fire exit having a crafty smoke. They had a waste basket wedging the fire exit door open so that they could get back in again.

Hearing his motorbike, they all looked his way. Wearing his skintight leather trousers and jacket, he took off his helmet and ran his hand through his hair. Looking towards the three women present, he saw their admiring glances and smiles to each other. Casually walking up to them, he smiled. 'Is Pete about?' he asked as he started to open the fire door.

'In his office or the back room,' said the oldest of the women. 'Shall I give him a shout for you?' She looked him up and down and took another drag of her cigarette. She was just about to drop it to the floor to stub it out with her shoe when Adam stopped her.

'No, you finish your cigarette properly. We don't want Pete

thinking you're out here having a crafty smoke and dropping your butts near the fire door, do we? Is it okay if I park my bike here?'

His sarcastic undertone seemed to hit a with a nerve with the older woman and she looked at the others furtively before nodding. 'Yeah, that's fine. We're coming in now anyway.'

Adam sauntered past them, avoiding any more questions. They knew they were in the wrong and although everyone did it, it was still frowned upon and the owner of the betting shop had asked them all frequently to smoke across the road, away from the building.

Adam couldn't believe the lack of security. Just because he had mentioned the owner's name, he had been allowed to walk straight in.

As he walked down the familiar corridor towards Pete's office, the fluorescent lighting made the dingy corridors feel even bleaker. He looked through the glass panes of the office to see if Pete was in there. Adam tried the door, which he noted was unlocked. Walking in, he saw that there was no sign of Pete, but he could hear the shuffle of feet of the three women returning from their cigarette break and heading back to their workstations. Sitting at Pete's desk and awaiting his return, Adam looked up as the women strained their necks to see what was going on. Nonchalantly, he smiled and waved at them like old friends. He knew one of them would tell Pete he was there, it was just a matter of time.

Adam didn't have to wait long before Pete came in looking hot and flustered and straightening his tie. 'Mr Lambrianu, no one said you were coming. Don't you usually telephone ahead?'

Looking Pete up and down, Adam took in his appearance. He was a youngish man, not much older than himself, possibly in his thirties. His work suit had seen better days, but Adam felt that was him just being snobby. Pete definitely felt he had something to prove and that was why Adam had decided to come today instead of Scarlet. She hated Pete and felt he was too big for his boots. The very mention of his name set her teeth on edge. Each week the protection money he paid got a little less and that annoyed her.

Pete's father owned the betting shops and had given Pete full run of the shops after wanting to enjoy his retirement. Everything had been okay until then, their protection money had been paid on time and there were no hassles. But Pete had a different point of view. He was stubborn and sullen in his attitude, complaining about having to pay for something that might never happen. It was now Adam's job to explain that nothing ever happened because their shops came under the Lambrianu 'umbrella'. They were protected and no one would interfere with their business.

Sitting down at his own side of the desk, Pete gave a weak smile. 'Well, I can guess why you're here. It's money, isn't it?' Reaching out for a packet of cigarettes amongst the numerous scattered on the desk, Pete lit a cigarette and blew smoke into the air, while sitting back in his swivel chair smugly.

'I was passing, Pete. But now you mention it, there are a lot of unpaid debts from yourself. How come you feel you don't need our, let's say "support", any more? Unless,' Adam joked, 'whilst I'm here, you're going to pay me in full. We all have times when money is a bit short and we appreciate that, but once you're on your feet again, we do expect to be paid. Don't you like to be paid for your services?' Adam's manner was very calm, friendly even. His low whispered monotone voice showed no malice.

'At least when your sister feels it necessary to come, Mr Lambrianu, I know what to expect. She shouts a lot and slaps me, but you're much harder to read,' Pete joked, trying to lighten the mood.

Shrugging slightly, Adam nodded. 'Well, that's my sister for you. But, as I say, it's just a friendly enquiry. We like to be kept in the loop if there is something you're not happy about.'

'Well, the thing is, I don't see why we should pay anything any more. A lot of gambling is done online now and although we get the usual stragglers in the shop who like to read the racing pages, most people gamble on their phones. So, what am I paying for? The protection of my computer?' Pete started to raise his voice to give himself an air of authority. 'We never have any trouble in here, so it's dead money I'm giving you. In fact, I'd go as far as saying we don't need your services at all any more.'

Adam kept calm, but he could feel his temper rising. His bright sapphire blue eyes clouded over and were almost dark as he looked at Pete. 'Has it ever occurred to you that nothing happens because *you are* protected by us? Isn't that how it should be? But, if you wish to end our agreement, that's fine by me. It's taking up too much manpower to chase you around for a few quid. Although, you are still in arrears for what is already owed to us, and for that I will pass your debt on to someone who has the time to waste.'

'Arrears my arse. I'm not paying anyone! And who are these bailiffs who are going to recover these so-called debts? I bet you don't want it spreading about that the great Lambrianus don't like to get their hands dirty and that they rip hard working people off. So no, Mr Lambrianu, give these so-called debts to who the fuck you like, but I'm not paying them!' Pete's face was flushed after his outburst, and he was almost out of breath.

Calmly, Adam reached out his hand to shake Pete's. 'Enough said, Pete. Our agreement is ended. Once I hand your debts over, you are no longer my problem. They will buy your debt off me, which means I get my money, and whatever interest they incur on top of that is their business... and yours.'

'What? How dare you come strutting into my office and threaten me. Get the fuck out! Do your worst. I'm not afraid of you!'

Adam's smooth, velvety voice drifted over the desk. 'I haven't threatened you, Pete. I have only informed you that I will be selling your debt on to a different recovery service. And please don't shout at me; I'm not shouting at you, am I? We're sat at the desk having a casual conversation and you have told me how you feel, and I have told you my plans. I'd better go now; I'd hate for us to fall out after all of these years. Goodbye Pete, good luck.'

Standing up, Adam fought hard to control his anger, but, unlike Scarlet, Adam always felt revenge was best served cold. He would wipe that smile off Pete's face and have him come begging at his door for mercy. As Adam walked out of the office, he heard the loud slam of the door behind him, which was Pete's last show of authority.

Adam walked towards his motorbike. The anger he felt rising inside of him made him want to scream. He wanted to go back in there and slit Pete's throat but thought better of it. There were too many witnesses and now wasn't the time. Revving up his motorbike louder than necessary, he rode off, ducking and diving through the traffic. He loved the freedom of the road on his motorbike and the speed. Scarlet said they were dangerous and that he was reckless but, to him, the bigger the bike the better. His Harley-Davidson was shiny and black with a bright red flame across it and he loved it.

He needed this ride to calm and soothe his anger before going to see his sister Katie. He wasn't looking forward to visiting the family home again and always did his best to avoid it. Even now, when he walked through the doors, he could still hear his mother's laughter and his father joking with him. Even all these years after their deaths, he felt the house was cold and subdued, almost in mourning for them. The house was full of painful ghosts which fuelled his anger even more. He felt cheated at times when he heard his sisters reminiscing about their mother and father – angry to have not been part of it.

Speeding up and dodging his way through the traffic gave him time to let off steam. All kinds of thoughts went through his mind, but most of all his attention was on Pete. He couldn't wait to wipe that smug grin off his face.

Arriving at the family home in Southend-on-Sea felt daunting as he rode through those familiar gates and saw the house. He had to give Scarlet full marks for effort. For all her bravado, she had kept the house in tip-top condition. You could see it had been freshly painted and the gardens looked as immaculate as ever. He parked his bike and took off his helmet, shaking out his hair, which was damp from sweat. He felt the sea breeze blow through it. Breathing in the coastal air felt good and it was always good to be away from London, even for a few hours. As he'd passed the seafront, he could see the donut shops with crowds gathering around and the smell of fish and chips wafted in the air. The amusement arcades were full of people enjoying themselves. Whatever painful memories he had, they didn't outweigh the good. This was home; this was where his heart was.

Opening the door, he could hear Scarlet and Katie gossiping again like they had never been parted. Hearing a man's laughter took him by surprise; he knew it wasn't Knuckles because he'd never heard him laugh in all the years he'd known him.

'Hello! Where is everyone?' he shouted as he walked down the long hallway towards the kitchen.

Katie popped her head around the kitchen door. 'Adam! My baby brother, come here love.' Adam winced as Katie nearly squeezed the life out of him. 'Blimey Adam, get out of those leathers. You will boil to death in them.'

'Don't you think I look good in skintight leather, Katie?' He winked and kissed her cheeks.

'Well, I see modesty hasn't caught up with you yet, you vain bugger. Yes, with your muscly torso and those trousers, you look like a member of a rock band.' She laughed.

'I don't know why he has to only wear a vest under that leather jacket! You'd think they hadn't invented shirts yet,' Scarlet snapped, but then she came across and hugged him. 'Bobby is here and Jack.'

Adam nodded. That solved the mystery of the male laughter. And it would be good to see Bobby, and Jake's son, Jack, again – it had been too long.

'Now why would I want to deprive all of those lovely women of seeing my tanned hard flesh, Scarlet?'

Katie and Scarlet linked their arms through his and walked into the kitchen. Pots and pans boiled on the stove and the smell of food reminded Adam he hadn't eaten anything since early that morning. It had been a hectic day. Adam looked around the room. 'Where is little Fredo? Haven't you brought him?'

Katie had five children, all from the ages of twenty years down, although two of them were twins. Fredo had been Katie's surprise. Just when everyone had thought she'd stopped being Mother Earth, she'd given birth to another boy.

Adam noticed Katie's faint blush. 'No, he's had a cold recently and Chris thought it was best if he stayed at home and recovered a little more. Anyway, I wanted to come alone. The others are living their own lives and Antonias is away at law school. He's not interested in the family business and prefers law instead, although I am sure Chris will try and make good use of that anyway...' Katie trailed off.

Adam cast a furtive glance towards Scarlet. It wasn't the first time they had noticed all was not well with Katie. She seemed a little withdrawn lately. Frowning, he smiled. 'Well, Fredo is only young; maybe it's for the best. Although it's a shame that the only time we get to see your happy brood together is when we're in Italy.'

Scarlet glared at Adam. She knew he was fishing for more information and didn't like it. Katie would tell them what was going on in her own good time, she was sure of it.

'Well, they have lives and jobs to do Adam, the same as you. Am I not enough?' Katie laughed.

'Of course you are sis,' Adam said. 'Come on, give me a hug.'

Their older stepbrother, Bobby, came striding forward. 'What's this? The prodigal son doesn't have a hug for his big brother?' Bobby wrapped his arms around Adam and hugged him. 'Good to see you, Adam. I'm sorry I haven't been around a lot, but you know where I am if you need me,' he whispered in his ear.

Jack, who was now head of the fire station he worked at, gave him a hug too. 'Can you believe it? Katie's only been here a few hours and Scarlet's got her cooking. Good to see you mate.' The mood was light and it was as though time had stood still in that house, because once again it was filled with laughter.

Jack and Bobby thrust a can of lager into Adam's hand and sat down. 'Come on then, Adam,' they laughed. 'How is life on the stud train? We hear the stories and see the magazines. Who's the latest squeeze?' They laughed and joked as Adam boasted about his conquests and made them all laugh. 'We're going to the men's room, Scarlet; some of this isn't good for your ears. After all, you're not getting any younger,' Bobby shouted as he, Jack and Adam walked down towards the basement where Francesca and Julie had built a 'man shed', bar and all. They could play pool, watch sports and talk men's talk to their hearts' content without the women.

Scarlet looked up at the mention of her name. 'Cheeky bugger. I've had no complaints.'

'Yeah, it's true what they say; there is life in the old dog yet!' Bobby laughed. 'Come on fellas, let's leave the women to bitch about us once we're out of the room.'

'What happened to that bedside manner of yours, Doctor Bobby? Life in the old dog, you cheeky bugger!'

Everyone was in high spirits, Scarlet most of all. This was home and with everyone in it like this, it felt like old times again. That was why she wanted to hold the same Sunday lunches with the family that her parents had done. No matter what anyone did during the week, Sunday was family day. That had gone by the wayside for years, but Scarlet felt as she'd got older that life had got in the way of family. She wanted to bring that tradition back to keep the family together.

'I'll shout when dinner's ready,' Katie called after them, but she knew it was too late. They had already gone to their man cave and shut the door.

'They'll turn up when they're hungry Katie.' Scarlet laughed. She wanted to choose her next words carefully. 'You know Katie, Adam is right. Whenever you come you never seem to come with all of the family. Is everything okay?'

Katie busied herself at the stove, turning away from Scarlet. 'It's just a coincidence Scarlet. I told you, Fredo has been ill recently.'

'Well, if he's been that ill, why have you come? I thought you were Mother Earth!' Scarlet snapped and then wanted to bite her tongue. She couldn't help her temper sometimes, and she knew it was her downfall. 'Sorry Katie, I didn't mean it to sound like that.'

'Fortunately, Scarlet, I know you.' Katie turned and put her arms around her sister. 'I know what you meant. You are the other half of me, after all. But, like I say, it's just coincidence. Next time, I promise. I didn't want to cancel my trip and Fredo is okay. It's just Chris being overly cautious.'

Scarlet smiled. She knew there was something else Katie wasn't telling her but she let the subject drop for now.

Eventually dinner was ready and Katie's roast beef and Yorkshire puddings filled the table. Instinctively, everyone sat where they had done as children, and no one was allowed to fill the empty space at the head of the table.

'Will Julie be joining us?' asked Katie.

Adam slapped his forehead. 'She said she would see you tomorrow, Katie. Sorry, I forgot to mention that.'

Katie smiled. 'I do hope Diana will come too.'

'Diana will probably be dragged out of whatever police station she's working at by Julie to go on a shopping trip with you, Katie. She still likes shopping and she is Julie's daughter, after all. She's doing really well but is a little work obsessed which is why Julie drags her away from all of that reality and goes shopping! That's Julie's answer to everything,' laughed Scarlet.

'Don't you find it strange,' laughed Bobby, 'that Julie has a daughter who could be a chief inspector in the police force? Now that is karma!' Everyone burst out laughing. 'And how is Ralph Junior doing? I haven't seen him for ages. Do you remember when Julie nearly had a heart attack when Diana called her only son Ralph. She said even Ralph hated his name so why had Diana embarrassed her only son with it.' Everyone burst out laughing again.

'He's with Josh in America. He likes it there and is doing well apparently. They come home from time to time to see "Grandma Julie", which he isn't allowed to call her, but they keep in touch.'

'I miss Josh,' mused Bobby. 'We had some great times together. Maybe me and the missus should go out there to surprise him. Life just gets in the way,' Bobby sighed.

Scarlet felt this was her moment to put her proposition to everyone. 'That's why I have been thinking about starting Mum and Dad's Sunday lunches again. It was one way of meeting up regularly; even you turned up when you could, Jack,' Scarlet stressed.

Bobby and Jack nodded in agreement. 'They were the good old days Scarlet, and you're right, maybe it's time to start again. We all looked forward to those Sunday lunches, it was the highlight of the week sometimes. And it was the only time Dad got to find out what was going on in his own family!'

'Oh my God, how many arguments have been over this table when Dad blew his top or Julie had a go at him? If this table could speak.' Katie laughed. 'It was over this table, Adam, we found out Mum was having you. They announced it over Sunday lunch. Me and Scarlet were eighteen. Do you remember that, Scarlet?'

Scarlet looked down at her plate. 'I do indeed. I remember saying it was disgusting that my parents still had sex at their age. I also remember Papa blowing a fuse. It was the first time in my life he really lost his temper with me.' As an afterthought, Scarlet looked up. 'Talking of losing your temper, Adam, you didn't say how you got on with the betting shop business. Did that little runt pay up?'

'No business at the table Scarlet, we're eating and having a family meal. Have a day off for once, eh? But for the record, no, he didn't, but it's all in hand. Now eat, Scarlet, before you get indigestion.'

Blushing at her slight reprimand, and changing the subject quickly, Scarlet said, 'For goodness' sake, is there a shortage of wine in this house? No wonder Julie hasn't come. Come on you lot, pour me some, my glass is empty. To us!' Scarlet raised her glass in the air and everyone joined in with her toast.

6

A WELCOME SURPRISE

While they all nursed their hangovers over brunch the next day, they heard the door open and a familiar voice call down the hallway, 'Oy pissheads, I hope you're up!'

Katie jumped out of her chair and ran to the kitchen door as Julie walked towards her. 'Julie! It's great to see you.'

'Look who's following me in.' Julie half turned and Diana, looking very businesslike in her long overcoat, flat black shoes and short black hair walked towards them. 'She looks as plain as a stump fence, doesn't she?'

'Diana!' Katie hugged her and the others got up to greet her. 'Come and have something to eat; you look tired.'

Yawning, Diana looked at her watch. 'I am tired. Mum was at the police station first thing this morning and after a twenty-four-hour shift. That's why I look as plain as a stump fence. I'm here in body if not in spirit.' She smiled. 'Quite the gathering of the clans, Scarlet.'

Scarlet stepped forward. 'It's good to see you Di. Thanks for coming.' She kissed her on the cheek. 'Come and have some coffee;

it will wake you up. Or would you rather go and have a shower or something first?'

'No, I'll eat if you don't mind, then I'll take a shower. If I smell it's Mum's fault!' she laughed.

Jokingly, Julie took her perfume out of her handbag and sprayed the air. 'See, a little camouflage works wonders, and stop moaning you. If you want to spend all night on the murder squad that's your problem. Why are you going for promotion if you're complaining you're tired?'

Picking up a slice of toast and sitting down, Diana crammed it into her mouth. She couldn't remember the last time she had properly eaten – it was usually just a sandwich on the go.

'No new husband on the horizon then, Diana?' asked Bobby.

Diana shook her head. 'Too busy Bobby. Anyway, one divorce is enough. We're better friends now than when we were married. Besides, I don't have time to eat, never mind anything else.'

Julie scoffed. 'Don't worry Adam, she still gets the odd "friends with benefits" out of John. I'm not stupid.'

'Mum we're just friends.' Diana blushed. 'It makes it good and civil for Ralph Junior that we can go on holidays together.'

'Don't get uppity with me miss. You're not too old for a clip around the ear,' Julie laughed. 'Would that come under police brutality or child abuse?'

While they all gathered around the table chatting to Diana, Julie pulled Adam aside. 'Me and Bruce made forty million yesterday. We took a million out of each of those forty accounts. It was pure heaven. Daylight robbery. God, I love that kid, he's got magic fingers.'

Adam raised his eyebrows in shock and nearly choked on his coffee. 'Forty million? I thought you said to keep it low profile.'

'Keep your voice down; it is low profile. They won't notice it yet. That broker has a lot of exclusive clients and I've made an appointment to go and see that broker firm of his. I want to see this man. I expect you at mine later, possibly tonight. I need to take Diana shopping first; she looks like shit!' Julie grimaced and looked towards the table where her daughter was sitting.

Adam couldn't help but laugh at Julie's maternal way of talking about her daughter, although he knew she meant well.

'Let's set up those watchers and get them on the case. This is big business now and you need to sort it. And we need to sort Bruce out as well. He wants to buy his mum a house and I presume something for himself. Bet he lives in a squat.'

'He doesn't live in a squat, Julie. He has a very nice studio flat.'

'That's what I said. Anything with less than eight bedrooms is a squat in my opinion. Where do you put all your rubbish? Fuck, I bet my shed is bigger than his flat.'

'Oy you two, what are you whispering about?' shouted Bobby. 'Can't you see we have guests?'

Julie dropped a wink. 'Just asking how Adam is. I haven't seen him for a while; he's usually buried under the duvet somewhere with some ugly woman!' Julie laughed and punched Adam on the shoulder.

'Right!' Adam rubbed his hands together. 'I'm going for a shower and then to work. Scarlet, why don't you take the day off and go shopping with the girls? I can sort things out at the club. What about you Knuckles, are you driving that lot or coming back with me?'

'He's going with you to the club!' Julie shouted. 'Do you really think I want Shrek driving us around the West End? Not a chance. I have my own driver outside. Incidentally, can someone take him a sausage sandwich or something?'

Much to Julie's annoyance, Knuckles never rose to her insults. He was used to them and they seemed to go over his head. She liked sarcastic banter and it was wasted on Knuckles.

'Girls? I like that, Adam.' Katie grinned. 'Being forty-seven doesn't agree with me and so "us girls" will go shopping and Scarlet will take the day off. We'll pop by the club later if you're about. Anyone else up for a drink this evening?'

Julie sipped her coffee and burst out laughing. 'Do you realise what you've just said, Katie?'

Everyone stopped what they were doing and looked towards Julie who was chuckling to herself as though sharing a private joke.

'No, what? Have I said something funny?'

'You said you were forty-seven, which means, as your twin, so is Scarlet who still tells everyone she's in her thirties! You've just blown her cover!' Julie found it hilarious, especially as she had heard Scarlet lie about her age constantly.

Blushing, Scarlet pouted. 'Well, you must be ninety if you're a day, so that still makes me a spring chicken!'

'Yeah Scarlet, but you're quickly catching me up.' Julie couldn't stop laughing and tears started to roll down her cheeks.

In Julie's mind, Scarlet had replaced Tony. She had loved having digs at him and torturing him with her comments and just like Scarlet, he would rise to it. Now this was fun!

'Well Julie, if you think surrounding yourself with all of those young men makes you look younger, it doesn't – it just makes you look like a paedo!' Scarlet spat out.

'It's better than having Shrek to look at first thing in a morning,' Julie joked. Everyone burst out laughing. They knew the only thing that got under Scarlet's skin was that she hated getting older.

Adam disappeared from the fun and games and went to take his shower. His mind was in a whirl – forty million pounds in one day! He felt like punching the air. He knew it could be done but now, in the cold light of day, he couldn't believe just how easy it had been. Jeez, that was a lot of money to be made while sitting at home drinking coffee. Letting the warm water rain down on him, he mused to himself that Bruce had never had that kind of money, which could cause suspicion. With him and Julie, it didn't matter so much, as everyone knew they had money, and so their main objective was to protect Bruce but still give him the chance to spend some of his ill-gotten gains. Making a mental note of it, Adam felt that was just one more thing to add to his list, but first was Pete the mouthy bookmaker. Today, Adam decided he would make Pete regret his decision to end their business relationship and open that surly mouth of his. An idea of revenge was forming in his brain.

* * *

Later that afternoon, two men in suits walked into the betting shop and turned the sign around on the door, indicating they were closed.

'Everybody out. Do you hear me? Get the fuck out!' one of them shouted.

Instantly, the gamblers reading the racing pages at the tables and looking at the monitors hoping their horse would win, turned and looked at the two men. Without a word they picked up their newspapers and walked towards the door. They didn't want trouble and these men in their black suits and ties could only mean one thing.

'You two ladies, go for your lunch break,' one of the men said to the women behind the counter. They stood frozen to the spot, not knowing what to do.

'I've got children,' one of them said without thinking. She was scared and didn't want to get hurt.

'Good, well go for your lunch break and they will still have a mother, won't they? Off you go now. And press the alarm if you want to, it's up to you. But you'll be dead before the police arrive.' He grinned.

As though by magic and much to the women's relief, Pete walked from the back office to the counter to see what was happening.

'Who the hell are you? Why is the shop closed? Where is everyone?' Seeing the women's frightened faces, he cocked his head to give them permission to leave. They pushed past him so quickly they nearly knocked him over. Pete straightened his tie and swallowed hard. 'Are you from Lambrianu?' he asked in a surly manner.

'Nope. He's sold your debt on to us and we want our money. We're here to introduce ourselves and collect our first payment.'

'Sold my debt? Don't you know the Lambrianus demand money with menace? They run protection rackets all over London. It's not a debt.' Spying them suspiciously, Pete took in their well-tailored suits and poker faces. These weren't bailiffs. This was not a debt recovery service.

'Tut tut Pete, you do have a lot to say for yourself. The Lambrianus are not our problem. You owe us ten grand and we want our first payment. Open the till, there's a good boy.'

'Like fuck I will. Now, I don't know who you are, but you can go back to the Lambrianus and tell them I'm paying nothing and sending you doesn't scare me.'

'If you don't want to listen to us, maybe you would like to speak to our friend?'

Bewildered, Pete looked around the betting shop; there was no one else there. 'Who?'

One of the men opened his jacket and showed the gun holster under his arm. 'This is my little friend and underneath his overcoat, he has a bigger friend. Now, we have bought your debt and we want paying... got it?'

Pete paled at the sight of the gun. He was tempted to press the alarm, but could see their eyes firmly fixed on him. 'What I owed the Lambrianus didn't come anywhere near ten grand. It's only a few grand. Is that what he told you?' Pete smiled. He knew if he dropped Adam in it, they would soon change their minds.

'We know how much it was for, Pete. But there's our introduction fee and admin costs, plus interest. Ten grand it is.'

Pete's jaw dropped. He couldn't believe what he was hearing. Surely this couldn't be true. He felt beads of sweat on his forehead and brushed them away with his hand. One of the men went behind the counter and stood at Pete's side, indicating he should open the cash register.

'There isn't much in it. It's been a slow day. I won't be able to do the day's takings until I see what the online bets are. That's what the women that work here do; they see the bets and pay the winnings online.'

'We know how it works Pete; you don't have to explain. We want a grand a week for ten weeks and if you miss a week the interest goes up.' The two men then looked at each other and smiled. 'Of course, there is a way you could work it off if you want.'

'Work it off?' Confused and scared, Pete looked at them both, not knowing what to say.

'We need something collecting from Tenerife. It includes a free holiday for you for a couple of days and you safely deliver our packages home to us. Not a bad few days' work.'

'You mean drugs, don't you? You want me to go through customs with drugs. You have to be joking. No way. That's a long stretch if you get caught.' Pete half laughed out of nervousness. He didn't know what else to say. He didn't know these men; they weren't from the Lambrianus, he knew that now. Opening the till, he could see there was a thousand in it and a bit of loose change. Scooping the money up, he cursed Adam. He hadn't expected this.

'Let's take a look in the safe, shall we Pete? I know you always have a bit extra in there in case someone has a big win. They want paying in cash the same as you do when they place their bet.'

'I've been to the bank; it's empty.' He was still talking when the man with him behind the counter scooped up the money from the till and turned to walk down the corridor towards his office. Adam had already told them about the sloppiness in security and that the doors were unlocked. He doubted whether the safe was kept locked, and when the man turned the handle, just like magic, it opened.

Pete had swiftly walked down the corridor behind him and seeing the man on his knees with the safe door open, his heart sank. 'Look fellas. Please don't take everything out of there. As you say, there are bets I need to pay. You said you only wanted a grand, well, you have it. Take that as the first instalment. That's all you wanted, wasn't it?' he pleaded.

The man by the safe stood up. 'So, you're entering into our agreement then? A grand a week. Slip up once Pete and the interest is 100 per cent. Don't forget that free holiday now. It's still on the table and a much easier way of paying off your bill. Three trips, that's all it takes and you get a nice suntan. But one late payment and my friend here will cut off your balls and use them as earrings *and* he will still want his money. Isn't your daughter called Sally?'

Pete rubbed his palms together. They felt hot and sweaty and he ran his finger between his collar and his neck. 'Yeah,' he stuttered, 'how do you know that?'

The man held up his mobile and spoke into it. 'You there, Jimmy?'

'Yeah boss. Just having a nice cup of tea and a biscuit with the ladies.'

Pete began to tremble; he felt he knew what was coming and his stomach churned. Almost hypnotised by the phone in the man's hand, he listened to the conversation on loud speaker. 'Put her on, Jimmy, let her say hello to her dad out with his friends.'

'Daddy!' Hearing her voice, Pete almost turned to stone. He

wanted to lash out, but he knew someone was with his family and didn't want to give them any cause to hurt them.

Swallowing hard, he ran his tongue across his lips to moisten them. 'Hey Sally, how are you doing love?' He was trying his best to sound casual and normal, but his legs felt weak.

'I'm okay Daddy. Your friend's come to visit. Mummy is making him some more tea. He wants to know when you're coming home?' In the background he could hear his wife asking this Jimmy person how many sugars he wanted in his tea. It all sounded so normal.

'I'll be home soon, I've just been held up at work.' Pete sighed as he realised what he had to do. He knew this debt would never be paid off. People like this always found a way to add interest. 'Did Uncle Jimmy tell you about the holiday I've booked to Tenerife?' Casting a glance at the man in the room with him, he saw him nod. He heard his daughter laugh and shout to her mum that they were going on holiday. Jimmy took over the phone. 'I might have to go before you get here, Pete. We'll catch up later. You enjoy your holiday and I will see you very, very soon.'

Pete's blood ran cold and he wanted to burst into tears. When the call disconnected, he turned back to the man beside him. 'You'd better not hurt them. I swear, if you do—'

'You'll do what, Pete? Your family are okay, you've heard that and that was a good decision you made about the holiday, good boy. We'll bring the tickets tomorrow morning and you leave tomorrow night. Oh, and for good measure Pete, hold this for me, would you?'

Pete's mind was spinning. He was about to say he couldn't leave tomorrow when the man took his gun out. 'Go on, take it in your hands. If you had the balls, you would fire it at us. Do you have the balls, Pete? Hold it!' the man demanded.

Pete's hand was shaking as he held it out.

Handing the gun over to Pete, the man grinned. 'I always wear gloves to work, which is why your fingerprints are now all over that gun. And should you try and double cross me and force me to harm your family, well, let's just say it won't be my fingerprints on the gun that killed them. See you tomorrow, Pete.'

Stunned, Pete watched them walk casually out of the shop with his thousand pounds. He wanted to be sick, but his first thought was to call home. His wife answered.

'Vicky, are you okay? Are you and Sally okay?' he almost shouted down the phone.

'Of course, love, why? What's the matter? You sound worried.'

Relief washed over him. 'Yeah, I'm fine love. You know you shouldn't let strange men into the house without me there.' He laughed.

'I didn't love; he said he used the key you gave him. He was here putting the kettle on when we got in from the shops. Is something wrong Pete? You sound awful.'

Pete closed his eyes and shook his head. Tears slowly ran down his cheeks. They had broken into his home. He could feel his legs weaken and sat down. 'Did he give you the key back?' Pete was doing his best to keep his voice steady, although he was choking back the tears.

'Oh my God, I forgot to ask. Well, you'll be seeing him before me so you can get it back then. He's even offered to feed the cat while we're away on our holiday. What a lovely surprise that was by the way!' Vicky sounded happy and pleased about their trip and carried on talking about how it was nice to meet some of his friends at last.

Pete felt sick to the stomach. He could feel the bile rising in his throat, leaving a bitter acid taste. Making an excuse, he ended the call. Sitting there, he stared blankly at the wall. He didn't know what to do and tomorrow those thugs would be back with his flight tickets. They had his fingerprints on the gun; he felt they might as well be holding it to his head. Burying his head in his hands, he burst into tears. He didn't know what to do. Then a thought occurred to him. If Adam Lambrianu could sell his debt to them, maybe he could buy it back. It was a long shot but worth a try. Dialling Adam's number, he desperately wanted him to answer. Adam was his last chance.

Adam sat at his desk and saw his mobile burst into life. When he saw Pete's name, he smiled. He knew what had happened and what Pete wanted so he let it ring a few more times to make him sweat before he casually answered.

'Adam, Adam, is that you mate?' Pete shouted down the phone. 'I'm sorry about the other day, I've been a bit stressed lately.' Pete wiped the snot and tears from his face with the sleeve of his shirt. 'Two blokes have just been here, Adam; they say you've sold my debt on to them. They want ten grand! Can you buy it off them and then we'll carry on with our usual arrangement? Our families have known each other for a long time, Adam. My dad has always been fair and square with you, hasn't he? Come on, Adam, I didn't mean anything.' Pete knew he was almost grovelling, but he didn't care. His and his family's life was on the line. He would do anything to sort it out amicably.

'Sorry, Pete. They don't sell debts, just buy them. Why would I help you when you almost threw me out of your office and trashed my sister? Sorry, this is all your own doing. You said you didn't need our protection and now you don't have it. Trust me though Pete, these men are not as reasonable as we have been. They will get their money back one way or another, especially with your prints all over that gun. Bye Pete.' Adam ended the call with a satisfied grin on his face and sat back in his chair.

Pete was still grasping his mobile, shocked by Adam's words. Adam Lambrianu had set him up. Pete crawled into a corner of his office and brought his knees up to his chest. Fear gripped him and the tears began to fall again. He'd thought he'd been so clever shouting at Adam that day, but now he was up to his neck in it. These men, whoever they were, meant business. They were cold-hearted killers threatening his family and emptying his cash register. The Lambrianus had never done that, he reasoned to himself. Neither his life nor his business would ever be the same again. What a bloody fool he had been!

* * *

Hearing the knock at the door, Scarlet removed her gold-rimmed glasses, put down her pen and folded her arms. She instinctively knew it was one of the employees complaining about something. After all, it usually was. 'Come in!'

'Well, that was a pretty loud shout Scarlet,' laughed Jimmy as he walked into her office.

Scarlet beamed. 'Jimmy! Oh my God, where have you been all this time? And look at that tan! Adam, look, the wanderer returns.'

'It's actually Adam I've come to see, Scarlet, although I am really pleased to see you, and you look more beautiful than ever,' he laughed as they both hugged.

'Adam? Well, that's a surprise. The last I heard you were living in Tenerife, living the high life with all those drug barons!'

'Nothing's changed Scarlet, which is why I'm here. Adam here, has been clever enough to find me a mule. Thanks Adam, I owe you one.'

Looking very pleased with himself, Adam sat back in his chair and put his arms around the back of his head. 'I take it all went well with our bookmaker friend? I've had him on the telephone pleading for mercy. What happens next?'

Jimmy sat down, while Scarlet poured each of them a drink. 'Well, his first visit to Tenerife will show us what he's made of. If he gets caught at customs, he ends up in prison doing a long stretch, which is something that wouldn't have happened if he'd had the protection of the Lambrianu family.' Jimmy laughed and winked at Scarlet. 'If he gets the stuff through, all's well and good and if he doesn't, that's his problem. Either way, he is on a downward slide. We've got his fingerprints on that gun if he ever steps out of line, which I doubt.' Jimmy laughed. 'Fuck, Adam, your father would be proud of you! You are one evil man thinking that one up and I appreciate you thinking about me. Things have been getting tight on my end and my regular lads want a cooling off period before the next drug run.'

'We've known each other too long, Jimmy. You're family. Does he know you're making him drive all the way to Manchester to drop the gear off?' Adam grinned.

'Nope and he isn't going to find out till it's too late. It's his own fault Adam; all he had to do was keep paying you and he would be protected. He wouldn't have my thugs crashing in there and demanding money with menace. His wife makes a nice cup of tea though,' Jimmy laughed.

Scarlet spun around to face Adam, rubbing her hands together excitedly. 'Of course, his dad will have to come out of retirement and put a manager in the shop. He will possibly want our old arrangement back if Pete ends up in prison.' Scarlet couldn't help laughing. 'How long are you staying in England, Jimmy? If you ever want your old job back as one of my getaway drivers, the door is always open.'

'Well, I'm here for a couple of days, then back to the wife and kids. Tenerife is good for them. Sunshine, beaches, the lot. I don't want to get my fingers dirty any more. If drugs are sold at my club, it's not my problem. Ignorance is bliss. I'm getting too old for all of that cloak and dagger stuff these days. I want to enjoy my retirement.'

'My dad would be proud of you Jimmy,' Scarlet's hug was

genuine as she wrapped her arms around her dad's old work acquaintance.

Adam ran his hands through his hair, satisfied. The smug grin on his face couldn't have been wider. 'Jimmy, if you lose any of your stuff because of Pete, I'll make good on it.'

'That's decent of you Adam, I appreciate that. You're a good bloke.'

Adam was glad Pete was going to get his comeuppance. He needed to know who was boss and his insults had made his teeth grind. Hearing him begging and pleading for help on the phone had really made his day. Whatever happened to him now was not his business. Good riddance!

Once Jimmy had left, Scarlet sat beside Adam. 'Well, you're one dark horse Adam. I thought we were partners.'

'We are Scarlet. More than that, we're brother and sister. You would have got Pete roughed up, but there would have been a next time. My way is final. He won't be shooting his mouth off about us again and if he does, it's nothing to do with us.'

Looking at her little brother, Scarlet nodded. 'I'm sorry Adam, sometimes I underestimate you. You're a clever man and you've earnt your stripes many times.' Reaching out, Scarlet tenderly ran her hands through Adam's hair. 'You're still my baby brother though and always will be.' She smiled. 'Let's have a drink to celebrate your victory. After all, when word gets out, I doubt any of our payments will be late again. Nobody wants their debt sold to those thugs. Cheers!' Scarlet chinked her glass of whisky against Adam's and they both burst out laughing.

7

A FINE ROMANCE

Scarlet was only in the office for a couple of hours, and no sooner had she left for her shopping trip with the others than Adam got to work. Julie's revelation about the money had him biting at the bit. Riding through the streets on his motorbike, he stopped at the traffic lights. Looking up, something crossed his mind. Before him was a supermarket. The very supermarket the bunch of women he'd met at the club said they worked at. Impulsively, he found himself riding into the car park and after parking up, walking through the doors. His excuse to himself was that Bruce rarely had any milk in or much of anything else for that matter so he would pick some up, although he knew he really wanted to catch sight of Jennifer, the young woman who had smuggled alcohol into the club for them all to share on their party night.

Aimlessly, he walked past the checkouts and down the aisles, but there was no sign of her. Disappointed, he picked up some milk. As he was leaving, he was about to pass a couple of women, when he realised one of them was Jennifer. Her long hair was brushed back into a ponytail and she had the supermarket logo on her fleece jacket.

He came to a stop next to her. 'Jennifer, isn't it? It's nice to see you again. You look much better in daylight,' he said with a smile.

For a moment, she looked puzzled and a frown crossed her brow, then her eyes met his and her face lit up. 'Our Christmas party at Lambrianu's! No one could forget those blue eyes,' she laughed and then remembering her friends at her side, she blushed. 'This is... erm, sorry, I forget your name,' she confessed.

'Adam, my name is Adam.' He held out his hand to shake hers. He had purposely omitted to tell her his full name.

'Nice to meet you again, Adam.' She smiled again and for a brief moment their eyes met.

Taking the bull by the horns, Adam felt this was his only chance. 'Do you want to go for a drink sometime?' Quickly, he cast a glance towards her hand to see if there was a wedding ring.

'See you in a minute Jen,' the other women interrupted, knowing at this moment they weren't needed. Jennifer watched them leave and looked up again into those blue hypnotic eyes.

'I'd like that Adam, but I have to go. What's your mobile number?' Taking out her phone, she quickly typed in Adam's number. 'Right, I'll text you and then you will have mine. You can call me and arrange something if you want to.' She smiled. 'Bye.'

Adam stood and watched her leave. As Jennifer walked away, Adam saw her turn back for one last look at him and he grinned. That meant she was interested. Suddenly his mobile burst into life and he answered it. 'You have my number now,' she said and ended the call. As he walked out of the supermarket, Adam felt that was the best bottle of milk he had ever bought!

Arriving at Bruce's, he handed him the milk. 'Put the kettle on and fill me in on the gossip.'

'Thank God you're here Adam. That Julie of yours does nothing but badger me. She's like a bloody firecracker.' Bruce ushered Adam into the kitchen, and put the kettle on. 'She's supposed to be going shopping or something, but she keeps texting me. She wants us to have a meeting at her place tonight. Are you okay with that?'

'Blimey, you have been busy Bruce,' Adam laughed, 'but yeah, once Julie has got the bit between her teeth, she's like a steam train. She's already filled me in on the meeting. What I want to know is about the money you've already creamed off the accounts.'

Bruce put their coffees on the kitchen table and sat down. Rubbing his face with his hands, he shook his head. 'Oh my God, it was so easy Adam. Even I couldn't believe it. We just transferred all that money into another account. Crafty Julie made up a new account in that Jamie's name and all the money has gone into it. By the way, she wants the truth out of you about how you came across Jamie and all this information. It's not my secret to tell Adam, so be warned.'

Taking a sip of his coffee, Adam nodded. 'I'll pick you up later and we'll go to hers together.' As an afterthought, Adam looked at Bruce over his coffee mug. 'You said she's been contacting you today – what does she want?'

Bruce sighed and shook his head. 'Apparently every shop she's going into she's asking if they take cryptocurrency. She's on a research trip. I'm sure we'll find out later. God, I'm afraid to look at my phone. Her brain is going at a hundred miles an hour and I can't keep up with her.'

Adam burst out laughing. 'Don't worry, you're not alone Bruce. No one can keep up with Julie. How her husband Ralph must have suffered. I'll see you later, and don't worry, she does have your best interests at heart. She isn't going to lose her star player.'

As Adam walked back to his bike, he took out his mobile and texted Jennifer.

What time do you finish work?

No sooner had he put his helmet on, his phone buzzed.

I don't finish until 10 p.m. It's the late shift. Sorry.

Not sure whether he was being given the brush-off, he texted back:

I can meet you then for a quick coffee, if you want?

Smiling, he read the reply.

That would be nice Adam. I'll meet you outside the front.

Musing to himself, Adam looked up at the bright sunny sky, even though it was still winter. Jennifer had no one to rush home to and no one was picking her up. And he could go and meet her after his meeting with Julie. Now it was time to get back to club business. Revving up his motorbike, he rode off feeling very pleased with himself.

* * *

As he rode up to the club, he noticed a couple of his bouncers-cum-henchmen outside having a smoke. He felt this was unusual because normally they went out the back of the club. As he rode up closer, he could see relief wash over their faces. 'Adam!' one shouted to him as he stopped. Slowly taking off his helmet, he watched as Ron walked up to him. 'Am I pleased to see you, Adam.' Dropping his cigarette, he stubbed it out with his shoe.

'Why do I feel this is bad news, Ron?'

'It's that bloody fool Loose-lipped Lenny... I said you should get rid of him. He's a bloody liability.'

Adam looked up and glared at him with his piercing blue eyes. 'I didn't ask for your opinion Ron, just spit it out.' Adam pushed his way past the other men at the front of the club and marched ahead with Ron hot on his heels. 'And for the record Ron, don't smoke outside the front of the club and don't drop your cigarettes on my part of the pavement or I will make you eat them – got it?'

Realising his mistake, Ron apologised. 'Sorry Adam, no offence. I will go and clear it up in a minute. But the thing is, the lads can't smoke out the back because Lenny is out there,' he explained.

Striding towards his office, Adam stopped. Taking a huge intake of breath and letting it out slowly, Adam turned to Ron and barked, 'In my office now!'

Ron knew that Adam would be angry when he told him his news. Embarrassed, he looked down at the floor, averting his gaze.

'Last night, Lenny was supposed to be doing a collection at one of the pubs. He strolled in there, pissed as a fart, demanding money off the landlord and waving a gun in his face in your name. Fuck knows where he got a gun from, but he's caused havoc. He's off his rocker.' Ron was almost breathless once he'd blurted out his story.

Running his hand through his hair, Adam listened to Ron and the more he spoke the angrier he felt. 'And how do you know all of this?'

'The landlord, Bill, called me. I've known him for years. Lenny hit him with the gun and then shot the mirrors behind the bar and all the bottles of booze, scaring a lot of people. The police will be onto it. You can't go waving a gun about these days. Lenny's off his head. He keeps repeating that you've betrayed him. Said he saw some bloke called Jimmy coming out of the club and he's Lenny's arch enemy apparently. I don't know...' Ron shrugged. 'Bill wanted me to speak to you first. I don't know about the other customers or if some bright spark has videoed it on their phone. Lenny made a quick getaway, after insulting everybody. Once I heard about it, I got one of the lads to drive around to his usual haunts and find him. He was as high as a kite and pissed, so we threw him in the car and shoved him in the outhouse in the yard.'

Adam's eyes clouded over and he glared at Ron. 'So to be absolutely clear, you brought a gunslinging drunk, potentially wanted by the police and with a pub full of witnesses, back to my club?' Lashing out fiercely, Adam slapped Ron so hard he staggered backwards. 'Why the hell would you do that? This is a respectable club. Why have we got him in our yard? Let the police have him; who cares?'

Ron stood rooted to the floor, his flushed face almost burning from the slap. Blinking hard, he shook his head to rouse himself from his dazed state. 'I didn't know what to do, boss,' he mumbled. 'But you don't call him Loose Lips for nothing. God knows what he would say to save his own skin. I just got him out of the way. I didn't think.'

'No, you didn't. I am on the end of a phone. Scarlet is on the end of a phone and yet you never called either of us you bloody fool. What do I care if that fool gets himself arrested and thrown in jail? Like I really give a fuck Ron. Everyone knows what business we're in. The police get their money and they're happy with it.' Adam's dark blue eyes pierced Ron's as he glared at him. 'Lenny is an old street soldier who collects money. What does he know about mine or Scarlet's business dealings? Unless the loose lips around here is you?' Adam looked him up and down. Ron knew a lot about their dealings. Was he to be trusted? Adam wondered to himself.

'No Adam, I'd never tell anyone what goes on behind the scenes here. Not my business...' Ron carried on speaking. 'But the money he got off Bill, well, he doesn't have it on him, and Bill swears he gave him it and I believe him Adam.'

'So, he's a gunslinging, thieving drunk, who you have brought here and landed on my doorstep. Is that what you're saying? Take me to him.'

Ron turned and walked ahead; he knew this could only end badly. Ron wished he had told Scarlet first – at least it would have all been over with now. She would have slapped him and cursed him and that would have been the end of it.

Adam walked into the yard. Hearing banging from inside the outhouse, Adam opened the wooden door and looked inside. He could see Lenny lying on the floor. He had been tied up with his hands behind his back and a gag in his mouth, making it hard from him to breathe properly. He was filthy and his clothes were blood-stained and torn. When he saw Adam, he stopped kicking at the door.

Calmly, Adam looked at the pitiful sight before him. Lenny had almost dislodged the toilet from the plumbing from his kicking and water was beginning to leak onto the floor, making his clothes wet. As Adam walked forward, Lenny cowered and shifted himself as far backwards as he could.

Reaching down, Adam ripped the gag from his mouth and threw it on the floor. While he waited, Lenny took several huge breaths.

'So, you're a cowboy now, Lenny? You walk into bars and start shooting the place up. Is that what I pay you for?' Adam calmly asked.

'It wasn't like that, boss. That landlord, Bill, he was giving me a lot of lip. And I saw you with that Jimmy bloke. He double crossed me once and I did time in prison for him. After everything I've done for you, how could you have that Jimmy here? You know we have history...'

'If an old friend of Scarlet's wishes to visit her at her premises, they can,' Adam emphasised. 'Where did you get the gun from, Lenny?'

'Dunno boss, really. I can't remember. I was out of it. What's going to happen to me?'

Looking at the pitiful creature before him, anger rose in Adam's stomach. Thankfully Lenny was a crap shot and had killed no one, but he had still been waving a gun about in public with witnesses. And Ron had brought Lenny here – why? The trail led straight back to Lambrianu's. Adam cast a sideways glance at Ron and suddenly, he realised what had happened. Ron knew Lenny and Jimmy had a history. Adam now realised that Ron had set Lenny up. He'd filled him full of booze sent him on a collection mission and given him the gun. The poison that must have dripped off Ron's tongue about Jimmy being in the vicinity would have wound this pitiful creature up. Adam was disgusted.

'You'd better get cleaned up, Lenny. You stink of piss and shit. Untie him Ron and drive him home. I'll sort this later.'

Looking up in surprise, Ron couldn't believe Adam's flippancy. 'Really boss? Is that all? Don't you want to ask him about the money?'

Fuming, Adam walked back to the office without saying another word. Scarlet looked over her gold-rimmed glasses at him. 'Is it raining?' She grinned as she looked down at his wet biker boots.

'How long have you been here?' enquired Adam.

'About ten minutes. Why? What's wrong? And don't say nothing because I know that flushed face and angry look.'

'I need a drink first, then I'll tell you.' Frowning, Adam waited until Scarlet had unscrewed the bottle of whisky and poured it into two glasses. 'I thought you were shopping with Katie and the others?'

'I am. Well, sort of, but I left my charger for my mobile here so, I've popped back to get it. What's going on?'

Taking a sip, Adam let the whisky soothe his throat and put his head back on the chair. Slowly he unravelled what had happened.

Scarlet banged her fist on the table and stood up. 'Let me go and see the little runt. I'll strangle him!' she shouted.

'No, you won't sister dear. This is my baby and I'll sort it out. Now go. Go and spend some time with Katie. Knuckles will be waiting. Seriously Scarlet, I'm not messing. Go and leave me to it.'

Calming down, Scarlet looked Adam up and down. Seeing the lack of smile on Adam's face, the anger left her and she nodded. Putting her charger in her bag, she ruffled his hair and was about to kiss him on the cheek when she remembered something. 'Adam, I'm not interfering, promise. But didn't Jimmy run off with Ron's wife? I'm not sure but something in the back of my mind says so.'

It was as though a light had been switched on in Adam's brain and closing his eyes, he remembered it too. 'Thank you, Scarlet. That's just what I needed. Go and have some fun for a change. I'll see you and Katie tomorrow. I have to be somewhere tonight.'

'A date, eh? Family before dates, Adam,' she scoffed and smiled.

'It's actually mates before dates, Scarlet!' Reaching over, he picked up the cushion from Scarlet's chair and threw it at her playfully. 'Now bloody go!'

When Scarlet had left, Adam sipped his drink and contemplated what to do next. First, he had to sort out the damage Lenny had caused at the pub. Bill would need compensating for the mess and breakages. He wondered if anyone had filmed it on their mobile phone as Ron had suggested. Or had Ron himself filmed it? Was that why he'd prompted that idea in Adam's brain? Gulping his drink back, Adam walked back out to the yard. Ron was cursing Lenny and kicking him while Lenny was curled up in a ball, begging for him to stop. This angered Adam.

Everyone knew Lenny wasn't the sharpest knife in the drawer. But he was okay for simple jobs and a lot of people knew him, even liked him.

'Ron! Do you have a problem following orders?' Adam shouted

and pushed him out of the way. Ron paled; he hadn't expected Adam to come out again. He'd been caught out like a naughty schoolboy and he didn't like it. Adam looked down at Lenny and saw tears were streaming down his face and he was holding his ribs. Blood was smeared over his face, where he had tried wiping it away. He looked pathetic.

'Just sorting him out Adam. Getting what he deserves after causing you embarrassment,' Ron said.

'And what do you deserve for bringing him here? Lenny, stand up if you can. You were okay standing up like a man last night with a gun in your hand, so stand up now you prat.' Turning to Ron, Adam wagged a finger in his face. 'No more stunts like this. After all, I haven't dealt with you yet. Now take him home like I said half an hour ago. Just do your fucking job while you have one!'

Ron paled then flushed with embarrassment in front of the other men who had been jeering him on. 'Sorry Adam mate.'

Adam turned swiftly; his ire was up. 'I am Mr Lambrianu to you, Ron. I am not your mate. I am your employer. Got it?'

Adam's sharp tongue cut through Ron like a knife. He had always been on good terms with Adam and called him by his name. 'Whatever you say, Mr Lambrianu,' Ron spat out before bending down to help Lenny up. 'Let's get you home, you waster.'

Adam watched as Ron and two others helped Lenny into a car.

Squinting one eye and holding up his finger and thumb in a gun shape towards Ron's back, Adam let out a low whistle to himself. 'Your time is up,' Adam whispered under his breath.

8

REPERCUSSIONS

Finishing off some paperwork, Adam could hear his stomach grumbling and realised he hadn't eaten since breakfast. A quirky smile crossed his face as he mused to himself that he owned restaurants but rarely got a chance to eat at them. Locking the office door, he checked to make sure there was no paperwork left around and put the alarm on before leaving.

Walking down the high street cleared his head. The sun was out and he welcomed the breeze that came with it. Popping into a local greasy spoon, he ordered a bacon sandwich.

'Mr Lambrianu, it's good to see you here. Sit down, I will make you one of my specials instead of a sandwich.' The owner smiled.

Adam looked at his watch. It was getting late. He wanted to fit in an hour at the gym before going to Julie's and a full English in his stomach wouldn't help. 'Sorry, not today, Gary. I'm going to the gym and then for a swim, but thank you. Another day, eh?'

'I will pack a few nibbles in a bag for when you finish.' Gary winked. 'I don't know you're always at the gymnasium; surely that six pack of yours doesn't need toning up any more? I suppose you do it for the ladies.' He grinned, while putting buns and sausage rolls in a bag for Adam. The cook brought Adam's sandwich through and Gary put everything on the counter.

'You're right. I would hate to disappoint the ladies, Gary.' Winking, he picked up the bags and walked out. The bacon sandwich barely touched the sides as he ate.

He'd thought about taking a car to Julie's and picking Bruce up on the way, but looking at the mounting traffic jams on the roads, he decided to take his motorbike. Bruce would have to ride pillion. He hated it, but it was the better option. At least on his bike he could dodge in and out of the traffic. Deciding to call Bruce in advance to let him know his plans, he took out his mobile. Instantly, Bruce answered and just as Adam was going to speak, Bruce blurted out, 'I'm already at Julie's.'

Surprised, Adam stood in the high street amidst all the shoppers. 'You're what? We're not due till later. I am on my way to the gym first.'

Bruce answered in a low whisper, 'She came and collected me. Feigned tiredness to the others on the shopping trip and turned up at my flat. Christ, Adam, I was in my dressing gown and she just walked in.'

Adam burst out laughing, imagining Bruce's embarrassment. 'I'm on my way.' Adam couldn't help smiling to himself as he walked back to the club. It was the only thing that had genuinely made him laugh all day. Poor Bruce. Now he was in Julie's clutches, there was no escape. But, on a more serious note, Adam knew Julie would look after him and put him at his ease. Or as much as possible considering Bruce was a nervous wreck around her.

Brushing his auburn, wavy hair back before he donned his black motorbike helmet, he pulled down the visor, revved up his bike and rode off into the traffic.

* * *

'Oh Katie, I miss you so much.' Scarlet reached over their table in Covent Garden and squeezed Katie's hand.

'I miss you too. But sometimes life gets in the way. Tell me about the business.'

Katie's weak smile bothered Scarlet and she swore she could see a tear in her eye. Scarlet's instincts told her all was not right in Katie's household. They were twins and she could sense something was very wrong with Katie but decided to leave it. This was not the time for an interrogation.

'Business is on the up, especially since Covid. The money is rolling in and Adam does most of the work. To be honest, Katie, and don't tell him I told you this, he's a very good partner. He's always coming up with new and fresh ideas.'

Katie sipped her white wine and smiled. It was nice just sitting here and having a drink with her sister. Not being mum or wife. 'You have to stop wrapping him in cotton wool, Scarlet. He's a grown man and the darling of the tabloids. Sometimes you treat him like a little boy.'

Picking up her own glass of wine, Scarlet shrugged. 'I can't help it. He's always been my little boy, even before we lost Mum and Dad. How can anyone resist those big blue eyes in that little face surrounded by his auburn hair? But I know what you mean. Knuckles has more or less said the same thing.'

'What? Knuckles strung a whole sentence together?' Katie laughed in mock surprise.

'Not exactly.' Scarlet grinned. 'He just said, "You suffocate him." So I presume that's what he meant.' Chinking their glasses together, they burst out laughing.

'Talking of Knuckles, he's looking quite the handsome man these days. Blimey, talk about making a silk purse out of a sow's ear. When I think back to how he used to look, he's definitely evolved now.'

Frowning, Scarlet looked up. 'Do you really think Knuckles is handsome?'

'Hey sis, not for me, but he is quite the eye catcher for a lot of women out there. And somewhere he must have a fortune stashed away, because he never spends anything. So, are you going to make an honest man of him?'

'Nobody could make an honest man out of Knuckles, Katie. He puts the devil to shame sometimes with all his shoplifting. Anyway, why would I marry him?'

'Come on Scarlet. Lie to the world, but not to me. You have his children. You have never remarried and we all know that Knuckles has taken up residency at your apartment. And to be honest, he's been a great dad. He loves those kids, especially when they read to him, 'cos he can hardly read,' laughed Katie. 'Crikey, he's looked after your kids more than you have, Scat. Be honest, Scarlet, how many school plays have you attended?' Katie held her hands up in submission, before Scarlet could interrupt. 'I know, not my business, but just don't take him for granted.'

A frown crossed Scarlet's brow. Katie was right, she did take Knuckles for granted. He was always there at her side and never complained. She'd never really thought about it before, but he was the only person she knew she could rely on. Maybe she had been blind. This had definitely given Scarlet food for thought.

'Come to the club tonight. Relive some good memories. Let's have dinner and drink the night away. The kids will be okay. Knuckles—' Scarlet stopped herself mid-speech, especially when she saw Katie's knowing look. She was going to say that Knuckles would keep an eye on them. 'The nanny will look after them,' she corrected herself.

'What about the others, are they coming?' asked Katie, ignoring Scarlet's slip of the tongue.

'Who knows? But they know where to find us. Adam has opted

out though; he has some young starlet to see.' Scarlet grinned. 'Diana might be able to pop by. It was good to see her today. It's so rare that we do these days, but she definitely enjoyed her shopping trip, even if Julie made her buy a leopard print top that she will never wear! She's more like Ralph than Julie realises.'

Katie nodded. 'True, Diana keeps a lot to herself and Julie misses Ralph more than she lets on. And I know she misses Mum and Dad, too. We all do, but she just hides it better.' They poured some more wine and burst out laughing.

* * *

No sooner had Adam got off his motorbike than Bruce was opening the door. 'Get in here before bloody Barbara Cartland shouts for me again!' Adam thought Bruce looked like a rabbit caught in the headlights. 'Do you know what she's done to me?' He grabbed Adam by the arm and dragged him into the hallway.

'Is it legal? You are past the age of consent.' Adam's shoulders shook with laughter. 'And what do you mean, Barbara Cartland?'

'With all her feather trimmed pink and leopard-skin kaftans, that's who she reminds me of, that author who wrote the romance books. Look at her, Adam.'

'I know of her Bruce, but it seems you know more about her than I do. Although I do see the resemblance now you mention it.'

'Oy, is he moaning about me again? Nice to see you, Adam. And you can take that sweaty leather jacket off, it doesn't impress me. You must boil to death in that. Skintight black leather with red flames shooting across it, and he thinks I dress badly.'

Adam unzipped his jacket and handed it to one of Julie's many 'companions'. Wearing only a black vest underneath, he did a twirl. 'Will this do Julie?'

Julie looked at Adam admiringly; he was indeed a handsome

man and sometimes when he caught the light he looked just like his mother. Other times, he was the spitting image of his father with those blue eyes and the cleft in his chin. 'Bloody hell, Adam, you've got muscles on top of muscles. Come on, we have business and it's very interesting thanks to my boy Brucey here.' Turning, Julie walked down the hallway into the lounge.

Bruce linked his arm through Adam's to get closer. 'She's said I'm one of her blokes, like that Lewis and the others. I'm a male prostitute for God's sake! My mother goes to church, Adam. She can't know about this.' Bruce paled as he looked at Adam.

Stunned at the news, Adam realised there had to be a perfectly good explanation for this, but for the life of him, he didn't know what it was. His eyes darted around the lounge as Julie sat lounging on the sofa with her small coffee cup.

'Oh, come in, scaredy cat. Well, it's for the best and he's just got a million pounds in his bank account.'

'Have I?' Bruce looked at Julie then back at Adam. Bruce took out his mobile and went onto his mobile banking. Sure enough, Julie had deposited a million pounds into his account.

'Well,' scoffed Adam, 'not a lot of male prostitutes get paid that, Bruce, so you must be good.'

'I have put him down as one of my employees, like the boys here. Also, if that's the case, no one will find it strange that he hangs around here a lot. I told you I would come up with something to give him his money and I have, so I will drip feed it in like wages and he will pay tax on it. Are you satisfied now, Bruce? You have some money for your mother to buy an organ for her church, for God's sake. Now, let's get on with business.'

Bruce was mesmerised by the number of zeros in his bank account. He had never had so much money in his life, and he knew there was more to come. Julie was just taking it easy.

Lewis came in holding a tray of fresh coffee with some shots of whisky on the side.

Julie looked up at Lewis and smiled. 'Lewis, Bruce thinks he's taking over your job as head boy. He's my newbie, so we will have to break him in gently.'

Lewis, with his black short back and sides and tanned muscly body looked Bruce up and down and smiled. 'Well Julie, it looks like my job's safe then.'

'You cheeky bugger. Go on, I will call you if I need you,' Julie laughed. Her fun nature was infectious. 'Right, Adam, first I want you to tell me where you met this Jamie's girlfriend and what she knows about you. I want the full story now, even the naughty bits.'

'It was quite a while ago now Julie. I popped into a wine bar in town to have a look at the competition and this woman sidled up to me with her empty cocktail glass. I offered her a drink, and in return for my drink she gave me her life story. Apparently, she'd had an argument with her boyfriend – our stockbroker friend, Jamie. I must confess I wasn't really listening at first, but one thing led to another and I ended up at her flat, hers and Jamie's flat. Afterwards, she starts trying to impress me about this boyfriend of hers who is a major stockbroker with lots of influential clients.' Adam waited for Julie to jump in and say something, especially as he had skirted over the naughty bits, but she didn't. She sat listening intently.

'Anyway, when she mentioned the money he earned my ears picked up. Then she went on to tell me that he brought his work home and that wasn't allowed because of data protection. She even showed me his laptop and she had the password, everything. The only problem was I couldn't get my hands on it. So as much as she bored me to death Julie, she gave me all of the information I wanted. There were photos of him around the flat and she told me how boring he was, going to work at the same time every day across London Bridge. My God, her mouth just ran away with her. I saw her a couple of times after that, but she started to get a bit clingy. You know me Julie, I'm not ready to settle down yet.' Adam laughed. 'In the meantime, a couple of the dealers from abroad had mentioned cryptocurrency to me. They were hinting that they would like to be paid that way rather than in cash. There are only so many places you can hide that amount of cash and banks are nosey, end of story. The rest you know, Julie.' Adam picked up his cup. His throat was dry.

'Well, the apple doesn't fall far from the tree, does it Adam?' Julie laughed. 'Are you still sleeping with her?'

Adam grinned. 'I've kept in touch. That way I knew this Jamie's whereabouts. She was my inside woman, if you like.'

'Inside and out by the sounds of it. Good. Keep it that way. Do it again and find out if he's been in touch with her and any suspicions he might have about his clients complaining about their losses.'

Adam nodded. 'I agree. We have to keep our finger on the pulse.'

'All the laptops are sorted now, too. Even Knuckles'... I got him a red one.' Bruce blushed. 'They are all ready to go. Let's watch those shares go up and down. Although, there is one thing you forgot to mention Julie.' Bruce looked up at Julie but she averted her eyes.

'Oh my God, yes!' Julie clapped her hands together. 'Bruce has been looking at those accounts and by the looks of it, that Jamie's already been creaming a little off the top. Not enough to notice, but the more Bruce delved into his financial affairs, the more we could see he's been a naughty boy, Adam. I will let you know how my appointment goes with his boss and I will say that Jamie has come recommended. After all, I am Julie Gold and his boss will lick my arse if I ask him because he knows I have so much money!'

Bruce coughed to interrupt. 'We're also official stock exchange brokers too now, so when it comes through, all transactions will go through the business and if it goes tits up, we just claim bankruptcy, like any other business.'

Amazed, Adam looked at them both grinning from ear to ear like Cheshire cats. 'Bloody hell, you have been busy. I don't know what to say to you both.'

'Nothing,' snapped Julie. 'We're partners and in it together.'

'Seriously though, Julie, thank you. Thank you for believing in my scam and helping. Me and Bruce knew we were on to something big. I owe you.'

'I saw a good opportunity and took it, the same as you did. But you will pay me back when the time is right.'

'Well, what is it you want, Julie? I would do anything for you, you know that.'

'In time, Adam. I have my own plans and you're going to help me.' She clapped her hands together. 'Enough of this serious talk, I thought you had a hot date to get to. And you, Bruce, don't you have something to plan with that windfall of yours?'

Adam looked at Julie strangely. He knew her of old by now and she had something on her mind. The way she had changed the subject after mentioning this 'thing' she wanted him to do concerned him. He suddenly had an awful feeling that she might ill. She wasn't getting any younger, so it was a possibility... but surely Julie Gold would live forever?

9

LAMBRIANU SPIRIT

Once Adam had said his farewell to Julie, kissing her fondly on the cheek, he put Bruce on the back of his motorbike and sped back into London, much to Bruce's dismay. He hated the way Adam weaved in and out of traffic and felt he went far too fast.

'Are you coming in for a coffee to talk things through? It's only 9 p.m.'

'No Bruce, there's something I have to do first. We'll catch up tomorrow.' Adam revved up his bike and leaving Bruce on the pavement, rode off.

'Evening Lenny. I just thought I would drop by and see how you are. Are you alone?' Adam asked. He had considered going to Loose-lipped Lenny's usual drinking holes, but thought better of it after the beating he had taken this morning.

'Adam. Yeah, I'm alone. No one comes to visit these days.' Lenny turned and leaving the door ajar for Adam, walked ahead into the lounge. Adam looked around at the pitiful surroundings. It was no more than a student bedsit. The wallpaper was peeling off the walls and there was damp coming through. Empty takeaway cartons were scattered on a table in the centre of the room and Adam felt queasy at the stench of the place. Although he couldn't understand it. He and Scarlet paid good wages for these street soldiers' services. If you paid them well, they didn't have the need to steal and that was what had puzzled Adam. Lenny had done a lot of jobs for him but he had never stolen money from him, and yet Ron had said Lenny had collected money from the landlord during his drunken shoot out – so where was it? He certainly hadn't spent it on his house.

Lenny looked nervous as he sat in an armchair that had seen better days and wrung his hands together. 'Do you mind if I smoke, Adam?' Adam shook his head and watched Lenny pick up an old tobacco tin and start rolling up a cigarette. 'What can I do for you? You've never been to visit before.'

Adam looked at the pathetic picture before him. 'It seems you have a problem with Jimmy visiting me. Well, let me tell you Lenny, whatever history is between you, I can't stop old friends visiting Scarlet, can I? But how did you see him when you weren't around that day? If I remember rightly, you were driving some of the strippers from the club to Scarlet's salon to have their sunbed top-ups, weren't you?'

Lenny took out a bottle of whisky that was stuffed down the side of his chair. Opening it, he took a gulp then offered it to Adam.

Adam shook his head. 'I'm on my bike Lenny. Answer the question please.'

'I went to prison for him, Adam. Two years I did and I kept my mouth shut. We did a robbery together and Jimmy grassed me to the police to save his own skin. He told them I'd took our booty to his house and left it there. He was charged as an accessory and got a suspended sentence. I did the jail time. He smiled at me when they took me out of the dock in court. Never sent me a penny to see me through those days. I thought you were stabbing me in the back, Adam.' Nervously, Lenny took another gulp of his whisky.

Adam's soothing voice wafted over to Lenny. 'I appreciate your loyalty, Lenny. Who told you Jimmy had popped into the club to see Scarlet, and more to the point, who gave you the gun?'

Lenny burst into tears and rubbed his face, embarrassed at falling apart in front of Adam. 'You know who, Adam, or you wouldn't be asking. You already have your answers. You're as crafty as a fox you are. So why are you asking?'

Adam nodded in agreement; they both understood each other without saying anything. 'Where is the money, Lenny? You took money off of Bill. So where is it?'

'I don't have it, Adam. I don't know, really, I don't. I'm not lying to you. I must have dropped it or lost it when I left the pub. I don't remember Adam, honestly, I don't.' Lenny's eyes filled with tears again and Adam watched as they ran down Lenny's swollen face.

'Okay, Lenny. I just needed to check. We go back a long way. Take the week off on full pay and not a word that I've been here. Get some sleep and I'll drop by a takeaway in the high street and get them to send you some food over.'

'Is that it, Mr Lambrianu? You're not going to kill me?' Wide eyed and shocked, Lenny put his hands to his swollen face and rubbed it.

'No, I'm not going to kill you, but answer me this: where is the gun now? What did you do with it when you left the pub?'

'I put it inside my coat, but it's not there now and I'm shitting myself because it will have my DNA all over it. I didn't shoot anyone. Too pissed, couldn't fire straight. I am sorry for causing you embarrassment, Mr Lambrianu.'

'You're going to work in south London for a while Lenny, out of the way. Everyone knows what you did and you need to keep your head down and your mouth shut. You owe me Lenny.'

'South London? They're evil bastards over there. Torture you if you step out of line.' Panicking, Lenny reached forward and grabbed Adam's hand, kissing the back of it. 'Please Mr Lambrianu, not with that lot, I wouldn't survive. I know you all work together, but those yardies who work for you are mean bastards – please Adam!' Lenny fell to his knees.

Adam mentally agreed with him. The yardies were a law unto themselves. His father had befriended and killed Marlon, the head of them, before taking over his turf and leaving his friend Angus to run it. Marlon's yardies had worked for his father and now worked for Scarlet and himself. They were good businessmen and there were no quarrels. 'I'll sort it Lenny, I promise. But you have to be out of the picture for a while.' Adam looked at his watch. He needed to leave to be able to get to Jennifer on time. But he had one last thing to do first.

Leaving a sobbing Lenny behind, Adam saw a Chinese take-away. Stopping, he put in his order and asked them to deliver it to Lenny's address as promised.

Then he decided to make his way over to Ron's house. When he got there, he parked down a side street. He could see people leaving Ron's and making their way home. As he walked closer to Ron's house he noticed his side gate was open and decided to go around the back. If there were people there, he mused to himself, then he would leave and wait for another time to pay Ron a visit.

Ron's garden was a bit of a mess. There were glasses and empty bottles of beer scattered around and, in the middle, he saw Ron with his back to him on his own, standing above a barbeque.

In the dimness of the garden with only a few fairy lights strewn about, Adam said, 'Hello Ron.' Adam kept his helmet on and just raised the visor so Ron could see him.

Startled, Ron turned around. 'Adam, what are you doing here? Or should I say, Mr Lambrianu?' he added sarcastically, obviously feeling braver now that he had been drinking.

'I saw people coming out of your house as I was passing and thought I would pop in to say hello and that the matter with Lenny has been sorted. Although there was something I wanted to ask you.'

Adam watched as Ron took the grill off the barbeque and threw it to the ground. The charcoal in the barbeque was still glowing red. 'I'm glad you sorted that Lenny out. You should have let me finish him off; he's nothing but a waster embarrassing you like that.'

Ignoring his comments, Adam walked closer. 'It looks like you've had a good night. What's the barbeque in aid of?'

'Just a neighbourly get together. It keeps the wife happy.'

'It's a bit early to finish a party, isn't it? Where is everyone?' Adam smiled.

'They've all got work in the morning and the wife has gone to pick up some more cigarettes from the garage up the road and left me to dowse the barbeque before bed. Christ, why is it no one ever comes around with their own fags? All night long they want to smoke and no one ever thinks of running home and picking up theirs. What do they think I am, a fucking tobacconist? But, as I say, it keeps the wife happy and in with the neighbours,' Ron scoffed.

Adam smiled to himself. Without thinking, Ron had just informed him he was on his own, but only for a few minutes; his wife would be back soon. That was long enough to finish what he'd started.

'I've come for my money, Ron. You know, the money you took off Lenny that he'd collected from that pub. I know you took it off him when you picked him up, and the only reason you went looking for him was to get your gun back.'

In disgust, Ron looked him in the face. Still holding the barbeque fork, he waved it in the air directly at Adam. 'I haven't taken anything from Lenny. He's a loose cannon and was pissed off about you betraying him. You can buy guns easily if you know the right people. So don't come around here accusing me. I was trying to protect your good name after his shambles attempt at frightening everyone. It was your money he was collecting.'

'And it was your wife that Jimmy ran off with. You had a bigger grudge to bear.' Adam could feel his hackles rising as he watched Ron pointing the long-handled fork towards him. 'Why does everyone think I'm a soft touch, Ron, just because I don't scream and shout like Scarlet? I find shouting a waste of precious time.'

Stepping even closer to Ron and the barbeque, Adam glared at Ron through the gap in his visor. 'And why the fuck are you lying to me and thinking you can get away with it?'

Still wearing his thick leather gloves, Adam reached out and grabbed Ron by the hair, making Ron lash out. 'No Adam, no!' Fear gripped Ron as he looked down at the red-hot coals. Forcefully, Adam pulled Ron's face down onto the burning charcoal and held it there. Ron's screams became muffled and the smell of his burning flesh and singeing hair filled Adam's nostrils, making him almost gag. Feeling a burning sensation through his thick gloves, Adam let go and watched as Ron fell into a heap on the floor. His body was spasming, and his face was unrecognisable with the melted, charred flesh.

Satisfied, Adam leaned over to get a better look at Ron in the dimly lit garden. He was still breathing slightly, although it was laboured. Calmly, Adam walked around the other side of the barbeque. The heat was so intense, Adam could feel the sweat pouring down his face inside his helmet as he kicked the barbeque over onto Ron's body. Surveying the scene, Adam realised it looked like a drunken accident. Much better and easier to explain.

He felt sorry for Lenny and knew he'd been a pawn in Ron's game but he couldn't have him walking the streets again bragging about how he'd got away with his drunken shootout. The yardies would see to that. He must remember to call them in the morning, he mused to himself. Lenny had had his last supper on him and that made him feel better, but as he'd been told many times by Scarlet, there was no sentiment in business.

Adam knew his alibis were tight; he had been with Julie, dropped off Bruce and was now on his way to meet Jennifer. Although, looking at his watch, he realised he would be later than he'd hoped, but only by minutes once he'd dodged the traffic.

Ron's shirt smouldered and ignited, and Adam left the burning corpse behind him and walked out of the garden. Carefully looking both ways up the street, Adam walked around the corner to his motorbike and revved it up. 'You will never look me in the face and lie to me again you bastard,' he muttered to himself as he rode off.

10

IT'S A KIND OF MAGIC

Glancing at his watch, Adam could see that he was fifteen minutes late. The supermarket was in darkness, and only a few cars littered what was usually a full car park. Cursing himself as he pulled up outside the supermarket, Adam took off his helmet, unzipped his leather jacket and welcomed the cool breeze upon his sweaty body. He could still smell the stench of Ron's burning flesh in his nostrils. Pushing his hand through his damp hair, he could feel it drying. Leaving his helmet on the seat, he walked around to the back of the motorbike and opened the box on the back of it. Taking out a bottle of aftershave, he put some in his hands and rubbed his face and under his arms, then ran his hands through his drying wavy hair. Then taking out a bottle of water, he quenched his thirst.

He was just about to put his helmet back on when he saw a light coming from the side of the supermarket. A wide grin crossed his face when he saw a group of women leaving the shop. At the back was Jennifer. She waved to the others before running into the car park and looking around. Adam flashed his headlights in her direction, and seeing him, she ran towards him.

Breathless, Jennifer stood before him. 'Oh my God, I am so

sorry Adam. I thought you might have left. Have you been waiting long? The supervisor wanted a quick word about our shifts. I am so sorry,' Jennifer blurted out.

Adam put his hand up to stop her. 'No matter, you're here now.'

His soothing, velvety voice calmed her and she smiled. 'Thank you for waiting.'

Adam went around the back of his bike and took out the spare helmet he carried. 'Are you okay to ride on the back? I thought we could go for a coffee or something, or would you prefer something stronger?' He smiled.

'I wouldn't mind a coffee. I've never ridden on the back of a bike before, but, if I'm going to, I might as well start with a Harley-Davidson, eh?' She laughed.

'It's always better to start at the top and work your way down in my opinion.' Adam grinned and gave her a sly wink before he put on his own helmet.

Waiting while she adjusted herself, he turned to look behind him. 'Hold on tight, this could be a rocky ride. Put your arms around my waist.' Pulling his visor down, Adam revved up his bike and going slightly faster than normal, he sped around the huge empty car park. He could feel Jennifer nervously wrapping her arms around his waist tightly. This was a rare experience for Adam. He had only had one or two people on the back of his bike, but normally the women he dated either met him at the club or expected to be picked up in a car. None of his starlets wanted to ruin their hair or smudge their make-up putting on a helmet. Adam liked the feeling of her body so close to his as she clung to him, and he could feel a tingling sensation as the speed of the bike began to excite him.

Adam made a point of stopping at a twenty-four-hour café. He was sorry it was such a short ride because he had enjoyed the nearness of her. 'That was amazing, although I feel you do go beyond the speed limit,' she said, passing Adam her helmet.

'Rules are meant to be broken. Are you hungry Jennifer?' he asked as he walked up to the tables.

'I'm starving, but aren't we supposed to have a drink first?' She giggled. 'A girl at work says you should go for drinks first, then if you get on, you order dinner or else you're stuck with your partner until the meal is served.'

'Well, why don't we rush in and bite the bullet? People have been known to walk out in the middle of dinner and I won't be offended if you do,' he laughed.

Sitting down and placing their food order, Adam looked at the beautiful young woman before him. She wore no make-up and her light brown hair had blonde highlights in it. Her warm brown eyes smiled when she did, and were surrounded by long lashes.

Adam took off his leather jacket. He was wearing only a black vest underneath and he saw the admiring glance in her eyes. He flexed the well-formed muscles in his tanned arms.

He grinned. 'I must say, you're a vision of loveliness.'

Adam watched her cheeks turn pink with embarrassment. 'I could say the same about you. You have beautiful blue eyes and that dimple in your chin sets off your whole face.' She blushed. 'I really shouldn't be saying that should I, or your ego will grow.' She laughed a warm, genuine laugh.

'My ego is already growing because I'm here with you.' Adam's soft, velvety voice floated towards her, and he could see she felt nervous. Changing the subject quickly, Adam commented on her suntan. 'Have you been on holiday recently? You look like you've been in the sun.'

'I go away a lot for work and it's usually in the sunshine.'

Adam frowned. 'Work? You get that much sunshine in a super-market?' He laughed.

'No, the supermarket is helping me pay for my master's degree. I'm a marine biologist. A very low paid one at the moment.' She grimaced. 'But when I get my master's, my prospects will improve.'

Adam looked at her in amazement. 'A marine biologist? Well, brains as well as beauty. So, I presume that means you go deep-sea diving amongst all the fish?'

'We spend a lot of time in the laboratory, but, yes, that is where my tan is from. My friends call me the eco warrior because I'm helping to save the planet. But I love it. I love the freedom of being underwater watching all the beautiful colours of the fish and coral. But it's an expensive degree and that's why I work odd shifts. I work a lot of nights so I can do my lectures during the day.' Adam watched as her eyes sparkled with excitement while she passionately talked about her work.

Realising she had let her mouth run away with itself, she looked down at the table. 'I'm sorry, I'm boring you, aren't I? Maybe we should have just ordered drinks.'

'No, you're not boring me Jennifer. On the contrary, you're a one-off. Obviously, there are marine biologists but you're definitely the first I've met. I've snorkelled before, and I do know what you mean about the freedom of the sea. Do you swim in a pool as well, or do you have to be surrounded by sharks and fish?' He laughed. Gazing at her, Adam mentally thought about how her slim figure would look in a bathing suit, but tried to dismiss the image as he could feel a swelling in his groin.

'Yes, I do and I have swum with dolphins, just not sharks yet. Maybe I should have been a fish.' She grinned.

Adam impulsively reached out and took her hand. 'I would say you're a beautiful mermaid. Captivating the sea bed with your beauty.' Adam smiled, showing a perfect set of white teeth.

Adam noticed she didn't pull her hand away but to his annoyance, the waitress appeared with their food and put the plates on the table, forcing him to move his hand away. When she'd left, Jennifer met his gaze. 'Well, I know you work at Lambrianu's, but what do you do there?' she asked.

Instantly Adam was on his guard. He didn't want to spoil the moment and tell her he owned it. He was enjoying himself, and felt that saying that would ruin the connection between them.

'I'm the gopher,' he laughed. 'I do whatever needs to be done, especially keeping an eye out for people smuggling in their own drinks.' As she laughed at his joke he felt that he had dodged a bullet.

'Well, if you're going to be the gopher Adam, you may as well do it in a swanky, top-class place like that. I could hardly believe it when we were told we were going there for the Christmas party. It's such a beautiful place, full of celebrities that you only see on the television. I swear,' she said excitedly, 'most of the evening me and the girls just sat there star spotting!'

Feeling uncomfortable with the conversation, Adam picked up his cutlery and began to eat. For the first time in his life, he didn't know what to say. Usually, the women he met at the club all knew who he was. Now he felt like the fish out of water!

After a few moments, Adam reached out and with his finger, wiped a little bit of food from the corner of her mouth, and licked his finger. Their eyes met as they looked at each other. It felt as though no one else was in the café, they were so engrossed in each other.

Adam felt at ease as the conversation moved away from his work. It made a nice change to not discuss business and to listen to normal day-to-day things in other people's lives. After a while, he felt it was time to bring up one subject that hadn't been mentioned. 'Are you seeing anyone in particular? I notice you're not wearing a wedding ring, but that doesn't mean a lot these days, does it?'

Jennifer shook her head vehemently. 'Of course not or I

wouldn't be here, would I? No partner and no children. That's the only downside to my job. There are times when I am away for weeks at a time and that doesn't help build a healthy relationship, does it? What about you? Is there a Mrs Adam waiting for you back at home? You must meet some beautiful women working in that club.'

'No and I don't have children either. Although I'm no virgin,' he laughed and hearing his warm, infectious laugh, so did Jennifer.

'Thank God, because neither am I.'

The hours seemed to fly by and in no time at all it was time to pay the bill. Taken aback and shocked, Adam saw Jennifer take out her purse. 'We'll go Dutch,' she said seriously.

'Dutch? What the hell are you doing?' he almost shouted at her. 'I invited you out. I don't remember saying to bring your purse!' Adam bit his tongue as he saw the smile drop from her face. 'Sorry, I just meant, this is my treat,' he reasoned. In all of his life he had never had a woman prepared to pay her half of the bill. He didn't even realise that actually happened. Half of him felt insulted that she felt he couldn't pay the bill and the other half cursed himself for flying off the handle. He didn't want to ruin this evening.

Blushing, Jennifer looked at him apologetically. 'I didn't mean any offence Adam. Let's make it my turn to pay next. That is if there is a next time?'

Adam's charming smile reassured her all was well. 'I would like to think there will be a next time, if you would like to meet up. And I will make sure I pick the most expensive restaurant in London if you're paying!' he laughed. 'Are you working tomorrow?'

'I have lectures from 11 a.m. til 2 p.m. and then I'm writing my notes up at home. I'm not back in work until the day after, when I'm supposed to be having a study at home day,' she sighed. Already, she felt it sounded like a lot of excuses and this had been her problem in the past. She was always busy and it was hard to find someone to slot into her lifestyle.

'Where is home? Do you live with your parents?' Adam asked.

'I share a flat with two other girls from university, in Croydon. We're not on the same courses, but it keeps the costs down. What about you, where do you live?'

For a moment Adam wasn't sure how to answer. He had his apartment above the club in the heart of the West End which he shared with no one, apart from the regular women that shared his bed. Or there was his family home in Southend with Lambrianu welded into the large iron gates. Thinking quickly, he decided on the latter. 'Southend.'

'Oh wow, right by the seaside. That must be lovely. All that fresh air,' she gushed. 'I want to live by the sea someday. And at least you don't have to go far for fish and chips.' She smiled. 'It's a long trek to work for you though, isn't it?'

'It's not too bad, especially by motorbike. At least I'm not sat in constant traffic all the time.' Swallowing hard and trying to think on his feet, Adam had no idea what was coming out of his mouth. 'I spend a lot of time at the club and there are living quarters above it if it gets too late.' Adam winced inside; the lies were growing and he hated it. Living quarters? It was a plush, three-bedroom apartment. Then Adam had a thought; it wasn't a lie and it was something else to talk about. 'Actually, I am starting up a coin exchange for cryptocurrency with my friend Bruce. We're just waiting for the registration to come through.'

'Cryptocurrency? I'm impressed. Does it make money?'

'It's like any normal currency, it goes up and down with inflation. But stay away from the cold callers. If you want to invest, go to a proper broker.'

'Maybe I will come to you and be your first customer, that is if I had any spare cash,' she laughed.

'That's a deal.' Adam knew they had to leave but he didn't want to and for the first time in his life he didn't want to rush this. More to the point, he couldn't. God knew he couldn't take her back to his place and it sounded like hers was crowded.

'Do you fancy a walk? Maybe we could ride up to the marina; it's lovely around there.'

Adam nearly choked on the last remnants of his Coke. 'A walk?'

'Yeah, it will help the food digest and it might be nice. Although it is late, so if you need to go home, I understand.'

Adam looked at her. Obviously she felt the same way as himself and didn't want the night to end. A walk hadn't exactly been what he'd had in mind. In fact, it was the first time a woman had ever asked him to go for a walk. This was definitely a new experience. He could see she was embarrassed and was probably kicking herself, considering how cold it was outside.

'A walk sounds good,' he said.

They left the café, got on his bike and rode off into the winter night.

* * *

'What the fuck are you doing?' Scarlet asked as she walked over to the corner of the bar where Knuckles was stood. Beside him was a woman talking to him. Suddenly everything that Katie had said earlier came to her mind. 'You're disturbing my employee while he's working. What is so important?' Scarlet spat out at the young woman.

'I was just talking; he was stood here all alone and I just thought I'd say hello. Christ, what's your problem?' The young woman, who was in a skintight, low-necked dress, flicked her long brown hair over her shoulder in a stubborn stance.

'My problem, dear, is that you're disturbing my employee, and flick those extensions at me once more and I will pull them out by the cheap clips they are held on with. Now fuck off.'

Tutting, the young woman walked away, and Scarlet moved closer to Knuckles. 'Since when could you string a sentence together and chat up women in my bar?'

'Wasn't. She was talking to me.' Knuckles picked up his orange juice and took a sip.

'About what? What did she say?' Scarlet stood there with her hands on both hips and demanded to know why Knuckles was entertaining a woman younger than herself in her own club.

'Dunno, I wasn't listening. Why?' he answered dryly. Knuckles' response put a half smile on her face, and she actually felt sorry for the poor woman who had been laughing and flirting to absolutely no avail. Trying to flirt with Knuckles was like putting oil on water; nothing happened.

'She asked me to dance,' Knuckles announced proudly and took another sip of his drink.

'I thought you said you weren't listening? Well, you bloody heard that, didn't you! Did you tell her that you wear a size-sixteen shoe, and your clod hoppers take up the whole dance floor?'

'Don't like dancing. Dance sometimes with Teddy though, she teaches me.' Teddy was their daughter and this was a piece of information Scarlet had missed. She had never seen him dance with Teddy and the news took the wind out of her sails.

Blushing slightly, Scarlet did her best to think of a retort. 'Well, twinkle toes, no wonder she's got flat feet!' Scarlet was glad it was dimly lit in the club; she could feel herself blushing with embarrassment as it dawned on her just how much she had neglected her duties as a parent. Katie was making her paranoid about Knuckles and for once she felt vulnerable. She had never considered her life without him.

Standing there beside him, Scarlet looked at Knuckles closely, something she hadn't done in a long time. He was always there, but she felt slightly ashamed that she hadn't really looked at him properly. Not in the way Katie had. Katie had seen what other women would see. He was indeed very tall, and wide, but definitely not fat. In his black tuxedo he cut quite the figure. His hair was more of a salt and pepper these days, rather than the black he'd had when they'd first met.

'Just do your job Knuckles and keep an eye on the place and those bouncers that seem to be taking longer breaks than usual.' Scarlet turned and walked back to her table to join Katie and Diana. Diana laughed and looked over her glass at Scarlet. 'If I didn't know you better Scarlet, I'd say you were jealous,' she laughed.

'Don't be ridiculous.' Scarlet blushed. 'He's just ignoring his duties and charming young women isn't what I pay him for,' she snapped.

Katie and Diana burst out laughing. It was almost a belly laugh from them both. 'Knuckles, charming the women!' they laughed again. 'That would be a first!'

'Well, maybe that's pushing it a little.' Scarlet had no explanation as to why she had made a scene. It was ridiculous. She would never be jealous over Knuckles... would she?

* * *

Walking along the marina with all the yachts and boats at the quayside, Adam felt Jennifer slip her hand into his. The moon shone on the water, lighting it up. Not a word was spoken between them, but as they walked further, Adam felt a sense of doom wash over him. Further up he could see Scarlet's yacht. Emblazoned on the side of it was 'Lambrianu', so there was no mistaking who it belonged to and he knew Jennifer would ask questions about the yacht and the owner of the club if she noticed it. This wasn't a conversation he wanted to get into. Not now, not tonight.

'It's getting late Jennifer, maybe it's time we walked back to the bike and I dropped you off home. Didn't you say you had lectures in the morning?'

'I suppose so,' she answered. 'I can't believe we've been out here for so long. I've definitely got my steps in!' Making light of the situation, Jennifer agreed that it was time to leave and slowly they walked back to the motorbike. Adam felt a chemistry that he couldn't explain, and the moment would have been perfect for a first kiss, but he thought better of it.

Riding through the empty streets, Adam's mind was in turmoil. He wanted to tell her the truth about who he really was, but he didn't want to break the spell and, he reasoned with himself, what did it matter? It had been a nice evening, like so many other nice evenings he had had. Why spoil things?

Jennifer handed him her helmet and watched him put it in the box at the back of the bike. She stood on the pavement, smiling at him, waiting for that first kiss. But Adam never took his helmet off. Instead, he told her to get some rest and thanked her for a nice evening. Seeing her face drop with disappointment, he waited while she turned and put her key in the door. Once she was safely indoors, he revved up his bike and rode off without a backward glance or a wave.

11

MISGIVINGS

'I'm interested in this cryptocurrency; it seems everyone is talking about it and your firm's name came up. Apparently, you have a very good worldwide reputation Mr Noakes.' Julie, wearing her best mink coat, stared at the suited man in front of her across the desk. She donned her diamonds and furs, knowing this would be the sprat to catch the mackerel.

Almost stammering and giving Julie a confident smile, Mr Noakes straightened his tie. 'You're right Mrs Gold, we have all of the inside knowledge you need to double your money. Of course,' he faltered, 'shares go up as much as they go down but we have vigilant staff who can advise you on this. I personally would look after your account.' He grinned. 'Just how much were you thinking of investing?'

'Oh, just a million pounds to start with. Better to start small than lose a fortune,' Julie purred. She watched as his eyes lit up. She knew he had done his homework and he knew who she was. He was almost salivating at the prospect of getting his greedy hands on her money. Julie smiled at him and with her long red fingernails, took out her gold cigarette case. 'Do you mind if I smoke? I always get nervous when I discuss money. I'm not always sure I am doing the right thing. It's awkward not having my husband around to advise me. I have to rely on the expertise of strangers.'

'No, no, go ahead.' Mr Noakes stood up and opened a window. Spying him, Julie knew he didn't particularly like the idea of her smoking, and it would probably set off the smoke alarms in the building, but he was prepared to sacrifice that to get his hands on her money. She could already see his eyes counting up the commission he would receive.

Her bright red painted lips blew the smoke from her long, gold cigarette holder into the air, almost making Mr Noakes cough and choke, which made her smile. 'While I was discussing this project with my friends, a name of one of your employees came up.' Julie tapped her chin with her red fingernails as though deep in thought. 'A Jamie something... I can't quite recall. Apparently, he had been looking after one of my associates and had done rather well for them. Maybe if he has that golden touch he could look after my investment, with your help of course, Mr Noakes. I'm sure your experience in these matters would be more than valuable.'

Wide eyed, Mr Noakes looked at her, and Julie could see he was in a blind panic trying to recall his employee who she'd mentioned. This confirmed her suspicions. This Jamie was nothing but a cog in the big wheels of the exchange. He was on the first step of a very long ladder and desperate to make a name for himself.

'Jamie, ah yes,' Mr Noakes said, 'one of our best,' he lied. 'He comes highly recommended. I would be more than happy for him to take you through the proceedings and help you.'

Unexpectedly, Julie stood up. 'Well, Mr Noakes, do you mind if I think about it for a day or two? I don't like to rush into things. As I say, I'm a widow and have no one to turn to for advice. I just want to make sure I'm doing the right thing – is that okay?' She reached out her diamond ringed hand to shake his. Reluctantly, he shook it and reassured her that she could take all the time she needed. He also gave her his well-rehearsed sales pitch about cryptocurrency and told her not to wait too long. After all, time was money, and she could be losing out on a fortune already.

Julie's bright red lips formed a smile across her face and she assured him she would be in touch soon. She spied his cheap suit and grey hair with distaste, wondering to herself why, if he was so good at business, he didn't buy himself a better suit. More to the point, why didn't he have his finger on the pulse and know his workforce and what they were doing? These offices smelled of bad management, but that just confirmed how easy it would be to rip them off. They might be good, but she was much, much better!

Mark, Julie's driver, got out to open the car door for her when he saw her coming out of the offices. He'd been Ralph's driver for many years and she trusted him implicitly. Once in the back of the car, he looked over his shoulder. 'How did it go?' he asked.

'The guy's a dickhead. He doesn't know that his firm is being ripped off for thousands of pounds by some junior no-mark, but odds on he will chase this meeting up to get his sticky hands on my money.'

'Working for Mrs Julie Gold will add a lot of weight to his client list. He will earn more than commission. He will be rubbing his hands together, wondering how many of your influential friends you will introduce him to,' Mark laughed.

Picking up her mobile, she dialled Bruce's number. 'You took your time answering. What are you doing?' she snapped.

'I'm at work, Julie. You know I work for a living,' he sighed. 'Can I call you back? I need somewhere more private to talk.'

'Okay, just letting you know I've had my meeting with old greedy bollocks. We'll speak later. How are your watchers doing? Are they earning their money?'

'I will check on them later Julie, but it's still early days. Let them concentrate on their jobs. Rome wasn't built in a day.'

'Well, it bloody would have been if I'd been there. Just make sure they're not falling asleep in front of those expensive laptops.' With that, Julie ended the call, then rested back on the seat. 'For God's sake, Mark, do I have to take care of everything?'

'No, but you like to Julie.' He looked in the rear-view mirror and smiled at her.

* * *

'Where the bloody hell is Adam?' Scarlet shouted down the corridor from her office. She didn't know who was down there, but she knew somebody would be listening. Nobody answered. Throwing down her pen, she got up from her desk and walked down the corridor. The cleaners were busy around the club, and two or three of the bouncers were hanging around talking to the strippers and having a coffee.

'Oy, you two,' Scarlet shouted towards the men. 'Didn't you hear me shouting? Where's Adam? Have you seen him? And you lot.' Scarlet pointed at the strippers. 'Why are you here this early?'

'It's measurement day, Scarlet... We always come in at the beginning of the month to check our rotas and make sure we haven't put on weight,' one snapped at her.

'Well, where is Linda?' Scarlet snapped back, embarrassed at having forgotten. 'Shouldn't she be putting you on the scales instead of watching you chat to these pair of monkeys? After all, I think your shifts might change looking at that arse of yours; it's starting to resemble the back end of the *Titanic*. Mind your mouth and remember who you're talking to.'

Lambrianu's was known for its prestige and perfection and so Scarlet and Adam left nothing to chance. The club had a good reputation and the last thing they wanted was overweight women with everything going south. The club provided the strippers with a rail of sequinned and diamante costumes to wear, but they were all one size, and if it didn't fit you were out.

Linda, the entertainment manager, had been employed by Adam. She had been a stripper at the club, but on reaching thirty-five had been made redundant. But Adam felt she was worth rehiring in a different capacity. She knew what was expected of the girls. She knew the ways of the club and she knew who thought they could chat up the punters for extra money, which was a no-go at the club, but they tried it anyway. She knew the bitchiness and the fights behind the scenes. Linda knew every trick in the book simply because she had done it all herself. Against Scarlet's protests, Adam had employed Linda as entertainment manager on probation and she had jumped at the chance, glad of still having a job, and if anything, she was more of a tyrant than himself or Scarlet could ever be. The regular punters liked seeing their old favourite walking amongst them in a full evening gown, playing hostess, asking them if they were having a good time while filling up their glasses with champagne, encouraging them to buy more. She was loyal and she was good at her job and ruled the strippers with a rod of iron and kept everything running smoothly.

Linda walked into the centre of the club floor with her clipboard and scales. Seeing Scarlet, she stopped, not wanting to interfere.

'I wondered where you were, Linda,' Scarlet snapped. 'These girls think it's speed dating night with my bouncers.'

'It's just turned 11 a.m. Ms Lambrianu, I always start my weigh-ins at 11 a.m. after the girls have had a late night.' Linda scowled at the women stood near the bouncers. 'If you're not here to work, leave now.'

Embarrassed, the women went and stood in line with the others who were queuing for their weigh-in. 'Good, then with your permission, Ms Lambrianu, I will begin. Are your bouncers staying to watch?'

Scarlet turned to the men. 'No, they bloody well aren't. You lot, fuck off and find something to do. Carry on, Linda. Incidentally, have you seen Adam?' Scarlet asked in a more civilised tone.

'I saw him at about 9 a.m. when I arrived, but I haven't seen him since,' replied Linda.

Nodding, Scarlet turned on her pink high-heeled court shoe and walked back down to the office, where Knuckles was waiting.

'Where have you been? I've had to wander around here looking for Adam myself.'

'Driving. Adam went out early,' he answered nonchalantly.

'Driving where? Christ, can't anyone give straight answers any more?' Exhausted and irritated, Scarlet sat back at her desk and yawned.

'Dropped kids off for their school trip.'

'Oh yeah, I'd forgotten. They are going skiing for the week aren't they?' Scarlet blushed. Yet again, without realising it, Knuckles had just scored another point. Knuckles had got up early and made a point to say goodbye to the kids before they left. Inwardly, Scarlet cursed herself.

'Did they get the school bus okay? They are flying from Gatwick, aren't they?' Scarlet asked.

'No, I drove them to Gatwick. Told the teachers.'

'Why the hell did you do that? That's all part of the trip, going with their friends and teachers on the coach to the airport. I presume you told the teachers where you would meet them?'

'My kids. Do what I want. Got there before the teachers.'

'That's because you're a getaway driver Knuckles. Coaches don't drive like you.' Exasperated, Scarlet shook her head. 'Never mind, as long as they got off safely and have plenty of spending money. I

gave them £500 each. I suppose you slipped them something extra?'
Scarlet spied him suspiciously. She knew he would have.

'Grand.'

'A grand each? For God's sake, Knuckles, they are only going for
a week!' Scarlet wanted to laugh, but felt the occasion didn't call
for it.

'My kids, my rules,' answered Knuckles with a shrug, and
walked out of the office leaving Scarlet shaking her head in dismay.

12

JEKYLL AND HYDE

'Bill, it's good to see you working hard this morning.' Adam gave a welcoming and reassuring smile as he walked into the pub. 'You really should keep the doors locked while you're bottling up on a morning; anyone could walk in.' Adam laughed.

Bill, the landlord of the pub where Lenny had caused chaos, was emptying the glasswasher and looked horrified to see Adam. He had dreaded this meeting and had been surprised it had taken so long.

'Mr Lambrianu, what brings you here? It's not collection day,' Bill stammered.

'Just a social visit, Bill. Just making sure everything's okay. After all, I wouldn't be doing my job if I didn't come round to see if you had any concerns, would I?'

Bill paled and knew there was trouble in store. Adam never visited for a social call; it was usually only ever at Bill's request. 'Can I get you a drink or something?' Noticing Adam's motorbike helmet in his hand, he smiled weakly. 'An orange juice maybe?'

'That would be nice Bill, thank you.' Adam smiled. His velvety voice unnerved Bill. He knew from old when Adam's voice was steady and soothing it usually came with a knife in your back. Swallowing hard, Bill picked up a glass, put some ice in it and poured from a carton of orange juice.

Making himself comfortable on the barstool, Adam took a sip of his drink. 'You know what's bothered me, Bill?' Adam questioned, and watched Bill shake his head. 'It's been a few days now since you had trouble in here and still there are no messages or missed calls on my mobile from you. Scarlet hasn't got any either, and you know we're always on call. So, tell me Bill, why haven't you told us you had a spot of trouble? Why have I had to come to you and find out?'

Bill averted his eyes from Adam's and began polishing a glass with his tea towel. 'Oh, that, well, I didn't want to bother you with that. I knew it would get sorted out one way or another. Ron took charge of the situation.'

Taking another sip of his drink, Adam put the glass down and smiled reassuringly. 'That's another thing that's bothered me. Why did you ring Ron? Myself, Scarlet and Knuckles decide what needs to be done and who to send. Why Ron?' Adam raised his eyebrows, waiting for an answer.

'I don't know, Mr Lambrianu; I just panicked, I suppose. I've known Ron a long time. I didn't think and I knew that Lenny prat worked for you. It wasn't like some stranger had come in, was it? You could see he was off his head on booze and the usual drugs he took.' Bill looked at Adam with contempt when he spoke of Lenny.

'Where's the money and the gun, Bill? Lenny didn't have either on him and doesn't know what happened to them. On that score I believe him. So, tell me, what did Ron promise his old buddy Bill?'

Bill almost dropped the glass in his hand and looked at Adam wide eyed. 'I haven't done anything Mr Lambrianu,' he stammered. 'I don't know what you're talking about, I swear. Whatever Ron told you is a lie!'

'Poor Ron, haven't you heard about him?' Adam beckoned Bill

with his finger. Frowning, Bill put his head closer to Adam's. Adam grasped his motorbike helmet in his hand and with one fleeting swoop, hit Bill over the head with it, knocking him off balance and making him fall to the floor.

Blood poured from the side of Bill's head. Dazed, he rubbed at it with the cloth he was still holding. Through blinking, watery eyes he looked up at Adam. The hard blow had almost knocked him senseless, although he felt that Adam could have hit him harder with it if he'd wanted to. His heart was pounding in his chest and the searing pain he felt made his head throb even more.

Nonchalantly, Adam picked up his drink and took a sip. 'I can see you're still conscious Bill, and so I am going to ask the same questions again and you're not going to lie to me. It really annoys me when people take me for a fool. So here goes.'

Bill staggered to his feet and held onto the bar for support. Trembling at his fate and Adam's wrath, Bill looked towards the doors, hoping that one of the staff would come through them, but as he looked, he realised that Adam had slid the bolt across. Whoever came now would have to knock to be let in. Dribble spilt from the side of Bill's mouth as he tried to collect himself and stand up straight. Swallowing hard, he looked at Adam. 'Ron set it up. He had some beef about you and some bloke. I don't know the details.' Holding his head in one hand, he continued mopping the blood away from his eyes. 'The gun is out the back; he said he would come back for it, but he hasn't shown his face.'

Ignoring Bill's obvious pain, Adam smiled. 'And who were the customers in the pub that night Bill, can you remember?' Adam let his eyes wander around the pub aimlessly, waiting for an answer.

'Why do you want to know about the customers?' Bill was starting to feel the fog disappear from his brain.

'Because people are nosey Bill and they like to share the gossip. They take photos of their meals out, their dog having a piss and their favourite flower in bloom, but not one person took a photo or video of some mad drunk waving a gun about in a pub and shared it online? It all seems very strange to me, don't you think?'

Bill shrugged. 'It was a quiet night, Mr Lambrianu; most of them were my old mates who just popped in for a pint. Some of the older blokes, like me, don't even have a mobile let alone know how to take photos on them. As for the money...' Bill stammered, looking down at the floor, 'I might as well own up, but Ron shared it with me. Things have been quiet lately, Mr Lambrianu and I have struggled making your payments. That bloody Ron, he said he would make everything okay and there would be no comeback. I'm sorry Mr Lambrianu,' Bill pleaded and walked closer towards the bar, leaning on it with his elbows.

Calmly, Adam listened to Bill's excuses and the truth this time. He wasn't telling him anything he hadn't already suspected. But none of it made sense. 'Well, you can keep the gun, I'm not interested in that, but I will take my money.' Then Adam looked directly into Bill's eyes. 'Ron's dead. Had an accident at a barbeque and burnt to death apparently. Barbeques can be hazardous things, almost like pubs with all those glasses and sharp objects about.'

Bill's blood ran cold, and the colour drained from his face. He knew what Adam was telling him. Rubbing his sweaty hands over his blood-stained shirt, he ran his tongue over his lips to moisten them. 'Ron's dead?'

'He is indeed. He wanted to bring trouble to my door and rob me, like you did. Not very nice.' Pursing his lips together, Adam slowly shook his head. 'Now Bill, what would you do if you were me? How should I deal with this betrayal of trust?'

Bill trembled. He knew that whatever he said would be wrong. Adam had him trapped. Bill looked deep into Adam's blue eyes, which had now clouded over. 'I'm not sure, Mr Lambrianu.' Bill could feel the lump in his throat rise up and down as he swallowed.

Adam drummed his fingers on his chin as though deep in thought. 'Well, if I kill you, I won't have any money coming in.' Adam took pleasure in watching Bill wince as he spoke. 'So I propose you show me how sorry you are yourself.'

Bill frowned, not quite understanding what Adam meant. 'How could I do that, Mr Lambrianu?'

'Firstly, give me the money Ron gave you, and make sure the next payment is on time and in full. If you were having trouble with payments you could have spoken to us. We're not animals, Bill, we listen to reason. Sometimes something is better than nothing, in the short term.' Accepting these terms, Bill staggered towards the cash register and opened it. Adam swiftly walked behind the bar and stood beside him. 'All of my money won't be in your morning's float for the day, Bill, so where is the rest?'

'In this cloth money bag at the side. I was going to pop out and bank it this morning,' Bill replied and Adam nodded.

'Now put your hand in the cash register Bill and slam it shut, hard mind. No half measures. I think you can cope with one broken hand for a while and it will always be a pleasant reminder of how you got away with your life. I'll tell you when to stop.' Adam put Bill's hand on the tray of the cash register and he took his other hand and put it behind the drawer. 'Go on Bill, or do you want me to show you how?'

Adam's request made Bill feel sick and he could feel the bile rising in his throat. 'Please Mr Lambrianu, no, no,' he pleaded.

Adam quickly slammed the drawer hard with Bill's hand inside of it. The scream that erupted from Bill was almost deafening and his eyes nearly popped out of his head. Adam opened the till and did the same again. With his hand still trapped in the drawer, Adam held it there tightly as Bill almost slumped to the ground in agony. Spit foamed from his mouth and tears ran down his face.

'Stand up! Be a man for fuck's sake. You weren't acting the

coward when you stole off me and set that poor bastard Lenny up!' Adam shouted.

Sweating profusely and groaning in pain, Bill tried standing up. Adam's eyes shone. 'Now you do it. Just once before I leave, then I will know you're sorry.' Adam let go of the drawer and waited.

Bill accepted his fate and trembling, he looked at his already swollen, throbbing hand. Tears ran down his cheeks and he begged for mercy, but he knew Adam had no mercy in him and this wouldn't be over unless he did as he was told. With all his might, he took a deep breath, wiped his forehead with the sleeve of his arm, and slammed the drawer shut on his own hand, screaming in pain and falling to the ground as he did.

Adam ignored his howls and picked up the money bag. 'I'll take this on account. Nice seeing you Bill.' Adam picked up his orange juice glass and put it in his pocket. He felt it safer to take it with him and get rid of it later, just in case Bill called the police, which he doubted. Adam heard a knock at the pub door and a woman shouting through it, and knew he had to make a hasty retreat. No one had seen him come in and no one had seen him leave and that was how he liked it. Looking up and down the ginnel as he left, Adam checked his helmet in case of any dents or scratches, got on his motorbike and revved it up. 'Time for a bacon sandwich now,' he mused to himself and rode off.

* * *

'Where the hell have you been? I've been looking for you all morning. And please don't tell me the last woman to go through your revolving door wouldn't let you out; I don't want to hear it,' Scarlet shouted the moment he stepped into the office.

'I take it you've missed me then sis.' He smiled and handed her one of the sandwiches he'd bought. 'Got you a chicken salad, just how you like it, from the deli. Got Knuckles a bacon sandwich with lots of brown sauce. Where is he?'

Scarlet smiled and picked up the packet with her sandwich in. 'He's around somewhere.' She shrugged. 'Do you want some coffee?'

'Mm, that would be nice. So how did your night with Katie go? Did she enjoy herself?'

'Yes, but it would have been nice if you'd shown your face. You are her little brother, after all.'

'Then we will have dinner together tonight and I will humbly apologise for my shortcomings,' Adam laughed.

'I wondered if you would take over here today. I want to spend some more time with Katie while she's here. Is that okay?'

'Goodness me Scat, are you going to leave the club in my incapable hands?' Wide eyed with mock surprise, Adam cocked his head to one side, waiting for an answer.

'I've never said that you're incapable. You're very capable, but I just wondered if you had anything else on today. We have a delivery coming this afternoon and one of us needs to be here. Do you have the money?'

'I'm not paying in cash and I've made my own arrangements with them; they are more than happy being paid in cryptocurrency.' Raising his eyebrows to prove his point, Adam carried on. 'Our Mexican and Cuban friends said that it was easier for them and causes them fewer problems.'

'Adam, I do hope you know what you're doing, because they don't like late payments and I don't want to have to see you in a body bag.'

'Trust me. I know you're not into this crypto stuff and you don't like the idea of me doing it, but believe me, they will be happy about it.'

'I don't really like the drug side of this, but if we don't do it, someone else will. Dad wouldn't touch the stuff, but times change and our celebrities who are whiter than white want more to put up their nose than a finger.' Disheartened, Scarlet felt ashamed she was dealing in drugs. She didn't want to get her hands dirty with it. It was true, her father wouldn't have liked it, but it seemed drugs were the in thing at the moment and everyone was doing it. And there was a lot of money to be made from it. Much to her relief, Adam had taken over that side of things.

Scarlet looked up at him from her desk as he stood in the doorway, eating his sandwich. 'Has Katie said anything to you? She just seems to have a lot on her mind lately and when I talk about Chris or Italy, she changes the subject... Maybe it's just me.' Scarlet dismissed her thoughts and shook her head. 'Never mind, Adam.'

'Actually, now you mention it, she doesn't seem quite herself. I thought that when I saw her and for whatever reason, Julie has seriously got the knife in Chris's back. She wouldn't come to the house until I reassured her he wasn't here. There's something going on we don't know about, but give it a few days and then bring the subject up with her before she leaves. Don't spoil her holiday or your time together, eh?'

'Julie?' Scarlet sat upright. 'What's Chris got to do with Julie?'

'I really don't know Scat, but there is definitely something wrong. You're the oldest, you find out.' Adam grinned. 'I'd better go and find Knuckles before he starves to death. It must be at least an hour since he's eaten.' Shoving his own sandwich in his mouth, he winked at Scarlet, who promptly rolled up the paper packaging from her own sandwich and threw it at him.

As he handed Knuckles his sandwich in the corridor, Adam's mobile burst into life. Looking at it, he saw that it was a call from Bruce.

'What's up mate?'

'I've just had three calls from our watchers. Bitcoin has just gone down. We need to sell. Are you going to call Julie, or are you going to make me do it?'

'Coward! I'll pass it on,' Adam laughed. 'How long ago did you get the calls?'

'About five minutes. Thanks Adam, I just can't face it today,' Bruce groaned.

'You are one of her boys Bruce. You're at her beck and call now,' Adam laughed. He found it hilarious that Julie had put him down as an employee of her household. Poor Bruce, labelled as a male escort. There wasn't a more unlikely candidate than Bruce!

'Shut the fuck up Adam! It's not funny! I can't believe I've sold my soul to the devil for a bank roll.'

'People have done it for less Bruce. Don't worry, it's all in hand and I don't think by looking at the others she has any designs on you. Speak later.' Ending the call, Adam rang Julie and told her what Bruce had said.

'That's good news because today we're going to sell it from those forty accounts. That way, it looks legitimate. They will know that there's been a drop in their investments, too. Where is Bruce? I thought he'd be coming today. I'll give him a call and get him around here and then he can work his magic. Incidentally, that broker firm keeps ringing me. I knew he would. Christ, my arse wasn't cold on his chair before that Jamie's boss rang me to see if everything was okay. And, you will like this Adam, he thinks it's a lot for me to take in, and keeps telling me that every day I spend thinking about it is a loss of earnings. Patronising bastard! I've told him I want that Jamie to come to the house and explain it in more detail to me. Now, I've got to go and ring Bruce before he escapes my clutches,' Julie cackled. She loved this cat and mouse game between her and Bruce.

'Treat him gently Julie!' Adam felt he should warn Bruce, but when he dialled his number, it was already engaged. Julie had beaten him to it!

During the rest of day, Adam kept looking at his mobile wondering if there would be a message from Jennifer. It had been an enjoyable evening, so why hadn't she called? He couldn't understand it and so decided he would text her himself later. A wide grin crossed his face and he carried on walking.

13

MORTALITY

Looking at himself in the full-length mirror as he straightened his purple tie while dressed in his formal grey suit, Adam felt older, much older. Running his hands through his still damp, collar-length hair, he shook it to let it fall into place and took a deep sigh. He liked the freedom of the road and his leathers, but business was business and he had to dress accordingly.

Getting into the back of the awaiting Rolls Royce, he made the short journey to the casino. The highly polished roulette tables greeted him first, then the delivery man who had a trolley with boxes of playing cards stacked on it. As he walked towards the lift that took him to the office, he saw a few other members of staff and greeted them. Thomas, the manager, was instructing the croupiers as always and taking them through their paces before their shifts. Turning, he spotted Adam and held out his hand. 'Mr Lambrianu, it's good to see you. I presume you have come to give us the "once-over"?'

'Not really Thomas, but I'd be shirking my duties if I didn't come and see you, wouldn't I? Anyway, I like to keep my finger on the pulse. How are things?'

'As you can see, everything is running smoothly and everyone is ready for inspection. If you have any concerns, please let me know.' Thomas held out his hand to reveal the line of people already forming and standing in a military fashion dressed in their black trousers, white shirts and pink bow ties. Adam walked down the line and greeted each of them, especially the older employees that seemed to have worked there forever. But something caught Adam's eye as he moved down the line and he quickly finished his inspection.

'Thomas, can I have a word...?' As Thomas moved closer, a frown crossed his brow. 'The fifth man on the way down looks like he's spilt something on his shirt while having his breakfast. Pay him for the day and get rid of him. Didn't you check them before I arrived?' Adam snapped.

Thomas's cheeks flushed pink and his eyes darted over to the line of people waiting to be dismissed. 'I never noticed, Mr Lambrianu; some of them have only just got here.'

Adam moved in closer to Thomas's ear. 'Do what you're paid for Thomas, or he won't be the only one looking for a job. Got it?' Seeing Thomas nod his head, Adam made his way to the glass lift angrily. Once it had reached the top floor he walked along the red carpeted hallway to his office. Opening the door, he could smell cigar smoke and opened it wide.

'Ola, Mr Lambrianu!' A swarthy man in his forties, with black hair and long sideburns, greeted him, a Cuban cigar firmly in the side of his mouth. Adam noticed he was sat in his chair and had made himself comfortable by putting his feet up on his desk. At either side of him were two tall, similar-looking men.

Frowning, Adam weighed up the men greeting him. These weren't the delivery men he was expecting, and he mentally cursed Thomas, because he hadn't told him someone was waiting for him in his office. He had been totally off his guard walking into this.

Quickly taking in the situation, Adam noticed a holdall beside the man sat on his chair. 'Hello, gentlemen. I do believe you are sitting in my chair.'

'You want your chair back? Sure, a chair is a chair. I am now taking over the deliveries for your enterprise.' The drawl of his voice and accent gave Adam the impression he was Cuban.

'Where are the usual men?' Adam's anger was rising, but he felt the need to stay calm.

'Unfortunately, they have been detained Mr Lambrianu. I am here to inform you that the price has gone up or this little bag stays with me.' The man grinned, revealing a mouth full of bad teeth, while tapping the zipped bag on the floor.

'I'm sorry, what is your name?' Adam smiled, although mentally, as he watched this greasy man with his filthy shoes on his desk, he wanted to strangle him.

'No names, it's not necessary. Now, where is your money? Don't tell me you have two million British pounds in your back pocket?' The man turned to his friends and spoke in Spanish to them and they laughed at his joke, although Adam knew *he* was the joke.

'Well, let's take out my wallet and see, shall we? You're earlier than expected.'

'No fast moves, I would hate for the authorities to find a dead body in your fancy casino.' Turning, the man took out his gun and coldly shot the man to the left of him. Watching the man slump to the ground in a pool of blood, Adam knew he was in trouble and needed to get to his own gun that was firmly buried in the back of the waistband of his trousers. Adam prepared himself for the worst.

The man at his desk grinned at him. 'Now, where is my money? Don't worry, I am not going to kill you yet.'

'There's no need for bad feeling. We're businessmen. Like I said, you're earlier than expected. I'll need to go to the casino safe.' Adam tried playing for time. One false move and he would be dead and this bastard would empty the casino safe anyway. 'How do I know you have anything worth buying in that bag of yours?' Adam smiled, nodding at the firmly zipped holdall.

The man at the desk glared at him for a moment. His brown eyes bored into Adam's. 'Don't businessmen trust each other? Here, I will show you,' he drawled. Nodding to the man at the right of him, he kicked the bag forward. 'Open it.'

Adam walked forward and put his hands on his waist, while slowly trying to feel for his own gun without being noticed. He leaned forward as the bag was unzipped. Bending forward, Adam looked inside. 'Is that all of it?' he asked.

'You filthy pig, are you calling me a thief?' Raising his steel toe-capped boot, he kicked Adam swiftly in the face, knocking him sideways. Dazed and struggling to hold himself upright, Adam could feel blood dripping down his chin. His head throbbed and his face stung as he wiped the blood away with the arm of his jacket, and spat blood out from his mouth onto the carpet.

'Not so pretty now, are you?' The man grinned, showing his row of bad teeth again, and chuckled to himself. 'No one calls me a thief, especially a pretty boy like you, with your airs and graces.'

Feeling the wind from the whistling bullet pass his ear, Adam ducked. Holding his nerve, he shook his head. 'Of course not, just checking,' he stammered. He still felt dazed, and blinked hard to bring himself out of his dazed state. Adam was angry at this man, but angrier at himself for walking into this trap. Realising this man meant business, he tried to remain calm, although his heart was pounding. His gun was out of reach and he cursed himself for not getting here earlier. Another gun was in the drawer of the desk that his assailant was firmly sat behind.

Adam looked at the man curiously. He didn't dare move but he thought he could see a red spot on the man's forehead. He instantly knew what it was. Someone had this man in their aim with their gun, ready to fire. As it was firmly fixed on the man at the desk, he knew it wasn't for him. The goon at the right side of the man sitting at the desk noticed it and spoke quickly in Spanish. Frowning, the man at the desk realised he was in someone's sights and cocked his gun to shoot Adam, who quickly reached for his own gun. But before he could, the door burst open and Knuckles shot the man at the desk in the head. Adam quickly fired at the man on the right side of him, watching him fall to the floor, before turning to Knuckles. His heart was pounding in his chest, but he managed to give Knuckles a weak smile. 'Am I glad to see you.'

'Press the fire alarm,' ordered Knuckles and Adam rushed forward and broke the glass on the fire alarm, watching as the casino staff rushed to the exit. Taking a deep breath and slowly letting it out, Adam sat down on the chair opposite the dead man.

'How did you know I was here?' Adam wiped his brow and looked up at Knuckles who had already put his gun back in his pocket. 'Scarlet.' Knuckles shrugged.

As though hearing her name, Scarlet ran in, breathless. Taking in the scene before her with the three dead men, she stared wide eyed at Knuckles and then at Adam. 'Shit! Your face, are you okay, Adam?' Seeing Adam nod and wipe his mouth again, Scarlet turned towards Knuckles. 'How did you get here so fast? The traffic's terrible.' She didn't know what else to say.

'Ran,' answered Knuckles nonchalantly.

'Well, you must be a fucking gold medallist running five streets ahead of a car. What the hell's gone on here, and why are those men bleeding on my carpet!' Scarlet walked forward to the man sat at the desk and grabbing him by the hair, raised his slumped head. 'Who is he, what did he want?'

'The same as everyone else... money.' Adam stood up. 'I'm going to tell the staff there's been an electrical fault. That might just convince them of the bangs they will have heard. Knuckles has a silencer on his gun, but mine hasn't and neither did his.' Adam nodded his head towards the dead man slumped at his desk and left the room.

Discarding his blood-stained jacket, Adam took the lift to the first floor and then walked down the rest of the staircase. He was expecting the fire brigade to turn up and he would apologise for their wasted journey.

Putting on his most charming smile, he walked out into the courtyard where everyone was gathered while the appointed fire wardens were checking everyone off their list. 'It's okay everyone, there seems to have been an electrical blow out somewhere. Everyone go home for the day while I get it sorted. Is everyone out of the building?' Turning towards Thomas and the fire wardens, he saw them nod their heads.

'We heard a noise Mr Lambrianu. Are you okay? You're bleeding.'

Adam nodded. 'Yes, I fell with the shock of the loud bang. Nothing to worry about. It looks worse than it is.'

Thomas frowned, but accepted the explanation. 'What about those men that went to your office? I can't see them out here. They said they had an appointment with you...'

Adam glared at him. Suddenly he felt his close shave with death was Thomas's fault. He had never mentioned the men and a warning would have saved a lot of effort. 'I wanted to talk to you about them, Thomas. They were just dropping off something for the club, but it would have been nice if you had told me I had people sniffing around my casino and office. How the hell did that slip your mind? Anyway, they already left – didn't you see them leave?' Adam enquired, wondering just how much Thomas had seen.

'No Mr Lambrianu, I was in the back sacking that croupier like you asked. And as for not telling you, it slipped my mind during your inspection. Sorry,' Thomas stammered and blushed.

As much as Adam wanted to slap him, he smiled. 'No harm done.' Gently tapping him on the shoulder in a friendly manner, Adam grinned. 'Go home while I get the problem fixed, and tell the fire brigade everything is in hand and no one's hurt,' Adam instructed as he walked away.

Going back into the office, he saw there was only Scarlet sat in the room amongst the dead men. 'Where's Knuckles?'

'Gone to get the van. We need to get rid of these bodies. Help me put them in the lift.' Standing up, Scarlet kicked off her high heels and padded towards one of the men on the floor. 'This one's a fat bastard, we'll take him first.'

Curiously, Adam stopped her. 'How did Knuckles know there was trouble here?'

'You have friends in low places Adam,' Scarlet spat. 'I got a call from some foreign bloke, I don't know. He said he'd been shot in the arm and needed to warn you trouble was on its way. He's possibly dead now, but thank God he called.'

Adam ran his hands through his hair. 'I swear I don't know these men Scarlet. I've never seen them before, and how come they knew where to find the others? We've been dealing with our usual guys for three years and there has never been any trouble. Why now?'

'Who gives a fuck, Adam? You were dead meat if Knuckles hadn't turned up. I'm not identifying my brother in the morgue. This drug stuff stops now. If people coming to the club need something extra to make their nights go with a swing, then they supply their own, got it?' Scarlet glared at him, her own piercing blue eyes matching his.

Realising his near miss with death, Adam agreed, but still found it confusing as to who these men were. How did they know about his arrangement? None of it made sense. Grabbing the man under each arm, the pair of them dragged him towards the lift. Scarlet noticed the long trail of blood across the floor as they dragged him. 'Shit, all of this is going to have to be replaced.'

'No it's not, it will take too long to organise. It needs a carpet cleaner for now. I'll do it myself, then I know it's done properly.'

'No, we'll do it together. That's what families do.' She smiled. 'But any broken nails and you're paying. Fuck, this one's a fat bastard, and his bladder was weak; I stink of piss!'

'It could be me Scarlet,' Adam laughed, 'I nearly pissed myself when his bullet whistled past my ear.' Pulling the dead man into the lift, they both stood up, mopped their brows, and took a breath. Adam wiped away the blood and sweat he could feel dripping down his face. Then they went back to the office to get the next one as Knuckles appeared.

'What you doing?'

'What the fuck does it look like?' snapped Scarlet.

'Looks like you're putting those dead bodies in the lift?' Knuckles shrugged.

Scarlet stood up straight with her hands on her hips and glared at Adam, then at Knuckles. 'You know I am never sure if he's just an idiot or a sarcastic bastard sometimes. I like to think it's the first one.'

Knuckles took off his jacket and walked up to the man at the desk and picked him up like a rag doll, throwing him over his shoulder and walking to the lift without breaking into a sweat. Adam and Scarlet looked on as he did the same with the third man. 'Should have waited for me.'

'Oh, just fuck off and get them into the back of the van,' answered Scarlet. 'Where are we going to put them?'

Knuckles rolled his eyes to the ceiling. 'New construction site in Walthamstow. Building some council houses.'

Flabbergasted, Scarlet looked up at him. 'Fucking know it all, he gets on my tits. How do you know what's happening in Walthamstow? It's not by reading the newspapers! And look at my dress, it's covered in blood.' Wagging her finger at both of them, she glared. 'I blame you two for this.'

Adam nearly burst out laughing, and would have done if his cut lip hadn't been so sore. He wasn't sure if it was just because he needed to let off steam, considering how close he had come to death, or the fact that Scarlet and Knuckles were such a comedy act without even realising it.

Once the dead men were safely in the van, Knuckles drove off, leaving Scarlet and Adam to clean up the mess at the casino. Adam went and looked through the cleaners' quarters and sure enough, found what he was looking for. 'Take your clothes off, Scarlet. I know you have spare clothes here but you need to go back to the club with the same clothes on. I'll put your suit in the washing machine while we're doing this.'

'My thousand-pound suit in a washing machine! For fuck's sake Adam, you seriously owe me.' Scarlet stood there in her bra and knickers while Adam went back to the cleaners' quarters in his boxer shorts. Finding two tabards, he brought them up and threw one at Scarlet. 'Thought this might hide your modesty.' He grinned.

Scarlet burst out laughing as she put the green tabard on and did a twirl. Then she looked at Adam in his. 'Oh my God Adam, definitely no selfies,' she laughed as they got to work.

14

DUCKING AND DIVING

Getting out of the shower, Adam felt much better. Just getting rid of the smell of cleaning fluid made him feel fresher. Now he had washed the blood from his face, he could see the damage. Already, his puffed eye was turning black and his lips were swollen, but at least his nose hadn't been broken. Hearing his mobile, he looked at it and saw it was Bruce calling. 'What's up Bruce, has Julie got you tied up in the cellar or something?'

'Better than that! Oh, no, I didn't mean that,' stammered Bruce, 'we've just emptied those accounts of twenty million! Fuck me, Adam. One account only has fifty grand left in it. Julie is wiping them out.'

Adam punched the air. Twenty million in one morning! 'Bruce, oh my God, I can't believe it.' Together they burst out laughing. 'What about her meeting? Is that still going ahead?'

In between excitement and laughter, Bruce confirmed it was. 'Anyway, on another note, how was your date last night?'

'Not sure Bruce. I haven't heard anything from her all day, so it can't have been that good.'

'Well, why haven't you called her? Surely it's up to you to call her and ask for a second date...?'

'Why would I call her?'

'Do you know how egotistical that sounds, Adam? You're so used to women chasing you that it's never occurred to you to do some chasing. If you like her, call her.'

Adam, realising his mistake, ended the call with Bruce and dialled Jennifer's number. She seemed pleased to hear his voice and chatted on about her day and the wonderful evening she'd had with him. Adam realised Bruce was right and he'd been an idiot.

'I left it later to call because I remember you saying you had lectures and I didn't want to interrupt,' Adam lied.

'Well, I did wonder. I thought maybe you didn't want to meet up again. I always feel like waiting for that second date call is the worst... Anyway, that doesn't matter now, does it. I'm working later, but I could meet you after if you want?'

Adam was just about to agree when he remembered he was having dinner with Katie and the family. He'd promised Scarlet and after today, he didn't want to break his promise. 'I have a family dinner tonight, Jennifer, I'm not sure what time it will finish. My sister has come from Italy and so it's a big deal. What are you doing tomorrow?'

The disappointment in Jennifer's voice was apparent. 'Tomorrow is good for me. No lectures as it's a study day, which means I'll be at home writing a thousand-word thesis and I'm not doing any shifts tomorrow night.'

'Tomorrow it is then. How about dinner? You will have worked up an appetite after all that studying. Will six thirty do you?'

'That sounds lovely Adam, I'd like that. Where shall I meet you?'

'I'll pick you up at your place.' Ending the call, he felt better.

And now he could get on with the rest of the day's work. Looking at his watch, he saw that it was only 3 p.m. and yet he felt shattered.

Wearing a navy-blue suit and lighter blue tie, he looked in the mirror. Pleased with himself, he left his apartment above the club and went to see if Scarlet was in the office yet. As he walked down the corridor, he saw Knuckles was back.

'Thank you for earlier, Knuckles.' As Adam looked up at him, he couldn't remember a time when Knuckles hadn't had his back. This great ape of a man had been the only real father figure in his life after his dad had died.

Knuckles slapped him on the back, making Adam stagger forward. 'Scarlet was worried about you last night.'

'I am a grown-up Knuckles and I'm not going to tell my sister if I have a date. I can look after myself.' Suddenly, Adam bit his tongue. He'd fallen right into Knuckles' trap.

'She worries,' Knuckles said sternly.

'You're right, Knuckles. I'll check in with her in the future.'

Knuckles walked away towards a group of bouncers who were waiting for their instructions for the evening. Musing to himself, Adam realised he could be selfish sometimes, but having to let everyone know where he was annoyed him. Nobody else told their sister where they were going. But as Scarlet always reminded him, *'You can write a text while having a piss and at least I know you haven't been shot or kidnapped.'*

'Julie's coming tonight to have dinner with Katie.' Scarlet stopped short when she looked up at Adam. 'What's the matter with you? You've got a face like a slapped arse, well, apart from the fact that it's taken a beating!'

Rolling his eyes, Adam ran a hand through his wavy hair. 'Just Knuckles giving me a lecture about keeping you informed of my whereabouts. He doesn't like you worrying.'

'What? He said all of that?' Taking on a serious note, Scarlet sat down. 'I'm not spying on you Adam, you're a grown man. It's just that you're a young, wealthy man and you have no one with you to watch your back. Dad had Jake and Ralph. I had Katie, now I have Knuckles with me. We all need a wingman or woman Adam. I know your bestie is Bruce, but he wouldn't be a lot of good in a fight, would he?'

'I see what you mean, but I have you and I don't want worry lines on your forehead. So yes, I will keep in touch, okay?'

Scarlet nodded. 'Right, so, back to business. That bookie whose debt you passed on to Jimmy. Well, I've just had his father on the phone. Apparently, the bookie's wife has been arrested. That bastard son of his gave the case with the drugs in to his wife to carry through customs and now she is banged up in some foreign jail. His dad wants our help.'

'He set her up. What a sleaze bag! How's she doing, did the old man say?' asked Adam.

'No idea. Once the wife was asked to go with the customs officers, her lovely hubby decided to make a hasty exit and has ended up with a bullet in his brain apparently. Jimmy wouldn't take the risk of him mouthing off to the authorities so Jimmy silenced him in the airport carpark before he could say anything. On a lighter note, his dad has to come out of retirement and take over the shops again and he would like to make our usual payment arrangements. I think he's a little afraid, now his son's been shot.'

Adam was intrigued. Jimmy must have had someone watching him at the airport, but he was never a man to leave things to chance.

'That's all I know. I'll pop and see the dad myself and make the arrangements.' As Scarlet busied herself and took out her lipstick to add another layer, Adam looked at the floor. A sideways grin crept on his face; he felt satisfied that justice had been served. That over-egotistical bookie had got his just desserts. Adam felt a sadness for the bookie's wife, but that was her husband's doing, not his. 'Well Scarlet, all men die, but not all men really live.'

'Christ Adam, that's a bit deep. I'm going to see the old man; what are you going to do?'

'I'll give the casino a final check over, make sure we haven't missed anything and then ring Thomas to open tonight.'

'Let them have the night off, Adam. They've all probably made arrangements anyway. Besides, the carpets won't be perfectly dry yet.'

'Fair point. What time is dinner tonight?'

'Seven, don't be late.' Scarlet wagged a well-manicured finger-nail at him.

Sauntering into the casino, Adam could smell the cleaning fluid. He decided to turn on the air conditioning. Hopefully, he thought, it might get rid of some of the smell. Back in his office, he reached for the switch, which was above the filing cabinet, and paused. A wide grin crossed his face as he reached out and grabbed the holdall the Cuban boss had brought with him that had been full of cocaine.

Quickly unzipping the bag, Adam checked to see that every-thing was still in there. Thank God he had come back to the casino to check things over, otherwise this would have been one hell of a find for the cleaners tomorrow. Picking up the bag, he gave the room a final once-over before locking the door behind him and leaving.

This little secret, he thought to himself, was one he would keep from Scarlet. As far as she knew, there were no drugs.

* * *

'Thank you for agreeing to see me, Mrs Gold. My boss said that you had asked for me in particular and that is quite a compliment.'

Jamie clutched his briefcase firmly to his chest. Standing in this manor house, which was beyond his wildest expectations, he felt slightly intimidated by all of the men wandering around the place.

He'd heard of Julie Gold, everyone had, and looking around the room full of antiques, he looked back at Julie and smiled. As far as he was concerned, his ship had well and truly come in. This woman was minted, he thought to himself, and the more shares he could sell her, the more commission he could make.

Spying him weighing up her house and everything in it, Julie wanted to laugh. A smile crept across her face as she mused to herself that this young fool thought she hadn't heard all of his compliments before. People had bowed and scraped to her for years hoping to get something in return. Now this young man standing before her saw only that she was a rich old woman, possibly thinking she was senile and gullible too. As much as Julie hated to admit it, she liked being old. It was a good mask to hide behind. People excused you for anything and you could snap at them, and they let it go because of your age. Men in particular. She had often wondered about how men thought of women. In your early years, you were grumpy because of your periods. Then you were grumpy because of the menopause and then you were senile and grumpy because of old age!

'Do sit down Jamie and I will have Lewis bring us some coffee, or do you prefer tea?' she drawled as she sat in her oversized wing-back chesterfield leather chair opposite him. She'd had it made specially oversized so it looked more like a throne. She was dressed in a bright red two-piece skirt suit with matching shoes, her face immaculately made-up as usual.

'Coffee please, Mrs Gold. I must say, your house is amazing,' he gushed.

'Thank you dear, we do our best.' Julie waited patiently while Jamie went on to thank her again. He had come to see her today, trying to make an impression but had failed dismally. His off-the-peg suit looked tired and worn, and his once-white shirt had been washed so many times it was a more off-white. His briefcase looked battered and had seen better days and his shoes were scuffed. If he had got up this morning thinking he would don his best clothes to impress her, she didn't want to think about what he wore on other days.

Lewis brought in the silver tray with its china coffee pot and cups. Julie waited while he poured the coffee and left the room before saying, 'Well, Jamie, I think it's time we got down to business.'

Taking a sip from his small china cup, Jamie nodded. Putting the cup down, he opened his briefcase and took out folders of paperwork. 'I've brought you some examples of just how much money we can help you make. Cryptocurrency is the only way forward these days, I can assure you of that.' Julie listened patiently as Jamie reeled off his perfectly practiced speech. 'So, Mrs Gold, how much were you looking to invest?' he asked eagerly.

This was the moment Julie had waited for. She had her own speech in mind, but not one he was expecting. 'Nothing really Jamie,' Julie answered nonchalantly and instantly watched the smile drop from Jamie's confused face.

His brows furrowed and his eyes darted around the room as he tried to think of something to say. 'Well, I was under the impression that you wanted to invest in cryptocurrency. The shares are doing very well, and you could double your money in no time,' he stammered.

Now the smile disappeared from Julie's face. 'Sonny, do I look like I need to double my money?' Julie gestured around her home. 'But what I do want is your services.'

Again, Jamie looked at Julie, confused, clearly not knowing what to say.

'My sources reveal that with the clients you have acquired, you have been helping yourself to some of their profits. I presume you've told them it's commission or something, but that doesn't interest me,' she scoffed.

Wide eyed, Jamie stared at her and his cheeks flushed pink. He was about to speak but Julie held her hand up to stop him. 'You've given your speech and I have sat here patiently and listened, and now it's my turn. You've been stealing your clients' money Jamie. In fact, you have been a very naughty boy in general.' Julie wagged her long red fingernail in his face and grinned.

Jamie's face burnt with embarrassment, and he reached for his coffee cup. His mouth felt dry, and his heart pounded in his chest. He wasn't sure whether to stand up and leave or proclaim his innocence. He wondered whether she was just testing him and decided to do the latter. 'I assure you Mrs Gold, everything the company does is legal and above board. We have all our clients' best interests at heart.'

'Your company does, Jamie love,' Julie drawled, 'but you don't. You've hit hard times recently, because according to my paperwork, you've only been scamming these people for a few months. You've impressed them with your honesty and so why should they question you now? Well, they will Jamie, because I've been emptying their accounts and you're going to help me cover my tracks. You are their trusted broker, and I'm sure a well-practiced thief like yourself will come up with something to excuse their losses. The clients you are dealing with have more money than they know what to do with and cryptocurrency is the new kid on the block. They want to experiment with it just to be fashionable. Personally, I've had to work hard for every penny and I know exactly where my money goes. I'm not greedy Jamie; you will get your share for your hard work and maybe... just maybe... you will get your girlfriend back.' Julie reached to the side of her chair and picked up her own portfolio and placed it on the table between them.

Jamie looked at her, flabbergasted. This old woman in front of him was as crafty as a fox. She'd played him and he had fallen for it. Mentally, he cursed her. How did she know all of this? He reached for the folder and opened it. Inside were fake statements he had sent to his clients. Intrigued, he looked up at Julie's poker face as she took out her gold cigarette holder and lit a cigarette. Jamie watched her blow the smoke into the air and then looked down again at the paperwork. Alongside each statement he had sent out to his clients informing them of their good fortune was his own encrypted statement showing exactly how much he'd stolen off them.

'Thieves should never keep records of their booty Jamie. That kind of bravado puts you behind bars,' Julie commented as she saw Jamie pale before her eyes.

Swallowing hard and moistening his lips, he spoke in a hushed whisper. 'How did you get these?'

'My husband taught me a couple of things which I've never forgotten. Number one is to never write anything down that could incriminate you. Number two, never trust anyone or anything, sometimes not even your own judgement. And number three, never presume people won't find out what you've done. Cover your back.'

Beaten and frightened, Jamie looked Julie squarely in the eyes. 'What do you want from me Mrs Gold? My boss will expect me to walk away from this meeting with some kind of investment from you, we both know that. I can't go back empty handed.'

'The bottom-line, Jamie love, is what lengths will you go to to save your neck? Lewis!' Julie shouted. Instantly, Lewis came into the room and stood beside Julie. 'Do you have your mobile handy?'

Julie had already told Lewis of her plan and he'd been on hand waiting for her call. Holding up his mobile, she nodded at Jamie.

'The number that is already typed in is your boss's, Mr Noakes. People like me with money to burn get his direct mobile number if needed. Now, I can either call him and say I have made a preliminary million-pound investment for the time being, and I am happy with the service provided. Or I could tell him you're a thief, embezzler and that I have documented proof. I could tell him how I am going to let the whole world know just what his company does with their clients' money. And of course, you would never get a job as a stockbroker again. Christ, you'd be behind bars, Jamie.'

Jamie looked up at Lewis holding the mobile. He could see there was a number typed in, but he didn't recognise it. Realising his whole career had just gone up in smoke, he cursed himself for being so stupid! 'What do you want, Mrs Gold?'

'What I want is for you to carry on doing what you're doing, but for me. You can take a percentage of your stolen booty, but I get the lion's share.' Julie held up her own piece of paper. 'But not for these paltry amounts. This isn't worth the effort. You ripped off a multi-millionaire for 300 quid? What the fuck, are you crazy? He'd probably spend more than that on a bottle of wine. You have to learn to think big, Jamie love. Also, I want you to get hold of other clients, the way you have these ones,' Julie drawled. 'So, find me some more Jamie. From each client, you take 100,000 pounds. You can have twenty-five for your trouble. I am sure that would stop your sofa surfing and impress that girlfriend of yours. After all, diamonds are a girl's best friend,' Julie laughed.

'A hundred thousand each time? Are you crazy? That would be picked up in no time. Someone would notice those kind of losses... surely?' Julie could already see the greed in his eyes, and she knew she had him hooked.

'All I want is to carry on as you are, Jamie. Nothing has changed, but we get richer, and they get poorer.'

Jamie's brows furrowed as he tried taking in what Julie was

saying. 'So, all I have to do is carry on informing them of their investments using the company name as their broker, but we take more, a bloody lot more, which is a risk and I get 25,000?'

'You got it, Jamie love. Your signature is on everything, as it is now, plus you will find more clients for us to steal off and you're going to live like a lord.'

'But why me, Mrs Gold? There are lots of brokers out there.' Jamie spied her suspiciously. This sounded too good to be true.

'Because most of the other thieves in your game are more experienced and more subtle. You are sloppy, but you will learn with me at your side.'

'What about the investment my boss is expecting, Mrs Gold? Are you going to put any investment his way?'

'As I've already told you, I will give you a million pounds and a glowing reference to Mr Noakes for helping me.'

'Very well, I'll do it.'

Julie looked up at Lewis and smiled, while Lewis pressed the button on his mobile. Instantly, Mr Noakes answered. Julie left it on loudspeaker for Jamie to hear.

'Mr Noakes, I just wanted to thank you personally for sending that nice Jamie chap. He couldn't speak highly enough of you and for everything you have taught him. I am investing a preliminary million pounds. I appreciate it's not much, but, as a woman on my own, I'm a little unsure of these things. I am sure you understand, being a man of the world. I would like Jamie to be my hands-on broker. I feel I know him already. Thank you Mr Noakes. Oh, and I will be sure to tell my friends about your excellent company.' Julie looked up and smiled at Jamie. Mr Noakes gushed and Julie could tell he was almost wetting himself at all the influential clients she could put his way – and she genuinely intended to. Because this way, she could rob them blind!

Once Mr Noakes had assured Julie that Jamie would be on-hand night and day, she ended the call. 'The million I am giving you Jamie, is without your 25,000. You don't rob off me, got it? I'm sure, Jamie love, you're going to be in for a big promotion and even get a better office if your boss thinks you can pull this off. So, you're on your way up already,' Julie laughed.

Jamie was mentally calculating what he could do with the money and yes, this old woman was right. Anyone dealing with influential clients wouldn't be stuck in a junior's office. They would have their own office with their name on the door. Jamie sat back, very pleased with himself. What Mrs Gold was asking of him was no more than he had already been doing, just on a bigger scale.

Once Julie had waved him off, she turned to Lewis and smiled.

'Not bad for a morning's work, eh Lewis? As his client, I am now putting all my trust in Jamie and his company. He's signing the statements and he's the one who will go to prison for embezzlement. The million I have given him is what I have already stolen off his clients. Sooner or later people are going to want answers, and he is the one they will turn to. He was too greedy and too quick to say yes to the deal Lewis. He will end up going to prison, because who is going to think an old lady like me could think of such a thing!' Julie let out a loud cackle.

'You're merciless Julie Gold, you know that, don't you?' Lewis laughed. 'Bloody merciless!'

15

FAMILY WARS

'Blimey Adam, your face looks like it's been run over by a steam train. What happened?' As Julie sat down to dinner in the restaurant above the nightclub, she couldn't help but notice Adam's bruised, swollen face.

'You know what it's like Julie, these things happen.' Adam laughed it off and shrugged.

Spying him curiously, Julie looked around the table at Katie, Scarlet and Diana. 'Is anyone else going to say anything, or am I the only one that's noticed?' Julie prompted.

Glancing at Adam and then back at Julie, Scarlet grinned. 'Of course we've noticed, we were just being polite and not pointing out the obvious, Julie!'

Julie reached over and stroked Adam's cheek. 'I suppose it won't be so bad once the swelling's gone down. Just as well the lighting's dim.'

Scarlet laughed and brushed it off. 'It's not the first fight he's been in Julie. He will heal and be as beautiful and vain as ever.'

'Unless,' Katie chimed in, 'he's found a woman who wrestles

him to the ground.' Everyone around the table laughed and chinked their wine glasses together.

'Or maybe some crazy, jealous Italian that wants him out of the way.' Julie's sarcasm dripped from her tongue as she looked over her glass at Katie.

A frown crossed Diana's face. 'That's a bit deep Mum, considering there are mainly Italians sat around the table. What do you know that we don't?' She laughed, trying to break the nervous tension. Suddenly, everyone had stopped what they were doing and was looking at Julie.

'A lot,' answered Julie, and letting out a sigh and painting her usual smile on her face, she grinned. This was not the time for what she had to say, but deep inside, her blood boiled with what she knew. Julie wondered about Adam's beaten, swollen face. She couldn't wait to get him on his own; she needed to know what had happened.

Eventually, the food and chatter flowed, and everyone seemed happy again. Julie watched them all and laughed at their jokes, wondering if they had all put her outburst down to her senility. But she knew better.

'Why don't we all go up to my flat and have our coffees, and then we're freeing this table and we can talk for longer,' Adam suggested. Secretly, he hated being in the spotlight. He could see the usual diners nudging and whispering to each other about his swollen face and wanted to leave.

Scarlet beamed. She loved having all the family together. 'What a good idea. And I know it's clean because I sent the cleaners up there this afternoon and there were no stray female bodies occupying it. Come on everyone, let's go kick our shoes off and relax.' Even though it was Adam's flat, Scarlet led the way.

'What about you, Diana? Can you spare us some more of your time?'

Diana cast a furtive glance towards Julie. Even though she did have an early start, she knew her mum had something on her mind. 'Yep, I'm in for a late night. After all, I call the shots now. They will call if I'm needed.' She gave her mum a crafty wink and followed the others upstairs to the flat.

Pleased with Diana's decision, Scarlet beckoned the waitress over. 'Send some champagne up to Adam's flat will you dear? Oh and some nibbles just in case.' Turning towards the others, she cocked her head and grinned. 'I know he has plenty of other alcohol up there because I got it restocked!'

'For God's sake, Scarlet, you sound like his mother. Come on,' laughed Katie and linked her arm through Scarlet's and Adam's.

In no time, they were all in the lavishly decorated apartment above the nightclub. Scarlet kicked off her shoes and flopped onto the leather sofa. 'Come on Adam, play host. There are thirsty women in here!'

Julie looked up at Adam from her chair. 'Is four the most women you've had in here at one time Adam?' she laughed. They all turned to face him as he poured the drinks and noticed the slightly pink blush to his cheeks, then they all burst out laughing.

'Oh my God, he's had orgies up here! You dirty bugger. Okay, I bet it's a first having so many old birds up here – and don't answer that,' she warned, while wagging her long red fingernail at him.

As usual when they were all together, they reminisced about the good old days. While Scarlet and Katie gossiped, Julie stood up. 'Come on Adam, I'll help you get some more ice for these drinks.' Adam dutifully followed her to the kitchen.

'I saw that Jamie guy and everything is sorted there. Come around tomorrow and I will fill you in.' She winked. 'So tell me, how did you get a beating Adam?'

'Greedy dealers Julie and greedy suppliers. It happens.' He shrugged and opened the freezer box so that no one could hear their conversation, although with all the laughter coming from the lounge, he doubted they could anyway.

'You have had the same satisfied dealers and suppliers for years Adam, why has it gone tits up now?'

'Someone else muscling in. I believe they killed, or at least tried to kill, my old, regular lot. Thankfully, they managed to warn Scarlet, but when I got to my office in the casino these men were already there waiting.'

'I know your dealings are a closed book, Adam, and your delivery dates too. That really doesn't add up, unless someone tipped them off?'

'I found it strange, but it's a shitty business Julie and you can't trust anyone, can you?'

'You could trust the suppliers you had Adam. After all, they tipped you off, didn't they?'

Frowning, Adam looked Julie squarely in the face. 'You have a point there Julie. I haven't really had a lot of time to think about it. What with that and then coming here tonight.'

'Watch your back Adam, and keep your enemies close. Take nothing for granted.'

Before he could answer, Katie popped her head around the door. 'For crying out loud you two. I thought you had gone to Switzerland to get that ice.' Swaying slightly and making her way back to the lounge, Katie flopped back in her seat beside Diana who was slightly tipsy herself and held her glass up for Adam to fill.

Adam sat watching them all laugh and crack jokes, but mentally he was pondering Julie's words. It had definitely been a warning.

'This is a lovely get together,' Katie mused. 'I wish I didn't have to leave tomorrow; it's been lovely, and tonight is the icing on the cake. Oh well,' she sighed, 'back to Italy and Chris tomorrow. But you will all come and see me soon, won't you?' Katie asked hopefully.

Julie couldn't help herself; this was the light to the touchpaper she needed. 'Why spoil a good evening by mentioning your husband?' Julie's voice was low and stern as she glared at Katie.

Scarlet stared from one to the other, almost sobering up. 'Why this grudge against Chris all of a sudden Julie? Didn't he send you your favourite perfume for Christmas?'

Julie's retort shocked them all. 'I wouldn't take a million-pound note off that backstabbing piece of shit.' Putting her glass down, Julie stood up. 'Sorry Scarlet, I won't spoil your evening, it's time I left.'

'No you don't Julie Gold. Sit down and apologise. I'm no fan of Chris, but he's Katie's husband and the father of her kids. Don't make her feel uncomfortable here!' Scarlet snapped.

Standing up beside Scarlet, Katie smiled. 'Come on you two. I think we've all had enough to drink. Let's have no cross words.'

Pulling her arm away from Katie's, Scarlet stood there defiantly, her face flushed with anger and her blue eyes shining like sapphires. 'No! Say what you have to say Julie Gold or piss off. You've hinted and sniped about Katie and Chris ever since she arrived. Come on, let's have it!'

Ignoring Scarlet's outburst and sitting down again, Julie looked directly at Katie. 'Did you know that it was on Chris's orders that Don Carlos was shot? Or was it Chris himself who shot him? I need to know if you knew, because Don Carlos was family to me and Ralph.' Her calm voice floated around the room, shocking them all into silence.

Scarlet sat open mouthed trying to take in what Julie had said, and she turned to look at Katie questioningly. Katie paled as she looked at them both. Slowly she shook her head. 'No, I don't know anything about it Julie, I swear. Are you sure?' Katie's brows crossed as she slowly sank back into her seat. 'That is a big accusation to make about the demise of a mafia boss. How do you know that Julie?' Her lips felt dry, and she moistened them with her tongue.

Each of them sat in silence, gathering their thoughts at this bombshell that Julie had just dropped.

Adam was the first to speak, choosing his words carefully. 'Julie, Chris is Don Carlos's nephew. They were family. Why would he kill him? Surely, you don't think Katie knows anything about this.'

'Seeing that shocked expression on her face Adam, I would say definitely not. But once Don Carlos made it clear that Chris would take over from him as mafia boss after his death, I knew he had signed his own death warrant. Don Carlos's house was built like a fortress. No one could get near him, unless it was someone he knew and trusted...' Julie cast a furtive glance towards Katie. 'I was told they had trouble with the alarm in the house the night he was killed. I also know that Chris had visited him that day.'

Lost for words, Scarlet looked at each and every one of them in turn. 'But how do you know this, Julie? No one knows who did it. They found one unknown dead man outside on the lawn that had been shot by one of Don Carlos's bodyguards but no one else. Do you realise what you're saying?' Scarlet sat back in her chair wearily.

'Don't treat me like a senile old lady, Scarlet. Ralph and I were friends with Don Carlos and the men that worked for him for over forty years. Do you think I still don't have inside information from those friends just because I'm an old lady? Don't you think that those who were closest to him want justice? Chris's name has popped up too many times, but who is going to do anything about it now that he has taken his seat as the mafia boss? No one is going to oppose him, except me. What have I got to lose?'

'Your life,' Adam commented.

'I've had my life Adam and most of yours. You were in line to take Don Carlos's place, did you know that? But Chris convinced him you were too young. That you didn't represent the good Italian family. You're a bachelor, still a young man.'

Adam was taken aback, totally shocked at Julie's revelation. 'Me?'

Scarlet and Katie's sharp intake of breath showed they had no knowledge of Don Carlos's plans either.

'You forget Julie, you have to be a full Italian to take over that rank as Godfather,' Adam laughed. 'I am half-English.'

'You're wrong Adam.' Julie shook her head. 'Believe me, I know. Your father married out of the circle and so did his father, but your roots are Italian and Sicilian. You are a Lambrianu, Adam. Everyone in Italy knows you. Just how much Italian do you need? The Godfather chooses who will be his successor. Chris steered Don Carlos away from choosing you.' Julie's eyes flashed at Katie. 'Did you know that? Did you know Chris robbed your own brother?'

'Shit Julie no, of course not.' Katie's eyes brimmed with tears at Julie's revelation. 'Chris and I don't live together much these days. In fact, we haven't for a while.' Katie bowed her head and blushed. This wasn't a secret she wanted to share, but, with all of these accusations she felt she had to defend herself. 'He wouldn't tell me anything as important as that Julie.'

Diana stood up and poured each of them a whisky. 'I think we all need a drink and time to think about this. Are you separated from Chris, Katie, is that what you're saying? If so, why all of the cloak and dagger?'

Scarlet jumped to Katie's defence. 'Will you all get off her back? What Chris has or hasn't done is none of her fault. Do you think she would come back and face us all if it was? Anyway, Julie, you seem very sure of yourself. Why have you said nothing sooner?'

'Biding my time, until I got all the proof I needed. But answer the question, Katie. Are you separated?'

Everyone turned towards Katie, waiting for an answer. 'Kind

of... I suppose.' Katie's blue eyes flashed at Scarlet and Julie, and she brushed a tear away. 'If you mean do we live in the same house? Not always. Do we share the same bed? Same answer. Our marriage is purely for appearances.'

Scarlet sat there gobsmacked; she couldn't believe her ears. This was her twin, the other half of her and yet she didn't know this. She felt angry and betrayed, because if Katie had confided in anyone it should have been her. Why hadn't she told her? She didn't know what to say.

It was Adam who spoke first to break the silence. He could see Scarlet was shocked, while Julie sat there with a smug look on her face. 'Why haven't you left him and come home Katie?' Running his hands through his hair and pushing it away from his face, he stared at his sister as though he didn't know her. 'You have family and money here. Chris has a percentage in the vineyard, but he doesn't own it. That's ours, Katie. Now, what the fuck is going on and more to the point, how long has this been going on for? Diana, can you pour some more drinks? I get the feeling it's going to be a long night.' Sharply, Adam turned towards Julie. 'And you can take that smug look off your face. If you knew our sister was unhappy, why didn't you say something? It's not like you to keep your big mouth shut!' he snapped.

Pondering the situation, Scarlet held up her hand. 'Stop it! I won't have us arguing amongst ourselves.' Scarlet looked around the room at them all as they looked to Katie for answers. 'What does he have over you, Katie? Adam is right, marriages come and go, so why haven't you separated properly and come home?'

Katie took a huge gulp of the whisky Diana had poured her. She had held in her secrets for so long, they had become part of her life and she didn't know where to begin. 'Julie is right, Chris holds a lot of power now. Even those that don't like him have to follow orders. That is the mafia, and he is the head of the family.'

It was Diana's turn to butt in. She had been quiet up until now but she had a gut feeling about this. 'Surely there is only one thing he can blackmail you over Katie, and that is about who killed Sharon, am I right?'

Sharon had been Jake's wife. Tired of being in the background, she had set them all up – Jake, Tony and even Ralph Gold – with the intention of taking over their business and putting them all behind bars. Jake had been ordered to kill Sharon, but instead, it had been Sharon who had shot Jake. Sharon had eventually been shot, but it was by Katie's hand.

The police had put the case on ice. No one knew who had done it. Only on seeing her father's distress had Katie confessed to killing Sharon. There were only a handful of people who knew the truth, and most of them were dead now... except for the people in this room.

'Yes, Diana. As soon as our marriage became a strain, I suggested we separate. It seemed it was for the best and for the children. All they ever heard was both of us arguing at some point. But Chris had his own plans. He knew it was me that killed Sharon and was prepared to tell the police to keep me in my place. I would go to prison for murder, which would mean leaving my children and possibly never seeing them again. At least this way, I have some freedom. But Chris is clever, he never lets me come back to England with all of the kids; it's his insurance to ensure I always go back. I have no choice. They are my kids, and if living a lie helps me keep them, then so be it.' Katie's voice wafted around the sea of confused faces. 'Chris still has the gun with my prints on it.'

'For Christ's sake, Katie, why didn't you tell me? This wasn't all your doing,' exclaimed Diana. Picking up her drink, she took a large gulp. 'Let me help you sort that bastard out. You should have told me!'

Scarlet and Julie cast furtive glances towards each other; it was as though there was another conversation going on in the room that they weren't privy to.

Suspiciously, Julie looked at Diana and then at Katie. 'Why are you so interested Diana? What has this got to do with you?'

'Because I was with Katie when Sharon got shot,' Diana confessed. 'Why do you think she had two bullets in her? One was from Lambrianu and the other one was from Gold!'

Julie paled. She hadn't expected this, but then a flash of memory came back to her. 'You know, Ralph always said there had to be two people in on it. He swore by that. So where were you, Diana?'

'Well, on duty Mum. Katie ran ahead and hailed a taxi and I just ambled along with my copper's hat on. Nobody looks a copper in the eye and no one thought anything of it. Katie gave Chris the gun at his insistence and now he has made her life a misery. Sorry Katie.'

Julie couldn't believe her ears. 'You and Katie concocted this murder between you? You could have lost your job and gone to prison. You were only just starting out in the police force. Why would you do it?'

Diana took out a cigarette and lit one, blowing the smoke in the air. 'Neither of us thought Jake would kill Sharon. He loved her too much and there was so much at stake. Don Carlos would have shot Jake for not having the balls to kill Sharon. We had no security, and our fathers would have ended up behind bars. Dad couldn't go to prison, he was a sick man. Someone had to get there and help Jake, but sadly we were too late. If only Jake's driver had kept his eye on the ball, he would probably still be alive now. I may be a copper Mum, but I have Gold blood running through my veins, and no one hurts our families. I'm sorry that Katie has covered for me all these years, and especially at Chris's hands. What a sly bastard he is.'

Taking another drag of her cigarette, Diana poured another drink for herself.

'Fuck, I never saw that one coming.' Julie shook her head in amazement and turned towards the others. 'Well, it looks like we are all in this together. So what next? Does Chris get his comeuppance and we make Katie a free woman? And you Adam, are you prepared to take your rightful place as a true Italian man who looks after his own? And you Diana...' She glared at her daughter. 'Are you with us?'

'Definitely Mum.' Diana held her hand out and Julie put her hand on top of hers. Scarlet and Adam did likewise. 'Gold and Lambrianu, fighting their battles together again,' said Diana very seriously. 'What do you want us to do, Mum? I'm sure you have a plan.'

'Too right I have, and I am going to make sure Chris dies an awful death before I leave this mortal coil, just as my Ralph would have done.'

16

THE ONLY WAY IS FORWARD

Bleary-eyed, Scarlet yawned and looked at the digital clock: 9 a.m. Turning to her left, she saw Katie still asleep with spit dribbling from her mouth. Her back ached from the sofa she had slept on, and she yawned again and looked around the room.

Someone had thrown a duvet over them both, possibly when they'd passed out from far too much alcohol. She had been sat more or less upright all night and her bum felt numb. Gently, she removed Katie's head from her shoulder, letting it flop onto the back of the sofa, and tried standing up, feeling her bones creak as she did. Katie didn't stir. Scarlet turned and looked at her twin and smiled. Reaching down, she stroked the side of her face, pushed the duvet around her more, and proceeded to walk into the kitchen.

Switching the kettle on and then walking quietly to the bathroom, Scarlet noticed her immaculate pink suit was now creased and looked like it hadn't been ironed in years, but her face looked worse! Black mascara was smeared across her cheeks and her hair looked like a bird's nest.

Searching through Adam's bathroom cabinet, she found what she was looking for – paracetamol! Her head felt as if there was a brass band inside it. Beside the painkillers, she found half a dozen brand-new toothbrushes. Running the tap, she cupped her hands and threw cold water over her face and hair. Ripping open the box, she brushed her teeth to bring some feeling back into her mouth, which felt like the bottom of a bird cage. Walking back into the kitchen, she made a coffee. Frowning, Scarlet wondered where the others were and out of curiosity walked through the apartment towards the bedrooms. Seeing one of the doors ajar, she pushed it gently open.

Julie was fast asleep in bed with Diana at her side. Scarlet smiled. The sight of them both gave her a pang in her stomach as she thought of her own mother. Diana was firmly cuddled up to Julie, almost childlike, while Julie's arm was wrapped protectively around her. Mother and daughter. It seemed strange to Scarlet that she had never thought of Julie like that, but she was a mother, after all. Julie just never shared that soft side of her.

Gently closing the door again, she peeked into Adam's bedroom. Adam was on top of his bed in his boxer shorts, snoring his head off.

The hot coffee soothed her dry throat as she sat at the breakfast bar sipping it. She didn't want to run the shower yet, for fear of waking everyone. Instead, she crept around Katie in the lounge and found her handbag containing her mobile.

Pressing the buttons, she messaged Knuckles to bring herself and Katie some clothing and some fresh underwear for Diana. His thumbs up emoji confirmed he'd received the message. Raising one eyebrow, Scarlet looked at his answer and shook her head. He was truly a man of few words, she thought to herself.

After another coffee and half an hour later, she heard a banging at the door. She knew it would be Knuckles, because only bailiffs knocked like that. So much for her creeping around to let everyone sleep!

Opening the door, she put her finger to her lips. 'Everyone is asleep, shush!'

Nodding, Knuckles handed over a holdall and turned to walk away. 'Oi,' Scarlet whispered, 'aren't you going to ask me if I'm okay or anything?'

Knuckles stood there and stared at her blankly. 'Are you okay?'

Exasperated, Scarlet ran her hands through her straggly hair. 'Oh, forget it. Make sure everyone is at the club, will you? I'll be another couple of hours.' Hearing a noise behind her, Scarlet turned and saw Katie in much the same state as herself wandering towards the kitchen.

'Scat, I hope that kettle's on, my mouth thinks my throat's been cut.' Hearing Katie's hoarse voice, she nodded, took one last look at Knuckles and shut the door. 'You look like I feel, Scat. Fuck, that was a heavy night last night. I haven't drunk like that in years.' Plonking herself onto a stool, Katie sat there with her head in her hands. Looking up, she saw Diana coming into the kitchen.

'Do I smell coffee?' Diana asked.

Scarlet threw the box of paracetamol onto the table. 'First come, first served.' She smiled and poured more coffee for the others. Both Katie and Diana scrambled for the paracetamol, moaning about their headaches and reaching for their mugs of coffee.

'Fuck, you kids are lightweights.' Sauntering into the kitchen, Julie looked at the three women. 'Pour me one of those, will you? I'm going to the bathroom. Oh here.' Julie threw a small leather bag towards Scarlet. 'I like my cocktail with my coffee first thing in the morning. Just mix it in. Time for a pee!'

They all stopped what they were doing and watched Scarlet open the little leather pouch. 'Oh my God, these aren't tea leaves. She has a bag of cannabis! What am I supposed to do with this?' Scarlet stepped forward and showed the others. If anyone had the shock factor it was Julie.

'Put it in my coffee, you silly cow. It will blend with the water, just stir it well!' Julie shouted from the bathroom.

'Does she ever take a leak without leaving the bathroom door open?' Katie asked.

Diana shook her head and smiled. 'Nope. Likes to hear everything and hates to miss parts of the conversation. Even her bladder doesn't allow her to stop being nosey!' Scarlet made the coffee cocktail and placed it on the table as Julie walked in. 'Nothing like a pick me up first thing in the morning. You should try it sometime. God, you all look like shit. I mean, I look like shit, but you three look worse. Where is Adam? Isn't he out of his pit yet? Adam! Get your scrawny arse out of bed,' Julie shouted, while the others held their heads and winced at the screaming banshee in the room.

They could hear mumblings and stirring coming from Adam's room and waited as they heard his footsteps padding down the hallway. He arrived in the doorway, yawning and scratching his head.

'Don't you dare scratch your balls in front of me,' Julie said. 'I had years of that with Ralph.' Taking a sip of her cocktail, Julie looked at the others. 'Why is it that men always scratch down there first thing in the morning? Us women don't do that.' She grimaced.

Stopping himself, Adam grinned. 'I wasn't going to, Julie, and you shouldn't be looking. You got one of those mugs of coffee for me Scat? I'm parched. God, that was a late one. What time did we get to bed?'

'God knows. All I remember is waking up at about 3 a.m. with Katie dribbling spit on me.'

Adam sat beside Julie at the breakfast bar.

Julie held her nose. 'Phew! You smell Adam. Go and put a dressing gown on or something, or better still, have a shower!'

'After this coffee Julie, or do you want to go first? Age before beauty.' He grinned.

'I need to ring Lewis. He can bring some things over for me. I'm not leaving a young man's flat in the morning with last night's clothes on. Christ, I haven't done that in years!'

'I doubt that Julie, with all those men living in your house,' Scarlet laughed.

Pokerfaced Julie looked around the breakfast bar at the dishevelled gathering. 'You lot really are stupid, aren't you. Those beautiful boys who live with me are all gay! Do you really think I would sleep with another man in Ralph's house? Don't be ridiculous,' she scoffed. Julie looked over the rim of her coffee cocktail.

'Bloody hell, why are all the good-looking blokes gay? Life isn't fair,' Diana laughed.

Katie was shocked. 'Why you little minx, Julie Gold! You do realise everyone else thinks you're bonking them. Why do you keep them around?'

'They just sort of turned up and I liked the company. They enjoy living in luxury. Seems fair to me.' Julie shrugged. All of them burst out laughing. This was hilarious news.

'You never fail to surprise me Julie,' laughed Adam.

'Good, I would hate to be predictable. They look after me and my business and I enjoy male company better than female. Women are so bitchy. Although you want to hear Lewis when he gets on his high horse!' she cackled. 'Right, off you go each of you and clean up. I am going to call Lewis and he can send my things on with the chauffeur. How you manage with one bathroom Adam is beyond me. Don't tell me it's the first time you've had four women in your house in the morning.' She winked.

'It's not, Julie, but they prefer to shower with me. It saves water!'

'Wait you lot.' Julie stopped them all as they started to move. 'I know you have hangovers and headaches, but do you remember the pact we made last night?'

Each of them looked at each other.

'We weren't that pissed, Mum. We all remember what we've agreed. Are you still with us, Katie? After all, it's your husband we're talking about,' asked Diana.

'I'm with you all of the way. This is my family, my kids. I will not let Chris rob me of them. It's time for action. I won't let him take over the vineyard, either. It's ours.'

'Life really is a circle,' mused Julie. 'I will sort things out at my end and let you know when we're ready to make a move. Are we agreed?' asked Julie sternly. Now she had got the bit between her teeth and the family onside, she wasn't going to let this drop.

Everyone looked at each other and nodded. 'We're all agreed. Just tell us where and when,' said Scarlet.

Adam's phone buzzed, informing him he had received a text. Looking at it he saw that it was from Jennifer.

Are we still on for tonight?

Adam looked at his bruised face in the mirror and sighed. In for a penny, he thought to himself.

Absolutely. See you then.

He wasn't sure if she would want to sit in a crowded restaurant with him once he had shown her his face, but he would cross that bridge when he came to it.

Scarlet raised an eyebrow and gave Adam a lopsided grin. 'Well, I think we all know that was a woman by the look on your face Adam. Which little starlet has the pleasure tonight?'

'No one you know. It's just a friend,' Adam lied.

'Thats a first,' she laughed. 'Right, I'm off to the bathroom first. Katie, Knuckles has brought some underwear and clothes for us. Diana there's spare underwear in there for you too. I'll ring the cleaners and get them to come in and sort out the mess we made last night.' As usual, Scarlet was in charge of the situation.

As Adam sped through the streets on his motorbike, he pondered his forthcoming evening with Jennifer. He knew from experience that his dates were usually out to impress him. They enjoyed the free champagne and the club life that Adam offered. They knew money was no object and once tired, Adam would pay them off with some trinket to avoid any bad feelings should they meet again.

But Jennifer was different. She still had no idea who he was.

And he had never been out with a woman he hadn't slept with on the first night before, yet he felt he should tread carefully with Jennifer. She had a mind of her own and could hold a conversation without fawning all over him and it made a pleasant change.

He had considered picking her up in his car but thought better of it. She was used to his motorbike and he didn't want to kill the illusion, well, not yet anyway. He was lying through his teeth and he knew it. Wearing his leathers over his suit and tie, he sped through the streets in the damp, drizzly darkness. Thankfully he had brought some leathers for Jennifer too, which were carefully packed away in the back of his bike.

Pulling up outside, he was about to text her when she ran out of the door to greet him. 'You're on your bike! I didn't know whether you would be on this rainy night.' She grinned.

Getting off his bike, he opened the box on the back and handed her the leathers. 'Put these on, they will keep you dry. I have to show you something else first and then you can make your mind up if you want to be seen in a restaurant with me.' Seeing her puzzled look, he lifted his helmet to show her his bruised face.

'Oh my God, Adam, what on earth happened? Were you

mugged?' Stroking his bruised face, she looked at him with concern.

'All part of the job, Jennifer. These things happen in a skirmish, but answer the question, do you want to be seen in public with my battered face?' He grinned.

Jennifer's heart skipped a beat as she looked at him. A swollen purple eye wasn't too bad; she'd seen worse. If anything, he looked even more rugged and handsome. 'It sounds like a dangerous job; I presume it was some drunk who took a swing at you?'

Adam smiled. He hadn't had to lie and deciding to end the conversation, he helped her onto his motorbike and rode off. Feeling her arms wrapped tightly around his waist gave him a warm feeling and he could feel a stirring inside of him.

The dimly lit restaurant made him feel better as he walked in; at least it helped to hide his bruises. Jennifer looked him up and down. His grey, well-fitting suit and tie made him look even more handsome and she couldn't help but admire him. 'You look very smart,' she commented as they were led to their table.

'And you look beautiful.' Jennifer looked down at her dress. She felt quite underdressed. She could see his suit was made to measure. It fitted him perfectly, showing the shape of his muscly arms.

She'd taken advice from her friends and worn her usual black thinly strapped dress with a 'v' neck. And she'd worn her hair in a ponytail, knowing that she would likely be wearing a helmet. Now, though, she took out the band holding it and let it fall about her shoulders. As she looked around the restaurant, she could see women glancing towards Adam as he sat down. Even with his black eye, he looked very sexy.

'Adam, it's good to see you.' Adam looked up, surprised, as the maître d' stood before him in his tuxedo and held out his hand to shake his vigorously.

'It's good to see you too.' Adam grinned, wishing he would leave. He didn't want to appear rude so he winked at the maître d', which indicated he wanted to be alone with his date. Taking the hint and grinning, the man looked towards Jennifer. 'You look beautiful madam. Maybe you would like some champagne before your order?'

Nervously, Jennifer looked towards Adam. She knew champagne was expensive but in a place like this she had no idea how much it would cost.

'That sounds perfect, I'll leave the choice in your capable hands,' interrupted Adam and then looked across the table at Jennifer to reassure her. Adam almost breathed a sigh of relief when the maître d' left the table.

'Can we afford it?' whispered Jennifer from behind her red velvet menu. 'Maybe we should leave.'

'Call it the perks of the job. We can afford it, at a discount. So, pick what you want.'

Looking at her in the candlelight, he could see she felt uncomfortable. This all seemed a little overwhelming to her. This was the norm for him and now he realised he had made a mistake. This wasn't her scene at all.

He could have kicked himself. Straightening his tie, he leaned forward. 'This place was recommended to me, although I do know the maître d'. I've met him a few times at the club. But I would have preferred an Indian or something. This menu is full of lobster and crème brulée.' He grinned, as though sharing a secret.

'I know,' she giggled. 'There's a steak house further up the road; they do two for one some week nights. Or there is an Indian up the high street, although I'm not sure about the spices and garlic...' She blushed and lowered her head.

Adam took the hint. Garlic was not the best thing for a kiss. 'The steak house it is then.'

'What about him?' Jennifer looked towards the maître d'.

'You go ahead, I'll have a quiet word with him and tell him something has come up.'

After squaring it with the staff and giving them a fifty-pound tip for their trouble, he joined Jennifer, who was already putting on her leathers.

The steak house she'd recommended wasn't too bad, even though the steak was a little overdone for his taste, and it was cheaper than what he had just tipped the waiters.

'I have to go away in two weeks, Adam. An opportunity has come up for me in the Caribbean. Someone dropped out last minute and they have offered it to me,' she blurted out mid-meal.

Trying to hide his shock, he smiled. 'Well, that sounds like a great opportunity. You must be very pleased.' The thought of her leaving before they had got to know each other saddened him.

'We have two weeks, though. Maybe we could still make the most of it?' she asked hopefully. 'I will only be gone for a few weeks...' She trailed off. Suddenly, her lovely steak felt sour in her mouth. She had worried all day about telling him and hoped he wouldn't take it as a brush-off.

Jennifer looked at Adam across the table. Even with his bruised face he looked handsome and as those blue eyes stared into hers, she felt her heart skip a beat. She hardly knew him and now she was leaving him. She knew it wouldn't be long before he found her replacement. With his perfectly formed chiselled features, the cleft in his chin and charming ways, he had swept her off her feet. Most attractive of all was his low, husky voice. He made every sentence sound like a romantic song.

'Well,' Adam said, 'a few weeks isn't so bad, is it? There are ways we can keep in touch if you have time?'

'I'd like that Adam, we can Zoom or something.' She grinned excitedly. 'But I am not sure about the time difference.' Giving him a nervous smile, Jennifer cursed herself. She didn't want to sound clingy.

'I'm sure we can work something out.' Under his long lashes, Adam looked into her eyes and reached over and put his hand on hers.

Adam asked her about her trip. He enjoyed the conversation; it was different from his usual brand of women. He enjoyed her company. She was funny and intelligent. They talked about a whole range of things and before they knew it, the meal had come to an end, and it was time to leave.

On the way home, Jennifer held him tighter around the waist than was necessary. She hadn't pulled down the visor on her helmet so she breathed in his aftershave. The only way she could describe this handsome man to herself was enigmatic. She realised that this whirlwind affair would be short-lived; after all, she had nothing to offer in particular and he would forget about her the moment she stepped on to the aeroplane. But tonight, as they sped along the streets, he was hers and hers alone.

As they pulled up outside her flat, Adam took off his helmet and shook his head to let his mane of hair free. Leaning forwards, Jennifer whispered into his ear, 'My flatmates are all out for the evening.'

Adam felt a familiar tingling through his body and a stirring in his manhood. Just then, his mobile rang. Sighing, Adam cursed himself for not turning it off. This really wasn't the moment to hear Scarlet barking down the phone.

Jennifer got off the bike. 'You'd better get that, it could be important,' she prompted and walked to the back of the bike to put her helmet in the box.

Reaching into his pocket, Adam looked at his mobile and frowned. It wasn't Scarlet's name that popped up on his phone, it was Julie's. Quickly, he answered.

'Adam, Jamie's girlfriend is in a wine bar in Chelsea. Get your arse over there and give her some of that Lambrianu magic. I want to know if Jamie has been in touch and boasted of his good fortune to try and win her back.'

Sighing, Adam cast a furtive glance towards Jennifer who was idly taking her time at the back of the bike to give him some privacy. 'What... now?'

'Yes, now! This is business, Adam. I need to know what that big mouth has said but she doesn't want to sleep with me, does she, or I would do it myself! Now get your arse into gear.'

'I'm kind of busy at the moment. Can't we do this tomorrow?'

'No, this is a golden opportunity. Whoever you're with, get rid of them. They'll wait if they're that interested!'

'Oh fuck,' Adam cursed loudly.

'Yep, exactly. Now go to it, Adam, I'm relying on you. Tell your girlfriend your arse is on fire, and you have to leave. Go!'

Knowing she was right, Adam ran his hands through his hair once again. His body ached and throbbed with anticipation as he looked at Jennifer's slim body, but business came first. His heart sank as he met her eyes.

'I'm afraid I have to go. Something's come up,' he apologised. Seeing the disappointment in her face made him curse Julie.

She gave him a weak smile. 'That's okay, I understand. It sounded important. I hope it's nothing serious?'

'Just work business.' Adam reached out and pulled her towards him. As their lips met, the ardency of her response sent chills through his body. He trailed his lips down her neck and felt her pert breasts through the thinness of her dress.

'How long do you have before you need to leave?' she murmured huskily.

'Not long.'

'Come on then, this won't take long.' Taking his hand, she

watched him get off his bike. Passion had consumed both of them, and Adam decided that tonight Julie could wait a little longer. Hurriedly, they ran through the door while discarding their clothing. Adam put his hand around the back of her neck and pulled her close, their lips meeting again. His hands roamed over her half-naked body, tweaking and arousing her pert nipples as he bent his head and flicked them with his moist tongue. Picking her up in his arms, he looked at her questioningly, and she pointed, breathlessly, to her bedroom.

He laid her on the bed and she opened her arms to welcome him as she marvelled at his well-muscled arms and body. His shoulders were wide and went into a 'v' shape at his waist.

Her eyes widened as he dropped his boxer shorts. 'Is that all yours? Was your father a donkey?'

'No Jennifer, it's half yours.' He grinned and threw himself on the bed.

Passion consumed them both and Adam could already feel her arousal as she moaned and murmured underneath him. Fireworks shot through her body as he entered her, and she gave a low moan, her hips rising up to meet each stroke. Adam moved faster as she began to reach her peak. Her cry as she grasped and clung onto his shoulders made him thrust even harder until he felt his body shudder in an orgasmic release. Collapsing at the side of her on the bed, they both struggled to breathe air into their lungs. Passion had consumed them both. Resting on her elbow, she turned to face him, and ran her hand through the fine hairs on his chest. 'Christ, that was good,' she panted.

Although Adam's body yearned for more of the same, Julie flashed through his mind. 'I'm sorry Jennifer, I have to go. Next time will be slower and more precise, I promise.' Turning to kiss her on the lips, he got off the bed and started searching for his clothes.

'I wish you didn't have to go,' she said. 'This is definitely a kiss and run.'

'I told you I didn't have long… but next time.' Raising his hand to his lips, he blew her a kiss and left. Breathing in the cool night air as he walked to his bike, he felt guilty about leaving Jennifer. But Julie was right. Business came first. Taking a backward look as he started up his bike, he saw Jennifer at the window waving. Waving back, he rode off to the wine bar in Chelsea and whatever waited for him there.

17

GUILTY FEELINGS

As the sun rose, Adam walked back to his motorbike. Guilt washed over him, although he had got the information that Julie wanted. Straddling his bike, he revved it up and rode off. The first port of call would be Julie's house. He knew he should go home and get washed and changed, but for now he wanted to ride on the open road and clear his head.

Lewis opened the door on his arrival. 'She's still in bed, Mr Lambrianu. She's not asleep but she likes her tea in bed while she watches the news. I'll let her know you're here. Can I get you some breakfast and coffee? You look like you need it. Would you like to freshen up first?' Taking in Adam's dishevelled look, Lewis couldn't help wondering if there was a problem.

'Coffee would be good and so would a shower.' Jokingly, Adam pretended to sniff his own armpits and rubbed the shadow on his chin.

'Good, let's get you sorted out first then we'll let Julie know you're here. Although I presume her ferret ears will have heard that monstrosity of a motorbike. Those things are too scary for me.' Lewis held his hands up in submission and laughed.

Adam followed the handsome man before him and wondered to himself why he had never seen it before. Julie's revelation that all of her male live-in friends were gay was more than obvious. Lewis was a kind and caring man, but seeing him acting as mother hen made it more than apparent. Julie was right, there was none so blind as those who cannot see.

Feeling the hot water run down his body made him feel instantly better. His thoughts ran to Jennifer and how he had left her so quickly and fallen into another woman's bed. The guilt he'd felt returned. It wasn't the first time he'd had more than one woman on the go, but Jennifer didn't know the rules and didn't deserve it. Adam decided it was better to let her down gently. She was going away soon, and the space would make things seem better in the cold light of day. She would forget about him, and he could carry on as normal without these horrible guilty feelings.

He hadn't known Jennifer long, but from their first meeting, he had liked what he saw and enjoyed her company. Although he did find it strange that she hadn't asked too many questions about him. Frowning, Adam let the soapy water run down the plug hole and turned off the shower. She had just had sex with someone, and she didn't even know his last name! Maybe she made a habit of sleeping around. After all, it had been herself who had suggested their encounter last night... Maybe she did know the rules, Adam thought to himself.

Feeling much better about the situation, he stepped out of the shower. Across the other side of the bathroom Adam saw that Lewis had been in and left two brand-new shirts still in their packaging and clean underwear for him. The fluffy white towels were hot from the radiator and there was an electric razor and toothbrush still in its packaging. A big grin crossed Adam's face as he looked in the mirror and picked up the razor.

'Well, you look a lot better than when you turned up with your hunched shoulders and slow walk. Was last night a total wash-out then?' Julie laughed. She was lying on her pink chaise lounge in her leopard print dressing gown drinking from a china cup. 'Lewis has made you breakfast. Have some coffee and something to eat while you fill me in on the gossip.'

Lewis appeared with a small tray loaded with bacon and eggs and a hot mug of coffee.

'You were right, Julie, that stupid bugger has been bragging about coming into some money soon. Apparently, he has an aunty who lives in the country that he wasn't aware of.' Adam laughed and chewed on his bacon. 'He's told her they could start again and get a better home and have a nice holiday. Whatever she wants. He's dangling the carrot to get her back. He loves her and to be honest, you've been his fairy godmother. You're giving him that opportunity so I think he will play your game and try and cream some more off the top.'

Putting down her coffee cup, Julie clapped her hands with glee. 'We're home and dry Adam. I must get hold of Bruce. We need to get some more out of those accounts while the clients think their shares are on the up. I want Jamie to convince them to invest more money.' Julie picked up her coffee cup and held it in their air, toasting Adam. Raising her eyebrows, Julie grinned. 'So I presume you had to sleep with this wonderful, loyal girlfriend then, and that she didn't take a lot of coaxing?'

'Not really,' Adam sighed. 'She was pleased to see me and two martinis and a packet of pork scratchings later we were on the way to her place.' As an afterthought, Adam looked at Julie, knowing she liked a bit of juicy gossip. 'She is a bit demanding though and she has some strange tastes.'

'Oh my God, does she like it on the rough side!' Julie laughed. 'Do tell me, Adam.' Julie's eyes lit up mischievously as Adam gave her snippets of his evening.

Once they had fulfilled Julie's appetite for gossip, she scrutinised Adam closely. 'So whose bed did you have to leave in the name of business? You seemed quite put out last night when I asked you to stop what you were doing and meet Miss Whiplash!' Julie laughed at her own joke, but she could see something weighed heavily on Adam's mind. She had known him for too long and had watched him hide behind a mask before.

'I've met someone. Someone different. It's early days and we've only seen each other a couple of times, but I enjoy her company. She's going away soon for work experience though, so it's best left.' Adam shrugged.

'Work experience? What is she, fourteen?' Julie was intrigued but shocked at the same time.

'No, she's at university. She's a marine biologist. But works at a local supermarket for extra cash.' Slowly but surely, Adam found himself telling Julie all about Jennifer. He hadn't intended to, but once he'd started, he couldn't stop, including his very hurried encounter before he went to meet Jamie's girlfriend.

'How do you know she doesn't know who you are? You're the darling of the tabloids, Adam. Most magazines publish what time of the day you fart! They're always publishing your naughty ways with some glamour puss on your arm. Does she live in a bubble? Doesn't she see the magazine rack at this supermarket she works at? She's waiting for you to be honest, Adam. She doesn't need to ask questions, because she knows all of the answers! You said yourself, she's not stupid, but she's playing the long game. Has she asked you for anything?' Julie laughed.

'Now that you mention it, no she hasn't. She even offers to go half on the bill if we eat out.' Adam blushed.

'Good. Because if she likes you genuinely, she has a lot to prove and the first thing is that she is not like the others. She's not a gold digger, unlike me of course. Crikey, if I hadn't hammered Ralph's credit card on a regular basis, he would have thought I'd been cloned by aliens.' Cackling out loud, Julie laughed at her own joke, so much so she nearly choked on her coffee.

Adam shrugged. 'We hardly know each other, Julie.'

'How long do you have to know someone if the feeling is right, Adam? There is no time limit.'

Adam gave a nervous laugh. 'I think you're jumping the gun a bit Julie. It's someone I've dated twice, no big deal.'

'Which is why you're sat here telling me all about her and how guilty you felt leaving her bed for another woman's. You're right Adam, it's no big deal.' Smugly, Julie sipped at her coffee and watched Adam almost squirm at her words.

Once he'd finished his breakfast, Adam bent to kiss Julie on the cheek and as he was leaving, he bumped into Bruce in the hallway. 'What are you doing here?'

'I've been summoned. She even sends a car for me now.' Bruce blushed.

'So, you really are one of her boys now.' Adam burst out laughing.

'It looks like it.' Bruce grinned. 'I've put in a bid for a house for my mother. Julie is going to deal with the paperwork. Mum loves it and I never thought I'd be able to do something like that for mum on my wage. I have a lot to thank Julie for. She scares the shit out of me, but her heart is in the right place. She's a strange character Adam but she understands me and accepts me for who I am.'

Bruce's heartfelt confession about Julie touched Adam. They had formed a bond and he was under Julie's umbrella now.

'How did your night go with Jamie's girlfriend? Did she come up with anything?'

'For fuck's sake. Is my sex life public knowledge? How did Julie know where she was anyway?'

'I'm tracking her. I met her friend the other night, Kim, the one that works with Jamie. They were having a drink together. I was telling her how to install something on her mobile and she handed it over to me. So, I worked my magic and I can now track her. That's how we knew she was in Chelsea.'

Adam pushed his hand through his hair, sweeping his wavy fringe from his face. 'You two are better than Russian spies! But I'm glad you're getting something out of this to fill your wallet and look after your mum.'

'The things we do for money, Adam. I would never have believed it if you'd told me this a year ago.' They both burst out laughing and hugged.

'Is that you Bruce?' Julie bellowed from the lounge. 'Come in for Christ's sake. I hate when people whisper in hallways and I don't know what they're saying.'

'You'd better go,' laughed Adam. 'Cruella de Vil is calling you.' They both laughed again as Adam left.

* * *

Once back in his apartment and freshened up with a suit and tie, he felt better. Now it was time to go and start the day's work with Scarlet. Suddenly his mobile burst into life with a text message. Looking at it, he could see it was from Jennifer and a smile crossed his face.

When are you ready for round two? Xx

I'm always ready x

Are you busy tonight, Adam? My shift finishes at 9 p.m.

I'll be there. See you soon x

Without realising it, Adam grinned all the way to the office, where Scarlet sat in her two-piece pink suit, her gold-rimmed glasses perched on the bridge of her nose. 'Have you just got out of bed? The day's half over, you lazy twat.'

'No Scat, I've had things to do. But I'm here now.'

'What are you grinning about? What's so funny?'

He sat in his leather chair beside her. 'Because you make me smile, Scat,' he lied.

'Don't use that flattery with me you old Romeo. I'm immune to it.' She smiled. 'Anyway, I had a call this morning. Did you know Loose-lipped Lenny is dead...? Well, presumed dead. Someone's saying it's the yardies. Wasn't he working with them?'

Wide eyed, Adam feigned innocence. 'He was working with them. What makes you think they've killed him?'

'Word on the street, and it's never wrong Adam. You know that.' Scarlet paused and gave Adam a knowing look, waiting for some kind of comment, but there wasn't any. 'He must have stepped out of line, because they only kill people if crossed. We've done business with them for years and had no problems. He's probably buried in concrete somewhere. I don't know any more.'

'Not our business, Scat. If it doesn't involve us, then why should we care?' He shrugged, although the mention of Lenny brought something to the forefront of Adam's mind. He still had that holdall full of cocaine. As Scarlet laid out the itinerary for the day, he wondered how much it was worth. Could he really be bothered to put the hard work in of trying to sell it under Scarlet's nose? That delivery had nearly cost him his life and wasn't worth the hassle. No, he decided to himself, while blocking his ears to Scarlet's rambling, he would sell it on to Jimmy for a fraction of the price and let him deal with it. Jimmy could sell it easily enough at his own clubs and would snatch the bargain out of his hands. Maybe it was time to take a rest from that side of things for a while and keep the heat off himself. With that sorted in his mind, he looked back up at Scarlet.

'You seem a bit down, Scarlet, what's wrong?'

Putting down her pen, Scarlet sat back and stretched her arms out. 'I always feel down when Katie goes home. She's part of me, and now I'm worried about her and Chris. He's been a real bastard right under our noses Adam. We need to free her of him.'

'And we will. Patience is a virtue, Scarlet. Julie seems to have everything in hand there. Katie has waited all these years, what's a little longer?'

'Mm, I suppose you're right. But we need to sort it soon. I don't like the idea that he thinks he's got one over on us. He needs to know who's boss.'

Adam burst out laughing. 'At the moment Scarlet he rules Italy and anywhere in between. He is the Don of the mafia, so I presume he is the boss. But you should be careful whose nose you put out of joint on the way up, because you always meet them on the way down. He'll get his comeuppance, but let Julie have this. She's taking it much more personally and demands her day in court, so to speak.'

Letting out a deep sigh, Scarlet nodded. She knew Adam was right and Julie wouldn't thank her for sticking her nose in. 'Okay, but let's hope it's soon, eh?' Squeezing Adam's arm for reassurance, she gave him a weak smile. She was about to say something else, when Knuckles entered the office. 'Can't you see we're talking? Have you ever heard of knocking!'

Knuckles walked out of the office and shut the door behind him, making both Adam and Scarlet glance at each other curiously. Suddenly, they heard a knock at the door. Automatically, Scarlet shouted, 'Come in,' and in walked Knuckles. Adam did his best to contain his laughter, but his telltale giveaway was his eyes.

Disgruntled, Scarlet elbowed him in the arm. 'I don't know

what you're laughing at. What do you want Knuckles, now you've learnt to knock on the door?'

'Boys are outside. It's payday.'

Scarlet sat even further back in her chair and rubbed her hands together. 'This part of the week always makes me smile. Show them in, Knuckles.'

One by one, each of the men that worked for them came through the door with a bag and emptied the contents on the floor in front of Scarlet and Adam.

'This is from some of those poxy stripper pubs in the East End.' Pouring his bag of money secured with elastic bands on the floor, the man looked up to see Scarlet's approval. 'Is it all there?' she asked.

'Every penny.' He grinned.

'Next!' she shouted.

Matt walked in with his bag and squeezed between the others. 'I had a bit of bother, nothing I can't handle though.'

Suddenly, Scarlet's hackles went up. 'What trouble?'

'Apparently there's some bloke and a couple of heavies loan-sharking on our turf. He's offering a better rate of interest, telling the tenants they don't need to pay us 'cos he will sort it out.' Looking down at the floor, Matt shuffled from one foot to the other with his head bowed. Quickly he glanced up at Scarlet and Adam.

Scarlet's face flushed to her roots. 'Well, we will send the boys in, that will sort this crap out. We've lent these people money and I want it back!'

Adam sat there nonchalantly listening to his sister's rantings. 'I'll go; there's no need to send anyone else. I'll give the warning to stay away and a warning to others if they try it again.'

'You?' Matt spied Adam curiously. 'The tenants in those tower blocks feel they have paid you double what they have borrowed in the past – that's the big problem. And this boss of theirs, Arthur something, is offering less.' Matt scratched his head, trying to remember the name one of the tenants had shouted at him when refusing to pay and slamming the door in his face.

'And you did nothing? You fucking wimp. Why am I paying you? You should have wrung their bloody necks!' Scarlet shouted.

'Now, now Scarlet.' Adam's soothing voice irritated Scarlet and she pulled her arm away from where he had patted it comfortingly. 'All I'm saying Scarlet, is let's not go in mob handed. There's no need. When does this Arthur bloke show his face, Matt?'

'Not sure.' Matt shrugged. 'But apparently he's got a couple of bruisers on his side.'

'Go back and have a word with that alcoholic bloke, Jerry. You know, the one with the squashed face. Apparently, he was a good boxer in his time until he found the pleasures of alcohol. He'll give us the information we need. Take a few bottles of whisky and a few quid in your pocket and he'll tell us everything we need to know. Then come back and tell me what you find out and I will sort it, got it?'

'Yes boss, I'll go back now.'

'And don't wear your suit, Matt. Jeans and T-shirt for this one. Let's not put Jerry under suspicion. He's a drunk, but a good drunk and he's a good pair of eyes and ears.' Adam nodded at Matt, indicating for him to leave and do as he was asked, then turned to Scarlet, smiling. 'Why don't you put those bundles of cash in the safe, Scat?'

Knuckles threw a glance at Adam. After so many years, he could see beyond Adam's charming mask and saw his eyes darken and the rage boiling up inside him.

Scarlet wagged a warning finger at Adam. 'Don't forget, it's the charity auction tonight for that MP and his friends. I want you in your best bib and tucker.'

Adam almost turned to stone. He had completely forgotten

about it and he was supposed to be meeting Jennifer, which seemed a much better prospect than sitting around drinking with peers of the realm. 'I don't really want my photo taken with them Scarlet, not when I don't look my best.' Rubbing his chin, Adam put on his best puppy-dog look.

'It looks okay to me. Swelling's gone down, just a bit yellow here and there. No excuses Adam, I want you there. This is what we do. These influential people keep us out of jail.'

Musing to himself, Adam knew she was right. Many a time she had pulled a favour in from these influential people. Their casino licence was always at the top of the pile when it needed renewing. Building permission was always granted and they never had any trouble from the police because most of the time they were inside their club dancing and drinking. It was always best to keep the devil on the right-hand side of you.

'I'll stay for a little while, but I want to find out more about this Arthur man. We need to strike while the iron is hot, Scat.' Lying through his teeth, Adam made excuses that he knew would appease Scarlet. If it was to do with business then he knew she would accept it.

'Mm, I see what you mean, although why you have to do it yourself is beyond me. We have people to do these things. Anyway, if you show your face for most of the evening, it will give you an alibi if you need one.'

He knew Scarlet was right, but he didn't want to cancel his evening with Jennifer. He decided he would put the ball in Jennifer's court and text her saying that he would be later than expected and if she cancelled, then that would be her choice.

* * *

Wearing his tuxedo, Adam admired himself in the mirror. Tonight, he looked like the businessman he was. His hair, although still with the fringe that had a life of its own, was groomed to perfection, and the cleft in his chin showed his perfectly chiselled jawline. Scarlet was right about the bruising on his face; it was hardly noticeable and the dimness of the club would do the rest.

Matt had been back to see him later that afternoon. He had got the information off Jerry as instructed. Apparently, Jerry had described Arthur as 'one mean bastard' and not to be trifled with, which had made Adam laugh. He was a man in his fifties, who had been a fence, served time, running the prison in the process, and had always been a wheeler and dealer. It sounded to him that this Arthur threatened the tenants to borrow money from him and had roughed up a few in the process. The best part of all was that Jerry had an idea where Arthur lived, because he knew him from the old days in the gym apparently. As far as Adam was concerned, that was a stupid move. You never let the left hand know what the right one was doing.

Taking out the piece of paper in his pocket, Adam stared at the address. It was in the posh part of London, but it was an apartment. That wouldn't be Arthur's home. He would have some country home in Kent or Essex, with some wife or girlfriend stashed away. Walking into the kitchen, Adam turned on the gas hob and set fire to the piece of paper and let it burn in the sink, whilst memorising the address.

Looking at his watch, he saw that it was 7 p.m. and time to make his appearance. Scarlet had laid on a hot and cold buffet at the back of the room. The champagne was on ice and the caviar was just waiting to be eaten. Taking one last glance in the mirror and brushing off invisible dust that was there, he made his way downstairs. The gathering was already in full swing, as the special auction was an early event. Friday nights were for the mistresses and Saturday nights were for the wives. Tonight was mistress night and tables were full of young women draped over their ageing MP dates, dressed in their diamonds.

Scarlet had made a point of having a few of the strippers there in evening gowns too, should any male be without an escort. It was good business and Scarlet thrived on it. As usual, Knuckles stood in the shaded area at the end of the bar whilst Scarlet played hostess, welcoming everyone personally.

Adam walked up to tables and shook hands with various people, joining them for a drink and moving on to work his charm on others. Everyone seemed pleased to see him as he made sure the waitresses filled their ice buckets of champagne, which in actual fact was a watered-down version, but everyone was in such high spirits they barely noticed.

Going to the bar to order his own drink, he heard a familiar voice as a tanned arm was draped around his waist. 'Where have you been Adam? I've missed you,' the woman whispered near his ear.

Glancing beside him, he knew it was one of the wannabee models who hung around the club looking for a sugar daddy, or the prospect of being spotted for some photo shoot. Sherry had done a fair bit of modelling and was well-known.

'Sherry, I agree it's been far too long. I take it you're not on your own?' Adam said, flashing her a smile.

Brushing her long blonde hair away from her face, she grimaced. 'Oh, I'm with some boring old fart, but I could meet you later?'

'I take it that same boring old fart is the one who bought you that diamond necklace and earrings?' He laughed. Sherry was a beautiful woman who liked the finer things in life, but who didn't want to pay for them herself.

'I need some proper sex, Adam, and you and that erection of

yours have never let me down before,' she purred. In the dimness of the bar, she trailed her hand gently over his crotch and stroked him. Instantly, Adam rose to the occasion. He couldn't help his male instincts; he had always been quick off the trigger when a beautiful woman approached him so willingly. Casually, he glanced around and spotted an elderly man, who he knew to be a politician, staring at them both at the bar.

'I think your date is waiting for you Sherry. Let's not upset anyone, eh? As for later, well, let's see how the night progresses. Come, I'll walk you to your table.'

Walking over with Sherry and a silver ice bucket with champagne, Adam smiled at the man sitting at the table. 'Welcome.' Putting the bucket on the table, Adam held out his hand to shake the man's. 'Sherry here has been informing me what she would like you to bid on at the auction. I hope you have a heavy wallet,' Adam laughed playfully.

Shaking his hand back, the man smiled. 'Will you join us for a drink, Mr Lambrianu? And then you can fill me in on how empty my pockets are going to be at the end of the night.'

Doing his duty, Adam sat at the table and drank a glass of champagne with them. 'Do call me Adam, all my friends do. And as for the auction, I will leave Sherry to surprise you with the details.' Adam spread his hand out towards the stage, which was piled high with trophies, jewellery and anything else people wanted to bid on to prove their wealth and donate to charity.

On leaving the table, Adam sent his text to Jennifer.

Something's come up, going to be late. Do you want to reschedule?

I was going to text you. The supermarket has asked me to stay later to stock the shelves. Can we do tomorrow? Sorry Adam, at least if we're both busy I'm not standing you up!

Adam smiled. Now he was off the hook, the stress left his shoulders. Looking over at Sherry sitting at the table, he raised his glass in a toast. 'Later,' he mouthed. Adam couldn't see why he should let a good opportunity pass him by and it would make the rest of the night interesting!

Once everyone had eaten, they settled down for the auction. This was what he had been waiting for. Everyone was engrossed in the bidding. Scarlet outbid everyone for the first item to get the ball rolling and soon everyone was silent, listening and waiting for the item they had earmarked to come up.

Walking up to the shaded part of the bar, Adam sidled up to Knuckles. 'I have to pop out, cover for me?' Seeing Knuckles nod his head, Adam left through the back doors without being seen. Climbing onto his motorbike, he rode to the address he had been given by Matt and Jerry. He had no idea what Arthur looked like, but presumed he would know him when he saw him – arrogant and full of self-importance.

Speeding through the well-known streets, he spotted the row of apartments. They would be hard to get into, as you had to press the buzzer to be allowed into the main building. Waiting for someone to come out or go in would take too long. So Adam decided to press all of the buttons in turn, pretending to be delivering a takeaway. At last someone pressed the door open, letting him into the building. After all, it was Friday night; someone would be waiting for a takeaway, wouldn't they? He ignored the hurl of abuse from the other intercoms of annoyed people that he had disturbed.

Checking that no one was around the lush, carpeted hallway, Adam proceeded to the lift. He didn't want anyone seeing him climb the stairs, especially the CCTV cameras, which he knew there would be in an apartment block like this. Keeping his helmet on, he got to the second floor and the flat number he wanted.

Pressing the doorbell, he waited and after a few minutes, a young woman answered wearing a bathrobe.

'Is Arthur at home?' Adam asked, wanting to make sure he still lived there.

'Who wants him?' the young woman snapped, satisfying Adam's enquiry.

'A friend.'

'Arthur, there's some arsehole here wanting to speak to you,' she shouted over her shoulder.

Adam didn't know how many other people would be in the apartment, and definitely didn't want them warned by her shouts to Arthur. Reaching into his pocket, he took out what looked like a perfume bottle. This had always been his best form of defence and now he was pleased he had it with him. Having the good sense to still be wearing his motorbike helmet with a scarf wrapped around his mouth and nose, in case he needed it, he smiled as the woman watched him spray a small squirt into the air near her face. Seeing her eyes flutter instantly, then close, he reached out for her as her legs buckled. She went limp in his arms and slid to the ground. Chloroform, Adam mused to himself. A short spray like that would put her to sleep for around twenty minutes. That was more than enough time for what he had to do.

There'd been no reply to the woman's shout, so Adam furtively looked around the empty lounge and proceeded to look in each room as he passed by. Then, he heard a noise. The shower was running. That was why he hadn't answered; he hadn't heard her!

Taking a deep breath and mentally crossing his fingers, he hoped the bathroom wasn't locked. Still wearing his biker gloves, he turned the handle and it opened. The room was full of steam, and through the large glass shower cubicle, he could see the back of a man with greying hair, letting the water fall down his body.

Adam swiftly walked up to the sliding door and opened it,

making Arthur turn in surprise. 'Who the fuck are you? And how did you get in here?' he snapped and reached out to turn the shower off.

Unzipping his jacket, Adam waited. 'I'm Adam Lambrianu. Are you Arthur?'

Without thinking, Arthur nodded. 'I bloody well am and you're a dead man.'

Taking out his gun with the silencer on it, Adam shot him in the head and then fired two bullets into his body. Reaching inside the shower and kicking Arthur's naked, lifeless body aside, Adam turned the shower back on and watched the crimson water flow down the drain. Looking around, Adam spotted two shower caps and proceeded to put them over his boots. That would hide any footprints as he walked back through to the lounge. The woman was still unconscious in the hallway. Putting his hands under her arms, he dragged her towards the now soaking wet bathroom as the water spewed out of the open cubicle. Laying her down, Adam put the gun into her droopy hand, making sure her prints were on it, and pressed the trigger, shooting another bullet into Arthur.

Adam saw a pile of towels near the sink and picking up two, he laid one out in front of him and stepped on it. Then he spread out the other one and stood on that, before picking up the previous towel. He repeated this process, almost like a chess game, until he got out of the front door. Once out of the front door, he shut it and heard it lock. Then he got onto his hands and knees, wiping all trace of his footprints away with the towels quickly while looking and listening to see if anyone had opened their doors. Still kneeling, he pressed the lift button and once the doors opened, he crawled on his knees inside it. Laying a towel down, he stood up. He'd left no traces of himself or his boots and the apartment door was locked. The only other person in there was the woman. Shame, Adam thought to himself, to hang all of this on her, but it was collateral and survival of the fittest. More to the point, Arthur would have done exactly the same if he'd been in his shoes!

Once outside, Adam furtively looked around to see if anyone was in the street, then pushed the towels into the box at the back of his bike and rode off to his apartment.

Quickly taking off his leather biker jacket and trousers, he changed back into his tuxedo. Looking at his watch, he realised he'd been gone just over an hour. Not too bad, he thought to himself. Taking a deep breath, he walked back downstairs into the club. He could hear laughing and cheering as the auction was in full swing. Standing beside Knuckles, Adam indicated to the barman for his usual drink.

'Any problems Knuckles?'

Knuckles shook his head, which Adam was pleased about. Everyone was so busy enjoying themselves, no one had noticed his absence. Gulping back his whisky, Adam saw that one of the police commissioners had won a bid and was shouting loudly and clapping, to make his presence known. Adam shouted to the bar staff to serve some free champagne for all the thirsty bidders.

Everyone clapped and cheered their approval at his generosity, and waited as the busy waitresses filled the ice buckets with more bottles. Adam took another drink from the barman. Smug satisfaction crossed his face at a job well done.

18

A NEW DAY

Jamie looked up from his desk and craned his neck to see if anyone was in his boss's office. It was five minutes before his boss left for the day and now was the perfect time to annoy him and get him to sign the paperwork agreeing to manage more funds from his rich investors. All he needed was Mr Noakes' signature and it would be signed and sealed.

'You can't bother him now Jamie, he'll bite your head off.'

'It needs signing Kim, and he won't use digital signatures. These clients need their rate of interest agreed or they will back off.'

Starting to clear her desk for the day, Kim shook her head in dismay. Jamie was facing the firing squad walking into their bad-tempered boss's office at this time of day.

With all his courage, Jamie knocked on the door and walked in. Mr Noakes was stood there with his coat on and was about to pick up his bag when he saw Jamie.

'Whatever it is, Jamie, it can wait until the morning. My train is due soon and I don't intend missing it for you.'

'But what about Mrs Gold, sir?'

A frown appeared on Mr Noakes' brow. 'What about her?'

'Well, you know she likes everything done yesterday and this is the paperwork agreeing to her terms of investment. She wants them by today or she'll withdraw her money. I think.' Jamie cleared his throat. 'If we miss her deadline, she won't introduce her friends to us.'

'And you've been sitting on this paperwork all bloody day? It should have been done first thing this morning.'

Jamie looked up at the clock. There were only a few minutes to go before Mr Noakes needed to leave the office. He felt the bulk of paperwork in his now sweaty hands and could feel perspiration on his brow. 'There are just a few signatures needed sir; it won't take a minute.'

Jamie had put all of Julie Gold's paperwork for the million pounds she was investing at the top and shuffled it amongst other investors' paperwork. His heart was pounding.

'Hand them over.' Looking at the pile of paperwork, Mr Noakes squirmed. 'For Christ's sake, Jamie. All of this is for Mrs Gold?'

Swallowing hard and trying to hide his nervousness, Jamie nodded. 'It's because she's a new client, sir. Everything has to be in order. Maybe you should do a digital signature and then we wouldn't have to bother you all the time.'

'I like to know what I'm signing. Anyone could use my digital signature. I'm old fashioned. I want my investors to trust me and know that I am thorough with their money.'

Jamie watched Mr Noakes pick up his pen and prayed to God he wouldn't check the other names on the pile of paperwork he had brought him. If he noticed, then he would have to confess and say the paperwork must have got mixed up and face Mr Noakes' wrath. But instead, while still standing, Mr Noakes looked at the first page, saw Julie Gold's name and scrawled his signature over each page quickly without even looking at the other paperwork. Afterwards,

Mr Noakes almost threw the paperwork at Jamie, letting it fly through the air and making him catch it.

Peering at the cheque that also needed signing, Mr Noakes looked up. 'What's the cheque for?'

'It's for the stockbroker; you know, the sub-contractor who works in the pits buying and selling our stock.' Feeling the sweat on his brow, Jamie brushed it away with the back of his shirt sleeve.

'For Christ's sake, everyone wants money. You go into the pits and bid next time. I can't afford to pay someone else when I'm also paying you. And the name's not even filled in, you imbecile. Sort it out, Jamie!' Jamie watched as Mr Noakes scrawled his signature over the cheque. 'Right, are we done?' Mr Noakes snapped.

'Yes sir, sorry sir. I wasn't sure of the spelling. I'll sort it out now, then people can't say we don't pay our debts on time. We need extra brokers with all these extra clients who are going to be investing.' Jamie smiled. 'Hope you don't miss your train.'

'So do I.' With that, Mr Noakes stormed out of the office. Jamie could feel his heart pounding; he thought he was going to have a heart attack. Apart from Julie's investment, the other pages – all forty of them – were informing their clients of a reduced rate of interest and how little money they had made on their investment with Bitcoin so far. Which was a total lie.

And then there was the cheque. He had purposely made a blank cheque out for 50,000 pounds. Now it had been signed he would put his own name on it. Smiling to himself, Jamie kissed the cheque. It was the easiest money he had ever made.

'You look pleased with yourself considering he looked like he was going to eat you alive.'

Gathering the paperwork together and placing it in his folder, he grinned like a Cheshire cat. 'Fancy a quick drink before your train? I'm buying.'

'Christ, that's a first. Well, just a quick one and then I have a date.'

'Who's the lucky man then?'

'Oh, just some teacher at the local university. He's nice, a bit timid, but it makes a change to cheesy one liners and cheating bastards, yourself excluded of course,' she laughed.

'One drink it is then, and let's make it a large one!' Jamie laughed. He couldn't hide his good fortune and felt on top of the world. Mentally, he thought how he would deposit the cheque first thing in the morning and in a couple of days he would be a rich man. He wondered to himself as they made their way to a wine bar close by, how many more cheques he could forge. Greed was getting the better of him and he was calculating how much he would also get from Julie Gold. 'Stupid old woman,' he thought to himself.

'If you're buying the drinks, I'm going to call my date and ask him to meet us here,' Kim joked. Picking up her mobile, she waited for an answer. 'Bruce, I'm at a wine bar in town if you fancy it. Maybe you could meet me here. My friend Jamie is buying the drinks and this is one occasion I don't want to miss out on. He's usually the one that avoids paying. You would think he's won the lottery. He's just ordered a bottle of champagne and I intend to drink it before he tells me he's forgotten his wallet and asks me to pay the bill.'

Bruce could hear Kim's light banter and realised it was Jamie she was talking about. Intrigued, he agreed to meet her at the wine bar. He wanted to know what was making Jamie so extravagant, considering he knew full well that Julie hadn't parted with a penny yet. Once he ended the call, Bruce rang Julie and told her.

'He's stolen some money, and by the sounds of it, quite a lot. He's becoming brave and greedy. Go and find out. Alcohol loosens lips Bruce and it sounds like he's fit to bursting. He'll definitely want to brag about his wealth to some potless teacher.'

Beaming, Julie put the phone down. Her plan was working. Next time she would clear all of the accounts and put them offshore into one of the many accounts she had set up. In the meantime, she would contact Mr Noakes and decide to invest more. After all, it wouldn't be her money she was investing. That way, she too would be a victim of Jamie's greed. She looked around the room, thinking, drumming her fingers on her chin. Things had sped up quicker than expected, but now was the time for action. This fool Jamie was a liability and she needed rid of him as soon as possible. Let him buy some outlandish things he couldn't afford; people would soon notice and start talking... Let him hang himself.

Once Bruce had arrived, they were on their second bottle of champagne.

'Oh God, you would think it was his birthday or something,' Kim laughed. A little tipsy by now, she introduced Bruce to Jamie.

'I hear you teach computers, Bruce?' Jamie asked. 'I know my way around a keyboard, but there are some things I am not sure of.' Waiting for Kim to go to the loo, he leaned in closer to Bruce. 'I need to set up a digital signature for my company; how easy would that be?'

'Very easy, people do it all the time, especially in business if one of the parties lives abroad or something – you're not going to travel just to sign something.' Suddenly Bruce realised what he was thinking. Jamie was going to forge Mr Noakes' signature and sign the paperwork that was needed. He most definitely was feeling brave now that Julie had put the wind beneath his wings. It was a paper trail, and would mean Mr Noakes would have to explain himself. After all, it was his signature Jamie was forging to steal money. Bruce realised that Jamie was becoming impatient. He didn't want to play the long game. He wanted more money now!

* * *

Looking up, Scarlet saw Adam coming into the office. 'Have you seen this?' Throwing the newspaper towards Adam, she showed him a news article about a man that had been found dead in his apartment, presumably murdered in cold blood by his hysterical girlfriend. 'Some neighbour or something heard a noise and reported it to the police.'

Adam picked up the newspaper and scanned the article. 'It happens every day Scat. Maybe he's been cheating on her. Who knows what goes through women's brains?' Adam shrugged. 'What's your interest in it?'

'Yes, well, you be careful about what goes through women's brains. That woman you disappeared with last night might have the same idea. I can't believe she left with that old man and came back on her own an hour later. God, I hope she had a shower first.' Scarlet grimaced at the thought.

'I'm sure she dropped off her booty of items and feigned a headache, definitely not what you're thinking. It would take that old man an hour to get an erection,' Adam laughed.

'Well, it's a shame your dick doesn't take an hour. You're ready at a minute's notice.'

'That's because I'm young and my dick, as you call it, appreciates beauty.'

'Mm, anyway, it says he was a known businessman and money lender. Bit of a rat by all accounts and his name is Arthur. I wondered if it was anything to do with the man Matt was talking about. It seems his girlfriend has done our job for us,' Scarlet laughed.

Flashing his charming smile, Adam sat beside her. He knew someone had tipped off the police that they had heard a disturbance, because he had done it anonymously himself. On the way back to the auction at the club, Adam had spotted one of the few telephone boxes left in the area and had made the call anonymously.

Suddenly, his mobile burst into life, indicating a message from Jennifer.

I'm free today if you are.

Lunch? I'll pick you up at 12.30.

I'm going to the swimming pool at the leisure centre in Croydon first, do you want to meet me there?

The very idea of seeing Jennifer in a bathing costume appealed to Adam and he made a note to get there earlier than planned.

The leisure centre it is then. See you later.

Disgusted, Scarlet turned to him. 'I can see the blood rushing through your veins Adam. And that telltale grin on your face. Was that her from last night?'

'No, I'm just organising a swim. I feel like a good stretch out. Now stop interfering and let's do some work.'

'Really? I have a pool; you could use that. Christ, why does everyone think I'm stupid.' Hearing a knock on the open office door, Scarlet looked up and saw Knuckles standing in the doorway. 'God, another late starter. Did you sort the kids out?'

'I knocked,' he answered and nodded his head.

'I want you to go to the casino and sort last night's takings out, Knuckles. Don't trust that lot. Oh, and pick up my dry cleaning on the way back.'

Adam watched Knuckles walk away now that he had been given his orders for the day.

'You treat him like your personal servant, Scat. Ease up, eh?'

'What else would he do if he didn't have me to sort his life out? Someone has got to organise him for the day or God knows what he'd get up to.'

'Indeed, Scat. He had a lot of admirers last night, though. Who knows what he'd get up to?' Letting the question hang in the air, he let Scarlet ponder on his words and proceeded to look through the pile of paperwork and invoices on his desk.

Musing to herself, Scarlet thought about Katie's comments regarding Knuckles and now Adam was hinting at the same thing. 'Has Knuckles mentioned he's got a girlfriend or something? Anyway, he hasn't got time for all of that. I keep him busy.'

'Well, he wouldn't tell me, would he.' A smile crept onto Adam's face as he watched Scarlet's face drop.

Scarlet had never considered Knuckles wandering off into the sunset with a girlfriend. He had been at her side for years, and she had taken it for granted that he would be for many more to come. The very thought of his leaving her made her feel sick inside, although she wouldn't admit it. Standing up, she saw Adam look at her curiously. 'There's something I need doing at the casino that I forgot to tell Knuckles about. Are you okay on your own for a while?'

Adam portrayed his best poker face. 'Oh I think I will manage Scarlet. Off you go.' He could see that the penny was finally dropping that Knuckles was human and maybe he did have a secret... yeah right! Adam laughed to himself as she left.

'You don't have to wait, Knuckles can drive me back,' Scarlet said to the chauffeur. Suddenly, she felt nervous. She wasn't sure if what she was doing was right or wrong, but everyone else seemed to think it was the right thing.

Walking into the casino, she could see it was already busy. Some people had all kinds of addictions and no sooner were they open than people turned up to try their luck. Nodding to the managers and smiling, she proceeded to the lift.

Knuckles was in the office with a couple of the managers and they were emptying the safe so that Knuckles could deposit last night's takings. Everything had to be signed for and witnessed, to prove everyone knew what had been taken out and who had taken it. This in itself made Scarlet smile as she stood in the doorway watching. Knuckles never signed his signature. He wouldn't put his name to anything that could be traced back to him. Old habits die hard. Instead, he put an 'X' and everyone knew who that was.

'I'll ride to the bank with you, Knuckles. There's something I want to talk to you about.' He looked up at her and nodded, while the other managers smiled and said hello.

Once Knuckles had put the special safety case in the back of the car, they drove off. Scarlet knew this was her chance to sound out Knuckles on her idea.

Sitting in the back of the Rolls Royce as he drove, she felt her mouth go dry and licked her lips. 'Knuckles... have you ever thought about marrying me?'

Seeing him glance at her in the rear-view mirror made her feel embarrassed. This wasn't a conversation she ever thought she would be having with him. But even though she had dined and flirted with men at the club and casino, she had never dated any of them. Knuckles always picked her up at the end of the evening and took her home. She thought about her disastrous marriage when she had been young. Maybe that was why it had never crossed her mind again.

Dominic had had charm, looks and everything a young girl wanted, but he hadn't liked her working at the club with her father. He hated the long hours and the fact that his dinner wasn't on the table at 5 p.m., even though he had known all of this before he married her. Suddenly, he had changed into a manipulating husband. Scarlet winced inside, remembering all of the arguments they had had. She hadn't seen him for years, but had heard he'd got married again and now had the life he wanted. The stay-at-home wife, the two kids and his dinner on the table.

Knuckles never made any demands on her. She argued with him daily, which was pointless because he never argued back. He was more like a sounding board and just let her get on with it.

They had twins together, which was more by accident than love. Once her divorce had come through from Dominic, she had been at a low ebb and had just needed to be held. She had gone to Knuckles' bedroom and got into his bed and he had indeed held her and made her feel better, and one thing had led to another... but Katie was right, he had turned out to be a good father despite his troubled past. No one particularly knew much about him, including herself, other than that he had been passed from pillar to post from children's institution to prison. That had been his life. Protection and getaway driving was all he knew, especially fighting. But with herself and the family, he had become part of a unit. Presumably something he had never had before.

'Nope.'

A frown crossed her brows as Knuckles' answer woke her from her thoughts. 'What, not even for the sake of the children? After all, we're their parents. I just wondered if you'd ever considered it. Or do you have a girlfriend?' she enquired.

Knuckles shrugged and shook his head. Presumably that meant no to both questions.

Feeling slightly frustrated at his lack of enthusiasm, she thought she would try again. 'Well, would you like to marry me? For the sake of the kids of course,' she stammered. She could feel her face flush with embarrassment.

'Suppose so. What do I have to do?'

'Well, you don't have to do anything. Nothing would change.

People do get married and sometimes it's even the man that asks the bloody question!' she snapped. 'I'd keep my own name and we'd just carry on as we are. It would make things simpler for the kids if anything happened to either of us, regarding a will or anything.' Scarlet was doing her best to make it sound like a business proposition, although she found it hard to wait for what she was saying to sink into his brain.

'Okay,' was his reply as they entered the bank car park. Feeling somewhat deflated, Scarlet didn't wait for him to open the car door for her and got out, slamming it behind her and storming into the bank, as Knuckles followed behind.

* * *

'Put that bloody phone down!' Scarlet screamed at Adam. Looking up and making his excuses on the phone, Adam could see things hadn't gone well and Scarlet's temper was always at the surface.

'I've just asked Knuckles if he had ever considered marrying me and all he could say was okay. Is that it? Okay!'

Adam burst out laughing and sat back in his chair. 'What did you expect? He's a man of few words, Scat. Surely you didn't expect a brass band or something. But, if he said okay, that means he's accepted your proposal, doesn't it?' Raising his eyebrows questioningly, Adam looked directly at her.

Slumping into the chair beside him, she kicked off her high-heeled court shoes which matched her suit. 'I suppose so. It's a bloody stupid idea now I think of it. I can't believe I let my mouth run away like that. Christ, Adam, what was I thinking?' Throwing her hand up in the air, she smiled. 'Maybe it's the menopause or something.'

'Well, are you going to go through with it Scarlet, menopause or not?'

'Mmm, we'll see. He might forget all about it and then I wouldn't have to do anything, would I? On the other hand, I've said it now and I can't really go back on my word, can I? Let's play it by ear, he probably doesn't even know what I'm talking about.'

'I think he does, Scarlet. Knuckles is far from stupid. He takes everything in and plays the long game.' Adam looked at his watch. 'It's nearly time I went for my swim. I'm not sure how long I'll be.' Adam was about to leave the room when he heard Scarlet muttering to herself.

'Christ, I must be wearing the wrong deodorant or something. Each man I've spoken to this morning ignores me.'

Hearing that she was back on form, Adam grinned to himself and made his way to his apartment, collected his swimwear and rode off to meet Jennifer.

* * *

Adam was shocked as he walked into the nearly empty adult pool. As he looked up at the diving board, there was his mermaid doing a backwards somersault into the pool. She had jumped so high in the air, it looked like she was on a trampoline. And she hardly made a splash as she dived into the water. Her plain black bathing costume and hat hadn't been what he had expected. Somewhere in his brain, he had presumed she would be bikini clad with her hair flowing. No, he mentally thought to himself. This was a professional swimmer and diver. How mistaken could he be.

'Jennifer!' he shouted once she'd surfaced. He waved at her to attract her attention.

A beaming smile, showing a perfect row of teeth, greeted him. Getting out, she raised the sides of her rubber swimming hat. 'You're early or I'm late!' she laughed.

'No, I'm early. I wanted to see my mermaid in action. Anyway, I could do with a swim myself.' Admiringly, he looked at her slim, petite body. There wasn't an ounce of fat on her, and he could still see her shapely pert breasts, which made him glad he was about to jump in the water before he embarrassed himself. Realising there was no point in impressing her with his jackknife dives, he just jumped in and started swimming, letting the pool cool his ardour.

As he swam, he noticed her glide past him, full of gusto and strength. Now, he thought to himself, he was the one who felt like a fish out of water. Reaching the end, he floated in the water beside her. 'You really are a mermaid, Jennifer. I always thought I was a fast swimmer, but you put me to shame,' he laughed.

'Come on, I've done my eighty laps. Let's get dressed and have that lunch. I've worked up quite an appetite.'

Adam was pleased at the suggestion; he had satisfied his curiosity, but felt like a learner in front of this Olympic swimmer.

Sat in the Greek taverna, he couldn't help noticing how young she looked. Her eyes shone and her face was still flushed from swimming. The long plait that hung down her back made her look almost like a schoolgirl. This was a far cry from the women he had dated in the past. They were always worried about smudging their lipstick and checking themselves in the mirror. But not Jennifer. Her fair complexion didn't have a blemish on it. She looked healthy and natural with a figure some women would die for. As she chatted away about her forthcoming trip, their hurried night of passion flashed through his mind, and he could feel a stirring in his body. As he listened to her excitement, he thought to himself how much he liked her, and the thought of her going away saddened him somewhat. He didn't like this feeling. It was alien to him. He had never thought twice in the past when one of his lady friends had said they were going on holiday. Usually, he was pleased because boredom had started setting in and he was glad to see the back of them without any hard feelings.

Impulsively, he took her hand. 'I tell you what. Before you go away, why don't we spend every day together, make the most of the time we have?'

'That would be lovely Adam, but what about your job? What about mine?' She laughed nervously.

'Surely we could fit something in around our schedules? I know I could.' He couldn't believe he had blurted that out, but he was also glad he had. These next few days could be when the boredom set in and he would be glad to wave her off. Only time would tell.

Picking up one of the olives off her plate, she popped it into his mouth. 'If you're sure Adam, then so am I. Let's make a list of the things we would both like to do. We could be tourists. I've lived in London for years, but you're so busy getting to where you need to be you never have time to look at this beautiful city. You can choose one thing to do and then I can. That way we're even. What do you think?' Instantly, she scrambled through her bag containing her wet towel and bathing costume and found a pad and pen. 'What's first on your agenda?'

Nearly choking on his olive, Adam burst out laughing. What was on his agenda? He really didn't want to write that down!

19

THE TRUTH WILL OUT

'Julie's Golden Boys!' The newspapers were full of photos and headlines of Julie as she'd been shopping with all her 'boys', including Bruce.

'I've got to go and sort out the strippers for tonight. Take a look at your friend Brucey's new profession. He's a dark horse,' Scarlet laughed. Intrigued, Adam looked at the local rag and nearly doubled up with laughter when he saw the headlines, tears streaming down his face. It was the funniest news they had belly laughed at in a long time, with photos of Julie at the front being followed like sheep by her army of men, Bruce amongst them. Adam couldn't resist calling Bruce. 'What the fuck are you doing Bruce? There are photos of you in line with Julie's boys shopping in Harrods. Tell me the story. Please,' he begged.

'It was for me actually Adam, and it's not that funny. Although what my boss and my mum will say scares me a little.'

'What, that you're a kept man? Christ, Bruce, there's men out there just begging for that place. But why was it for you?'

'Julie understands that for all of my hard work I can't go advertising money I couldn't possibly have earned, and yet it's there sitting in my account. So now everyone now knows I am part of the Gold empire, so no one will take any notice if I walk around with a Rolex watch or a new car. What I have in my bank account may raise eyebrows but it wouldn't rouse suspicions. Everyone knows Julie pays her boys generously. Personally, I think it's quite clever. The best way to hide is in the public eye.' Once Adam had stopped laughing, he could see the common sense in it. It was a foolproof plan of Julie's.

No one would take notice of Bruce's good fortune now. He might be the talk of the town and people may whisper about him, but they would make up their own minds about what he was doing for his bank balance. 'Actually Bruce, that's quite clever. How do you feel about it?'

'Well, it feels a bit weird being in the newspapers and I know people are gossiping about me, but then they always have. Everyone thinks I'm a bit weird so what's the difference? This time I'm a weirdo with a bank balance.'

'You're not weird, Bruce. You're just different and you're my best mate. Seriously though, as long as you're okay with it and you're not being railroaded, that's all that matters.'

'Julie understands me, Adam. She doesn't laugh at my odd ways; in fact, she ignores them. She's going out of her way to make sure I get my share. She has made offshore accounts for us all. It's all going to go tits up soon anyway, especially now that Jamie has got his boss's digital signature and is signing all kinds of cheques. When they do an audit, he is seriously for the high jump.'

'Digital signature? When did that happen?' asked Adam. He didn't know anything about this.

Bruce went on and filled Adam in on Jamie's corruption. 'The minute I told Julie, she got me emptying those accounts. That is where the offshore accounts come in. Time is not on our side Adam. He's even booked a cruise for him and his girlfriend who is all over him like a rash at the moment. Apparently, she never stopped loving him!'

Frowning and confused, Adam couldn't believe what he was hearing. 'How do you know he's going on a cruise?'

'He's told Kim, who is a friend of his girlfriend's by the way, and she in turn told me. He's not covering his tracks and his money is burning a hole in his pocket. He's renting a flat in Chelsea, or in the process of doing so.'

'I'm sorry Bruce,' Adam apologised. The fun and laughter had now left him and he felt guilty. 'I've left you to deal with a lot on your own these past few days, haven't I?'

'There's nothing you could do, apart from be kept up to speed. It's all in hand. Julie has contacted Jamie and he is signing off imaginary clients who don't exist, embezzling money. She has kept her word and paid him but the clever cow has paid him in cash. There's no bank transfer from her with her name on it. I would love to have seen his face when she handed over 25,000 in cash! I bet he wet himself. The interest and the commission he's handing over to these imaginary clients is outrageous, apart from what he's stealing for himself. I would say another week and we will have emptied the accounts and then questions are going to be asked and we will be well out of it. Worse for him though, with his pending trip it will look like he has absconded,' Bruce chuckled.

Adam let out a slow whistle. 'Christ, you have been busy. I should have been with you.' Adam thought about the last couple of carefree days he'd had and he was being brought back to earth with a thump. He had neglected business, all for the sake of a bit of fun and frolic. The last couple of days had been good fun, and the nights even better.

'Adam, don't beat yourself up about this. You're entitled to a life. It's all in hand. What could you have done?'

'I see your point, Bruce; it's just been a little hectic lately. We should meet up later for a drink – you could come to the club. I know you don't like it, but let's catch up.'

'No. Not now Adam. We need to keep our distance for now. On another note, our registration to start our own coin brokerage has come through. And so has my deed poll for change of name. I haven't mentioned it to Mum, but my money is in the name of Bruce Sinclair.'

'Do we even need to start a coin brokerage now? Sounds like that Jamie has done all of the work for us. It's not exactly how we planned it in the beginning.'

'If others can do it, why not us? It's a legitimate business opportunity and the bookie always wins. Either way, we get paid; all we need is customers and Julie can provide those. Christ, she is like Father Christmas. She can provide everything.' Bruce laughed.

'It sounds like you have a soft spot for Cougar Julie.' Adam giggled.

'She makes a lot of sense, and she has been good to me. And shopping with her is an experience in itself. As soon as she walked in, staff pulled out chairs for her and waited on her hand and foot. She was like a famous movie star.'

Adam laughed. 'Are you going to keep your job at the university?'

'If they will let me. There's bound to be gossip and I presume I'll be held over the coals for my private life. But that's just it, isn't it. It's my private life. I haven't killed anyone. I'll have to cross that bridge when I come to it. We'll speak soon Adam. I have to go to work and face the firing squad in the canteen when they have read the papers.'

'Take care, Bruce and any trouble, get back to me.' Adam ended the call and sat down. He was glad the office was empty for once. He needed time to think. He was supposed to be seeing Jennifer as planned today, but he wasn't sure if he should go.

His time alone was short-lived. Scarlet arrived soon after and stood in the doorway with her arms folded. She could see something was troubling Adam. 'Well, well, well, I was going to put you on the missing persons' list. Three days you've been out and about while I've been slogging my guts out here.'

'Do I moan when you go on holiday?' Adam snapped. He hadn't meant to but it had just come out wrong.

'Hey, I was just messing. What's up?' Walking past him towards her chair, she ran her hand absently through his hair. 'Tell big sis what's on your mind, or who?'

'Nothing. Sorry Scat. Sometimes I feel I just need to get away from it all, clear my head, that's all.'

Scarlet could see there was more to it than met the eye, but she was determined not to pry. 'You're right, being couped up in nightclubs, strippers and casinos doesn't exactly do much for the complexion, does it? Why don't you go out today and get some fresh air? There isn't a lot going on today.'

'I might, but first I need to sort out those money lenders. I'd like to be there to meet them.'

'You got the bit between your teeth Adam? Off you go then, and then go for a swim or something. You looked like a new man after your swim the other day,' she laughed.

A smile crept onto Adam's troubled face when he remembered that day. And Scarlet knew she had said the right thing.

Just as Adam was leaving, Knuckles walked in. 'Oh God, what do you want?' Curiously, Scarlet watched Knuckles as he bent down on his knees.

'Have you dropped something?' she asked, irritated by his scrambling around on the floor.

Whilst on both knees, Knuckles turned to her and handed her a ring box. 'For you.'

Shocked, Scarlet realised this was Knuckles' proposal. It had taken a few days for him to think about it, and to be honest, she'd thought he'd forgotten about it. Gobsmacked, she took the ring box from him and looked inside. It was a huge sapphire surrounded by diamonds – a ring she would have picked herself.

'Like your eyes,' he said, then reached into his pocket and took a receipt out.

'What's this? You're giving me a ring and now you're giving me the bloody bill for it?' she snapped.

'Proof I paid for it.'

Blushing slightly, Scarlet looked at the ring and the receipt. Considering Knuckles pleaded poverty, she was surprised at how many thousands he had spent on the ring. She felt a warm glow inside her. Knuckles never paid for anything he could steal, and yet this was his grand gesture. He looked prouder of the receipt than he did the ring. He had bought this ring out of his own money and shown her the receipt to prove it. This was his ultimate commitment.

Scarlet frowned. 'So, is it a special sapphire ring, or just a ring with a sapphire in it?' she asked, but she could see the confusion cross Knuckles' brows. 'What I mean Knuckles, is what is it for?' she prompted. 'Say the fucking words!'

Again, Knuckles paused. He wasn't sure what she wanted him to say.

'Okay, number one: are you asking me to marry you? Number two: is it my birthday and you've bought me a present? Number three: are you just showing me what you've bought for someone else?' She rolled her eyes to the ceiling. 'Give me bloody strength.'

'Number one,' he answered, looking quite pleased with himself.

'Well ask me then! And it's on one knee, not both. You're not scrubbing the bloody floor.'

Changing his stance, Knuckles moved and knelt on one knee as instructed. 'Do you still want to get married?' Knuckles looked down at the floor and Scarlet thought she saw him blush a little. Emotion and Knuckles were not compatible. He seemed to wait for her laughter that it had all been a joke and the rebuff to go with it.

Sighing with exasperation, Scarlet waited for a moment, then said, 'Repeat after me you baboon! Scarlet Lambrianu, will you marry me? Shit,' she scoffed, 'my father would turn in his grave if he could see me now!'

'Scarlet Lambrianu, will you marry me?' Knuckles looked up and met her eyes.

'My goodness Knuckles, I'm shocked.' Wide eyed and full of mock surprise, she added, 'I never expected your sudden proposal of marriage. I wasn't aware you were crazy in love with me.' Mocking him slightly and feigning surprise, Scarlet looked at him and realised her acting didn't impress him. 'Yeah, course I will, if only to get you off your knees for Christ's sake. Give me that ring and it had better fit!'

'Took one out of your jewellery box for size,' he mumbled.

'Well, I hope you put it back. Going through my jewellery box indeed! That's worse than my knicker draw.' Clearing her throat, it was back to business mode for Scarlet. 'Right, now that's settled. I don't want a big wedding, I've done that. Just close family and friends. Do you have anyone you want to invite?' Scarlet watched him shrug. 'Well, I'll sort it out. All you need to know is what time to get there and to have your suit fitted. Now, go and do some work Knuckles. I think Adam might want your help.'

Watching the huge bulk of a man get off his knees almost made Scarlet laugh. She had expected a bit more enthusiasm, but she had known him long enough to know that was never going to happen. Sitting back in her chair, she put the huge sapphire ring on her finger and admired it. She squirmed at the thought of telling Julie about this and her sarcastic comments were already running through her mind. Biting her bottom lip, she toyed with the idea of telling her now and getting it over with, but instead Scarlet decided to ring Katie. At least there she knew she would get kind words.

* * *

Adam sat in the back of the car; he knew he was okay for time meeting Jennifer because she was working today.

As he was about to drive off, Knuckles walked up and knocked on the car door. Winding the window down, Adam waited. 'I'll drive.'

Raising his eyebrows, Adam laughed. 'Has Scarlet sent you to keep an eye on me Knuckles?'

Ignoring him, Knuckles walked around the car to the driver's seat. He was slightly confused when he saw Matt was driving. Knuckles glanced towards Adam. 'Get out,' he ordered.

'No, Knuckles, Matt is coming with me. I'm going to see those collectors on the estate and he can point them out to me. He can sit in the front with you if you insist on driving.'

Accepting his explanation, Knuckles opened the driver's door and waited for Matt to get out.

Driving onto the estate, Adam was pleasantly surprised. It was the usual council tower blocks and looked grey from the outside, but other than that, it was clean and tidy. Not what he had expected at all.

Turning towards the back seat, Matt pointed his finger towards the entrance. 'There's one. He's the big bruiser I saw the other day. The one with the leather jacket beside him must be another one. Christ, he's built like a brick shithouse isn't he?'

'If you say so Matt. Are there any others?' Adam's calm voice filled the car, showing no emotion or excitement at finding the collectors so easily. Knuckles looked into the rear-view mirror at him questioningly.

'Drive into that tunnel that joins these tower blocks, Knuckles. We can park the car there. There are too many windows open for what I have in mind.'

'What do you have in mind, boss? We going to have a punch up and show them who's boss around here?' Matt's eyes glistened with excitement, but Adam ignored his question. Then Knuckles turned his head towards Adam. 'Two more there.' He nodded.

'Do you reckon there's two or more for each tower block Knuckles?' Adam asked. Seeing Knuckles nod his head in confirmation, they drove off to the concrete tunnel that connected the tower blocks. Adam looked around. It was more of a concrete passageway, possibly a shortcut for the residents to save them having to walk around each tower block to get to the main road.

'Where are all the cars, Knuckles? There must be someone on this estate with a car.' From the back seat, Adam leaned forward in the shady tunnel and looked around.

'There.' Knuckles pointed. Adam craned his neck forward and at the end of the tunnel he could see a residents' car park, full to the brim.

'I doubt the collectors come in separate cars, unless they are going to different places afterwards. I think they all come together and if there's six or more, it has to be a van.' Weighing up the situation to himself, Adam was speaking out loud. 'One will start collecting at the top of the block and the other from the bottom. They will do each floor and then they will meet in the middle and leave together with their cash for safety. That's what we do, isn't it?' Adam's question was fired at Knuckles, who nodded.

'Matt, go and see if the lift is working,' Adam instructed. If nothing else he wanted him out of the car.

'Sure thing, boss.' Matt excitedly opened the door, then turned to Adam. 'Do you want me to go up and beat one of them up boss?'

'You should have done that when you had the chance, which is

222

GILLIAN GODDEN

why I'm now here.' Adam's sarcasm stopped Matt in his tracks. Shutting the door, he walked off towards the flats. 'Come with me Knuckles. I want to see what vans are parked around here.'

Adam and Knuckles got out of the car and walked towards the car park. It was mainly cars, and the odd vans they spotted had logos on the side advertising plumbing or carpet fitting. From experience, Knuckles knew what he was looking for. 'That one,' he said, pointing. Adam surveyed the vehicle and smiled. It was a lone white transit van parked in a disabled area without any kind of logo.

'Good. Right, when I get the keys off these goons, bring it around to the front Knuckles and then let Matt get into the driving seat.' His blue eyes looked up towards Knuckles as Matt ran towards them.

'Boss! Boss!' Matt shouted, almost out of breath as he hurried towards them. 'The lift is working, and those blokes are already knocking on doors and threatening people. Once the lift door opened on the third floor, I heard them shouting and barging into people's flats. Thats when I pressed the button and came straight down again to tell you.'

In his excitement, Matt failed to notice Adam's eyes cloud over with disgust. He glared at the man in front of him. 'Did they see you, Matt?'

'No, I stood at the back of the lift when the doors opened and came straight down again. They will probably think it was just kids messing around,' he explained.

'So you're a mind reader now as well, Matt? I didn't realise you had so many talents. If it was me, I would be suspicious of a lift door opening and no one getting out.'

Laughing at his joke, Matt shrugged. 'No one would get out of that lift with all the commotion that's going on up there. And kids press lift buttons all the time, that's why they are always breaking down. Do you want me to make sure the other lifts are working, boss?'

'Yeah, why not. Unless you already know with your mind reading skills.' Adam's velvety sarcastic voice was lost on Matt who was far too excited about what they were going to do now he had back-up.

'Right, now he's gone, we'll go in.' Casually Adam walked alongside Knuckles into the flats. Adam made his way to the fourth floor, leaving Knuckles to man the entrance. He could hear a banging as he looked out the lift doors as they opened. He could see one of the men he had seen earlier kicking someone's front door and shouting.

The man looked at Adam, smartly dressed in his suit and tie, curiously. 'Whatever it is you're selling, I want my money first,' he shouted and turned towards the door again and started hammering on it with his fist.

Standing beside the lift door casually, Adam watched and waited until the man turned to him again. 'If you know what's good for you, you'll fuck off!' he threatened.

Scanning the corridor, Adam noticed every door was shut. He could hear children crying and shouting from inside, but outside it was just as he liked it – no witnesses. Taking out his gun while the man stood with his back to him, Adam fired into the back of the man's leg. Hearing him cry out and slump to the ground, Adam watched the blood pour out of his leg and run along the corridor. Panting and clearly in pain, sweat appeared on his brow as the man clung to his leg.

'You bastard,' he howled. The man started to crawl towards Adam, dragging his body through the pool of blood to get revenge as Adam walked back into the lift. Holding the doors open with the button, Adam stood back and watched the man crawl inside the lift, doing his best to hold his leg while trying to reach out to Adam. 'You won't get away with this. There's blood everywhere!'

Smiling, Adam looked down at his shoes. Adam had already planned for this and had wrapped clingfilm around his shoes. His own footprints were nowhere to be found. Blood gushed out of the man's leg as Adam pressed the lift button to the next floor.

Adam held out his gun. 'Stay still now. One false move and the next one is in your head.'

'My mate's up there. You just fucking wait. We'll string you up by the balls!' he panted before lying down on the lift floor and holding his leg. He could feel the wooziness in his head as everything became distorted and he blacked out. Reaching down, Adam stuffed the bottom of his trousers into his socks so they wouldn't get blood on them. He then searched through the man's pockets and found what he was looking for. It was a set of car keys, presumably for the van.

As he looked out of the lift doors as they opened on another floor, he saw another man shouting at some poor unsuspecting tenant who had stupidly opened their door. It was a woman with a crying young baby in her arms and the man was threatening that he would take half a payment now but wanted double next week. Anger boiled inside Adam; the poor woman looked terrified.

'Hey!' Adam shouted. 'Is this your mate? I think he's been shot. There's blood everywhere in this lift!'

Swiftly turning, the man ran towards Adam, looked down at his mate and then back up to Adam. He was about to speak when Adam raised his hand and hit him on the head with the butt of his gun, knocking him senseless. Adam stepped to one side as the man fell into the lift on top of his friend. Peering out of the lift door, Adam looked at the woman and put his finger to his lips to stop her speaking. Seeing him, she nodded and shut her door.

Pressing the button again to go back down to the ground floor,

Adam hit the man on the back of the head again, knocking him out for sure this time. As he got to the bottom, he saw Knuckles standing at the tower block entrance and threw him the keys.

Knuckles went to the car park and pressed the button on the key ring. Just as he had said, the lights flashed on the van parked in the disabled bay and he got in, driving it the entrance to the flats. He saw some people milling around and wondered where Adam was, then he heard him. He was standing in front of the lift doors trying to hide the men inside with his body. 'Lift's broken,' Adam shouted.

'What are you doing with the door half open then?' a woman shouted at him.

'I'm from the council, we've been called out to check it. Maintenance is on their way.'

Looking Adam up and down in his suit, she muttered some insult about the council and then proceeded through the doors to the staircase, followed by everyone else with their bags of shopping.

Knuckles walked towards him.

'That was close Knuckles. Let's get these two into the back of the van.'

Picking one up, Knuckles heaved him over his shoulder and pushed him into the van. While he did this, Adam reached into his jacket pocket and took out a roll of clingfilm and started wrapping it around the man's leg to stop any more blood escaping. By now, Adam's and Knuckles' jackets were smeared with blood.

Running around the corner to their own car, Adam opened the boot and took out a crowbar, then threw his jacket inside. Matt was already standing beside the car. 'I wondered where you'd got to. All the other lifts are working, and there are two blokes in each block.'

'What? And you never came to look to see if we were hurt?' Disgusted, Adam glared at him. 'You get into the front of the van so you can drive off once we have the others in the back. We'll need to take the car back.'

Adam walked towards the next tower block, while Knuckles walked to the third. This time, when he saw one of the men down the corridors he just hit him over the head with a crowbar. It was far less messy than a gun.

Between them, Adam and Knuckles loaded the back of the van with all six men. Some were bleeding from their heads, but not too much. Adam smiled and looked up at Knuckles. 'You didn't need a crowbar then, just that iron hand of yours. Maybe I should get one.'

Panting to catch his breath slightly, Adam bent over near the van to get some air into his lungs. Taking out his gun with the silencer on, he fired at the petrol tank and watched as it started to leak fuel. Banging his hand on the side of the van, he shouted, 'Start driving back, Matt. We'll meet you there.'

Oblivious to the leaking petrol, Matt started the engine up, smiling as he started to drive off.

Adam and Knuckles could see the trail of petrol as Matt was indicating to turn onto the main road. Adam took out a cigarette and lit it. Once he had taken a couple of drags and saw the red glow on the end, he threw it towards the petrol line. Grabbing Knuckles by the arm, they both ran towards the tunnel where their own car was parked safely. Suddenly, they heard an almighty bang and the sound of windows smashing as the van exploded.

Knuckles drove directly out the other side, and as they looked over, they could see smoke and fumes billow into the air and another explosion. Leaving the chaos behind them, Knuckles drove on.

'Phew, that was close. I can't have a wimpy bastard like Matt afraid of a couple of fat bastards working for us, Knuckles. He could have sorted this with the lads the other day. Why come back empty handed full of excuses? He had to go; he knew too much about our operation. Now, the only problem is the blood in the lift and down that corridor.' Adam burst out laughing maniacally. 'Christ, what a bloody mess!'

'Jerry,' muttered Knuckles, while keeping his eye on the road.

'You're right, Knuckles, Jerry. He'll get there before our cleaners and with all of that commotion, no one will notice.'

Adam made the call to Jerry, who agreed to sort it.

Ten minutes later, Jerry called back to check what floor Adam had said and wanted it confirming because as far as he could see, the corridor was clean. 'You could see it had been recently mopped by the wetness of it. The lift is a bit of a mess though, I'll mop that out with some bleach,' he half shouted down the phone.

Adam frowned and told Knuckles. 'That's weird... unless?' Adam wondered if whoever was inside had come out once the thumping on their door had stopped to investigate and cleaned it up.

'Jerry's already starting on the lift, and if any blood is found, people will think it was just a war between those money lenders. Send one of the lads around later and take Jerry a couple of bottles as a bonus. As for that lot burnt to a crisp, they aren't going to say anything.' Adam threw his head back and laughed. 'You see, Knuckles. Smoking kills. Remember that.'

20

A DOUBLE LIFE

'It's been a lovely week, Adam. I didn't realise London was such a beautiful place with so much to offer, and we've been blessed with the weather.' Reaching out for Adam's hand, Jennifer squeezed it.

'I agree. Look at us sat outside Covent Garden surrounded by tourists and all that London has to offer. You've made it special, Jennifer.' Impulsively, Adam squeezed her hand back, although he felt a little embarrassed. He wasn't one to show emotion, but he couldn't help it. Adam looked under his long lashes towards her. He'd surprised himself. Seeing the Victoria and Albert Museum and all the other places she had dragged him to had been fun and interesting. He'd done all kinds of things he would never have dreamed of and had enjoyed it.

'What would you like to do tonight, or tomorrow if you have to work?' Looking down at her food and toying with it, Jennifer waited for Adam's response. She didn't want the day to end.

'I'm not working tonight; I'm owed a little time off and so I'm taking it tonight, to be with you.' Adam still felt they were walking around each other on eggshells. The nights they had spent together had been more intense than he had felt with any other woman.

With Jennifer he felt a connection, but something inside made him want to dismiss it.

She was going away soon, and life would return to normal, whatever normal was, he mused to himself. While she chatted on, he observed her: the sun seemed to make her hair blonder and her eyes shone with excitement at the days and nights to come.

'Actually, I'm a little tired. Why don't we just have a chill night? See what's on Netflix, get a takeaway and see what happens.' He flashed her his charming smile. She bowed her head and her cheeks flushed.

'That sounds like a great idea. I'm sure my flatmates could do a disappearing act for the night. Anyway, Shannon spends most of her time at her boyfriend's. I don't know why she just doesn't move in with him.'

'Probably because he hasn't asked her yet!' Adam laughed. 'What about the other one?' Adam tried to recall the other flatmate's name but couldn't.

'Marianne,' Jennifer prompted him. 'Oh, she's going on a hen night, so God only knows when she'll turn up!'

'So it's just us two, then?' Reaching for her hand, Adam kissed the back of it.

'That sounds great. How about a swim to work up an appetite?'

Adam's eyes pierced her own. 'I can think of better ways to work up an appetite.' The blood was pulsing through his veins, and he could see by the way she exhaled and blushed she felt the same. Tonight was just for them. Over the week they'd had sex, but he had left before her roommates came home. Tonight, he thought to himself, he had no intention of leaving early. 'I have some things to do later this afternoon. Why don't we finish up here and I'll meet you at yours later, about 8 p.m. That will give you time to get rid of everyone.' He grinned.

Jennifer looked at him; he was beautiful and everything any

woman would want and yet here he was with her. She knew she was punching way above her weight, which was why she had wanted to spend every waking moment with him before their wild affair dwindled and he got bored. Time was running out, and she knew that. Breathing in his aftershave, she felt her chest rise and exhaled deeply.

'You come whenever you want. I'll be waiting.'

Waving the waiter over, Adam paid the bill and stood up, passing Jennifer her helmet. 'While you're waiting, you can decide what you'd like to do tomorrow.' Walking towards his motorbike, he felt Jennifer reach out and hold his hand as they walked. Although he felt slightly uncomfortable, as though everyone was watching him, he liked it. He liked her. He liked the way her eyes lit up when she laughed. It was a deep throaty, genuine laugh.

'I've already thought of that. I'd like to go to the beach. Go to the amusements and eat fish and chips. How does that sound?'

Wincing inside, Adam felt a flutter of butterflies in his stomach. He had been raised at the seaside. Those kinds of things were the norm to him, but he hadn't done any of those things since he'd been a kid with his mother. And revisiting those memories was painful. How on earth, he wondered to himself, was he going to get out of this one?

'You said let's explore London. The seaside is hardly London, is it?' Adam was trying hard to sway her from that thought without disappointing her.

'Oh, you know me and water, but you're right. What about a picnic in Hyde Park or something?' Not wanting to push the subject further, she backtracked. 'Actually, there is a fun fair at Tooting Bec Common. That could be fun. There will be candy floss and toffee apples – yummy!' Licking her lips with enthusiasm, she grinned.

'Well, that sounds like an expensive trip to the dentist, but, yeah, that sounds good.' Without thinking, Adam swept her off her feet, his arms tightly around her waist, and kissed her. She was almost on tiptoes as she responded to his slow meaningful kiss. He felt confused. His emotions and body seemed to have a life of their own. He had never had any kind of commitment before; he didn't like it. The closer you got to people, the more pain you felt when they left.

* * *

'Where the bloody hell do you keep disappearing to? You turn up for work when you feel like it with that stupid grin on your face. I take it it's a woman, but who?' Scarlet's brows crossed and she drummed her well-manicured fingernail on her chin. 'I'm damned sure it's not one of your local bimbos. Last night, they were asking about you and I told them to take their turn in line. So come on leather boy, who is it?'

'It's someone you don't know and someone who isn't going to be around for a while, so there is no point in introductions. And as for my smile, well, that is just for you Scat.' Adam walked over and gave her a kiss on the cheek. Looking down, he saw her hand. 'Wow! That is some rock. Did Knuckles steal it for you?' he laughed.

Sticking out her chin stubbornly, she looked at the ring again. 'Actually, he spent his own money and bought it. He even gave me the receipt. And as for your smile, you cheeky bugger, no one smiles like that for their older sister. Go on, have fun, it doesn't matter that I'm here working my socks off and I have a wedding to arrange!'

'You work so much better under stress Scarlet; you love the adrenaline.' Adam held up her hand and admired the ring again. 'So, he finally popped the question. I take it you're having your engagement party here?'

'Not sure about popping the question, but yeah we're going to get married. I hadn't really thought about an engagement party... I don't think Knuckles is much of a party man...' Absently, Scarlet looked around the room, pondering. She still hadn't told Julie and before it was made public, she wanted to get it over with. Locked in her own thoughts, she still felt a little embarrassed about the whole idea; she wasn't sure what other people would think.

She looked up at Adam and sighed. 'Do you think people will laugh at me marrying Knuckles after all these years?'

'What do you care? You've never cared about what other people think before. If you're unsure, Scarlet, don't do it. There's no pressure. And why should people laugh? Everyone knows you have a couple of kids together. It's not exactly a secret, is it?'

'Things changed when I married Dominic. What if Knuckles turns out to be the same? I know he's a brainless oaf, but he's been loyal and puts up with my rantings. People will think I could do better for myself, but I'm not so sure. He's always been there for me, even though we don't know a lot about him after all these years. But he's not having half of my share of the club or casino. I'd want one of those prenuptials.'

Adam put his arms around her and hugged her. For the first time he could see the vulnerable side of Scarlet. A side of her that she rarely allowed people to see.

'Knuckles doesn't want anything, Scat. As for his past, well, I think that's something he would rather forget, and the people in it. You and the kids are his family and future. Okay, so he doesn't have the social skills of a charming husband sweeping you off your feet, but he's handsome – in the right lighting.' Adam smiled. 'Personally, I think things would just carry on as they are, but it would be legal with a ring. I think you should talk through your concerns with him. You might even get an answer.'

'Maybe I should.' Scarlet pondered Adam's words. 'It's just happened a bit fast. Maybe I was a little impulsive.'

'Nobody said you had to get married tomorrow, Scarlet. It could be a long engagement. I don't think Knuckles cares either way. He is part of your life, and he's happy with that. And if you keep frowning with stress, you'll get wrinkles.' He laughed to lighten the mood. He could see her eyes glaze over as she became lost in her own thoughts. She had a lot to think about and only she could come up with the answers.

Pulling herself together and exhaling deeply, Scarlet was back in business mode. 'On another note, I've had Matt's wife on the phone asking if I know anything about his whereabouts. What do you know, Adam?' Pulling her glasses down her nose, she peered at him closely, her bright blue eyes burning into his own.

'Why don't you ask her if he's still cheating on her with that barmaid with the big tits he's always sniffing around? Maybe he's held up there somewhere. How would I know? He only works here.' Adam shrugged innocently. 'I tell you what, Scat, as you have a lot on your mind, I'll make the call to his wife.'

'And what about that explosion they're investigating near the block of flats that we've had trouble with? Do you know anything about that? I know you do, Adam.'

'Yes, I solved that problem and now everything is back to normal. I said I would sort it and I have. Those collectors would have carried on threatening and taking those people's money on our turf. Nobody fucks with us Scarlet unless they can back it up. Those tenants owe *us* money, and no one steals off us. We have a reputation to uphold.' Pursing his lips together, Adam's eyes flashed with anger.

'You sound like our father; it would have pissed him off too. You're more like him than you realise, you know. But be careful Adam.' Scarlet could see his anger rising and decided to change the subject. She had made her point. 'How's that crypto thing going? You haven't said much about it. Has it fallen on its arse?'

A great big smile washed over Adam's face. 'On the contrary,

Scat. It's working a treat.' Smugly, Adam stood up. 'Well, I'm going to leave you with your thoughts, as I have things to do. I might not be around for the next few days. But things will return to normality soon.'

Raising her eyebrows, Scarlet smiled at him. 'I take it it's your mystery woman? I'm impressed Adam. Nothing holds your attention for long apart from business. Just be on the end of your mobile if I need you.' Wagging her finger at him before he left, she continued. 'Business always comes first, I don't care who you're sleeping with.'

* * *

Adam got into his car and called Julie to find out how things were progressing with their plans.

'Nearly sorted Adam. That prat is signing cheques here, there and everywhere. We're going to pull the lot soon and close down all the accounts, including my own. We have the pin numbers of all those digital wallets. Then I'm going to go to his boss's office when Jamie isn't there and enquire as to why my account is closed. That will spread suspicion. Greedy bastard! He would try blackmailing us anyway, Adam, so we need to jump before we're pushed. All the offshore accounts are set up and running and that Jamie thinks we're only going through him now. As if we would be that stupid! Come when you can, and we'll go through it properly.' Julie had nearly run out of breath with everything she had just blurted out. 'Christ, I need to light another cigarette,' she laughed, and with that, Julie ended the call, which Adam thought was strange. Usually, Julie had loads of gossip and you found it hard to get her off the phone.

The day passed through its normal business routine and he went to the casino to see how things were progressing, although his mind wasn't on it. He couldn't help looking at his watch and feeling butterflies in his stomach when he thought about his date with Jennifer.

Tonight, he'd opted for a black silk shirt, which highlighted his blue eyes. When she opened the door, he could see that she too had made a special effort. Her hair hung softly around her shoulders. Her minimal make-up highlighted her cheekbones. Adam couldn't help but stare for a moment and take in her appearance with her black and red floral dress with its button-up front, just teasing him with a hint of her breasts. She was a beautiful woman.

'I've missed you.' She blushed and opened the door wider for him to enter.

'So soon? It hasn't been that long.' He grinned and held out the two bottles of wine he'd brought, with his own name branded on the label at the back. Walking into the lounge and sitting down, he waited while she looked for a corkscrew in the kitchen and then came through.

'What do you want me to order from the takeaway Adam? There are a couple of menus on the table. Do you have anything special in mind?'

'I've already sorted that, and it should be here in an hour or so. I've chosen Italian, and no, before you ask, it's not a pizza.' He could feel the blood rushing through his veins as she bent over the table and poured the wine. The glimpse of her cleavage captivated him. Taking a sip of wine, he put down his glass and embraced her. Their lips met as each other's passion surfaced, and each kiss became more ardent. His hands roamed all over her body as she clung to him tightly, pushing her body closer to his, while running her hands over the silkiness of his shirt and down to his crotch. His erection was apparent as she stroked him. 'Come to bed,' she whispered huskily, flushing with excitement. They both made their way to the bedroom.

With every tender kiss and stroke of each other's body, they undressed each other slowly, while Adam flicked and teased her nipple with the tip of his tongue, making it more erect. As she lay beneath him, encouraging him, Jenny whispered, 'Now, Adam, I want you now.' She moaned and opened her legs to greet him, feeling her own moistness as she writhed beneath him.

'Not yet,' he panted, and trailed his tongue along her thigh, making her moan with ecstasy and pleasure as she ran her hands through his hair. Fireworks shot through her body at his first thrust inside her and they both cried out with sheer pleasure. Waiting while Jennifer reached her peak, Adam threw his head back, gasping for air to fill his lungs. Then he cried out, almost dizzy from the spent force within him. Later, lying beside her, their hot and sweaty bodies clung to each other, almost trembling. They were both panting, trying to catch their breaths, their hunger for each other satiated in their lovemaking.

The doorbell rang, breaking the spell of the moment. 'That will be the food,' Adam whispered huskily and rolled off the bed. He picked up her pink dressing gown off the back of the door and wrapped it around him and headed for the door, his legs still feeling weak beneath him.

Joining him in the hallway wearing his shirt, with her face still flushed, Jennifer held her hand out. 'Leave that for the microwave later. Come back to bed.' Flashing her a smile, Adam put the bags containing the food on the floor and followed her back into the bedroom.

Their chemistry was electric and each time they made love, their bodies entwined with each other, the passion and excitement rising beyond heights neither of them had known before. Straddling him and satiating her own needs, eventually Jennifer almost collapsed in a heap beside him as she nestled her head upon his chest.

Sometime later, Adam opened his eyes and looked at the wall clock in the bedroom – it was nearly midnight. Turning his head slightly, he saw that Jennifer was still asleep. He traced his finger along her lips adoringly, waking her.

'I must have fallen asleep,' she murmured and kissed his chest.

'We both did after that marathon. Come on, woman, let's use that microwave. I need a drink and food. You've drained me!' he chuckled.

'I don't think anyone could drain you Adam, you're a stallion, and let's be honest, you were blessed by the gods.' She laughed contentedly. 'Come on though, I'm starving.' She tweaked his nipple.

Relaxed and content, they both ate and drank their fill, talking and laughing with each other as though they had known each other for years. 'Where have you been all my life Jennifer?' Adam spoke tenderly, sweeping her hair from her face.

Looking into his hypnotic blue eyes, she whispered, 'Waiting for you, Adam.' Eagerly, she sought his lips once more, embracing their need for each other.

The next morning, the sunlight broke through the blinds and woke Adam. He blinked hard and saw that it was after 8 a.m. He knew Jennifer's flatmates would be turning up soon, and he had to get washed and changed before work, too. Carefully removing the duvet from himself, he got out of bed and got dressed.

'You don't have to leave like a thief in the night you know.' Propping herself up on one elbow, she blew him a kiss.

'You looked so peaceful; I didn't want to wake you. I'll see you later.' Leaning over, he pecked her on the lips. 'Maybe we could still go to that fun fair later if you fancy it?'

'Mm, maybe, but I think I've had all the pleasure rides I can deal with at the moment, don't you?' She laughed and picking up a pillow, she threw it towards him as he ducked to avoid it.

'I'll call you later, Jen.' With that, Adam forced himself to leave. He didn't want to leave her lying in bed on her own. He could still smell the nearness of her on his shirt from where she had worn it last night. Her perfume surrounded him, almost like an embrace.

Driving along, he opened all the car windows to wake himself up with the morning air. His mind wandered back and forth to their love making and their time together and he couldn't help smiling and feeling a skip in his step as he sang along with the radio. Life was good, he thought to himself. No, it was bloody brilliant!

21

___

HAPPY DAYS

Days and glorious passionate nights turned into a week, and the time was drawing closer to Jennifer leaving. Adam had a sick feeling in his stomach when he thought about it. Emotions he had never felt before washed over him. Neither had made any kind of commitment; it was a friend with benefits kind of relationship, although Adam knew it was deeper than that. It was time to come clean and tell her who he was and let her make her own mind up about him.

Looking himself up and down in his grey tailored suit and tie and sweeping his hair back away from his face, he felt satisfied. Before he left his apartment he fed Fred, the goldfish they had won at the fun fair. Last night had been their last night together. Tonight, she was having a girl's night out with the girls from the supermarket to wish her well in her travels. He had felt disappointed when she had told him, angry even. She had chosen to spend the night with her friends instead of him. He wasn't used to being passed over.

Letting out a deep sigh, he checked himself again, noting that his hair had a life of its own and his wavy fringe had fallen out of place. His anger flared up. 'To hell with her,' he shouted at the mirror and left for the waiting chauffeur at his car.

Lewis opened the door at Julie's before Adam had got out of the car. 'Morning Mr Lambrianu.'

'Oh don't call me Mr Lambrianu,' snapped Adam. 'Call me Adam; you do to Julie when I'm not here.' Adam walked past him into Julie's lounge where she was lying on a chaise lounge in a bright red chiffon dressing gown trimmed with feather boa. Her make-up was perfect as always.

'Adam, come and have some coffee. Are you ready for today?' she cackled. Her eyes flashed with devilment. 'There is talk about Jamie. I don't suppose you've seen him lately, but me and Bruce have. Oh my God, Adam, he's ridiculous. He looks like he's won the lottery. Expensive suits and he's flashing the cash. That girlfriend of his is lapping it up,' Julie drawled and raised an eyebrow. 'She's back on the scene. No surprise there then,' she scoffed. 'Kim told Bruce she was worried about Jamie and his outlandish ways. It seems he's attracting attention. Today we wipe the accounts, Adam. Close everything down. I've been in touch with Jamie and told him we're pulling out, but we want one last set of signatures.'

A frown crossed Adam's face. 'Why on earth would you tell him that? We can close the accounts on our own; we don't need him.'

'No, but we can use him. He's going to notify all of these clients that the company has gone into bankruptcy. That their money no longer exists.'

'And how are you going to make him do that Julie? Even he isn't that stupid.'

'No but he's greedy. Look in that holdall near the fireplace.' Adam saw the bag she spoke of. Curiously, he stood up and unzipped it and saw that it was full of money. 'Bloody hell Julie, how much is in there?' Adam ran his hand along the piles of money in the bag.

'Well, if it impresses someone like you who has been surrounded by money his whole life, just think what it will do to Jamie. He'd sign his own mother's death warrant!' Cackling loudly, Julie laughed at her own joke. 'Seriously Adam, he will do whatever we say just to get his sticky hands on that. He'll have his own plans for it I'm sure, or I am sure his girlfriend will.' Giving Adam one of her wise, knowing looks, she put a cigarette in her long gold cigarette holder and lit it.

Adam looked up as Bruce walked in. 'Here we are. The three amigos.' Julie clapped her hands together with glee. 'Right Bruce, let's work our magic. Clear those accounts out, then get rid of that laptop. Adam, get rid of all the other laptops your faithful watchers have had. They have been very good, ferrying information back and forth. They deserve a bonus. They must have been glued to those screens. Even Knuckles is a dab hand, excuse the pun, considering he only has one.' Again, Julie laughed.

Instantly the mood changed, and Bruce pulled up a chair beside Julie. Lewis came through, handing them each a laptop and Adam started following Bruce's lead. 'It's easier with more of us, it will be quicker,' explained Julie.

Each in turn they emptied each client's account. Millions turned into nothing but zero. All the crypto money out of the wallets was put on the coin exchange and sold for a lot less than it was worth and people were buying it up. Suddenly, it was turned into 'clean' money and sent off to the offshore accounts. The lounge was silent apart from the tapping of the keyboards. The tension in the air was electric and no one spoke a word. Eventually, all of the money in their offshore accounts was clean, legal money.

'How much have we ended up with Bruce?' Eagerly, Julie looked over his shoulder.

'All in all, plus what we have bought in goods, I would say about eighty million.' Bruce grinned at Julie.

Adam let out a low whistle. Each of them sat there in silence after hours of hard concentration and deliberated over what they had done. It had been easier than robbing a bank. There were no casualties, and no police chasing them up the high road with their sirens blazing. Instead, they had all sat in Julie's lounge full of nervous tension and clouds of nicotine, being served coffee and biscuits by one of Julie's many men and had taken eighty million...

Hearing the doorbell, Julie looked at the clock. 'That will be Jamie. Right, Bruce, get out of here. Go with the boys to the kitchen and have some dinner. Both of you bugger off!'

Worried, Adam looked from Julie to Bruce. 'We can't leave you on your own Julie. Fuck that, we're in this together.'

'You will do as you're told for once in your life Adam. Me and Lewis can sort this. Go! Both of you!' she ordered. 'Lewis, go and answer the door. Tidy yourself up a bit first though, you look like shit. Adam, pick up your jacket. You've done your bit and now it's my turn. Fuck off!'

Reluctantly they did as they were told, while Julie sprayed her perfume in the air to cover the smell of sweat and cigarettes.

Lewis showed Jamie into the lounge. Julie couldn't help but notice his appearance. He had a well-tailored suit on and thick gold jewellery on his wrist and around his neck, which matched the expensive gold watch he now wore. Personally, Julie thought he looked like a pimp.

'Would you like a drink Jamie?' Turning towards Lewis, Julie beckoned him. 'You're forgetting your manners. Get our guest a drink of his choice.'

Lewis handed him the large whisky he requested and raised an eyebrow at Julie. 'I have something for you Jamie as you've been so loyal in your work. I have written something out that I want you to put on your computer and sign digitally.'

Julie handed the note she had written out to Lewis, who in turn handed it to Jamie. Carefully, he read Julie's scrawl. 'This is a letter to the clients informing them the business is bankrupt.' Jamie nearly threw her letter back at her in disgust. 'I can't do that. What happens when they find out it hasn't gone bankrupt?'

'Mistakes are made all the time Jamie. It could just be another typing error. Lewis, bring that bag over here and give it to Jamie.'

'You want me to inform important clients that there is no money in their accounts and that the company has gone bust? Forgive me, Mrs Gold, but I can't do that.'

Jamie was intrigued as Lewis heaved the heavy holdall in front of him and unzipped it. Gobsmacked, he stared silently at the contents. 'There is three million in that bag. All in cash and all for you, if you write up the letter and sign Mr Noakes' name on it. Oh, we can soon retract it and say it has all been some big mistake. But this is just a ploy to make shares flood the market and go up. It will work, trust me. Everyone will want to buy shares cheaply if they think a company is going bust. Everyone loves a bargain, Jamie. Then, we retract, but we'll have made our money, won't we? And I mean we Jamie love,' Julie drawled. Treacle almost dripped from her mouth with her sweetness. Casting a furtive glance at Lewis, she gave him a wink.

It didn't matter what she was saying, Jamie wasn't listening. He was bedazzled by the contents of the bag. Julie could already see him mentally spending it. 'You could go on a lovely holiday Jamie, or even buy a holiday home to escape to when things get stressful. I'm sure any lady in your life would appreciate it; I know I would.' Julie dangled the carrot in front of him and she could see him drooling.

Moistening his lips, he looked at Julie, then down at the bag again. 'Just a letter informing them of the company's troubles and that they could lose their shares. Maybe encourage a meeting with them all or something?'

Julie knew he would try and backpedal a little, and she had counted on it. Saying the company was going bust was a bit drastic, and she knew he would settle for telling them the company merely had some troubles and that their investments could be at risk. As far as Julie was concerned, it all meant the same thing.

Bruce and Adam stood in the next room, craning their necks near the doorway to try and hear the conversation. They hardly dared breathe as they listened. They could hear Julie's calm voice, flattering and friendly. They could also hear the apprehension in Jamie's.

'I will do it, Mrs Gold. As you say, people make these errors all the time. It would soon settle down once everyone realises everything is okay.'

Silently, Adam and Bruce punched the air. Everything was going as planned. Julie and Lewis sat patiently as Jamie took out his work laptop, which he shouldn't have out of the office in the first place. Julie looked at Lewis smugly as Jamie quickly typed away, before turning the laptop towards Julie to check it. Scrutinising it carefully, she could see the office letter heading emblazoned with its logo informing all of the clients that their shares were in danger. She nodded and waited while he digitally signed it from Mr Noakes CEO.

Julie and Lewis both watched as he pressed 'send' and smugly they looked at each other. Julie heard a noise on her own mobile and ignored it for the time being. 'Well, Jamie darling, that should shake up a few investors so we can buy up their shares.' She smiled. Then she asked to check his laptop and looked into the 'sent' section to make sure the email had gone, and he hadn't tried tricking her. Sure enough, he had sent it to all of his rich clientele. 'Now that business is over with for the time being Jamie, would you like a drink before you leave? That is quite a heavy bag. Would you like me to get my chauffeur to drive you back to London?'

'No, that's fine Mrs Gold. I have my own car now. I'll skip the drink if you don't mind and just head off.' He grinned and held out his hand to shake hers.

Shaking his hand and promising to speak soon, she waited while Lewis showed him out. Then she went to the window and peered out. His little red sports car sat in her drive and Lewis helped him put the bag of money in the tiny boot. She wanted to laugh out loud. The fool, the bloody fool, she thought to herself. He was leaving a blazing trail behind him.

Bruce and Adam walked into the lounge. 'Phew! That was nerve-wracking. I didn't think he was going to do it,' exclaimed Bruce.

'Of course he was going to do it. Did you really think his morals and principles would leave that lovely bag of money in my lounge? Of course not. As soon as his clients see that email, the first thing they will do is check their accounts and see that there is nothing in them, but Jamie doesn't know that, does he?' Nudging Adam in the ribs, Julie laughed. 'Fuck, I would love to be a fly on the wall when Mr Noakes gets all those angry emails and telephone calls. Lewis, pour us all a drink, we need to celebrate. Crack open the champagne for Christ's sake!'

'We need to wait and make sure they all have the emails first, Julie.' Adam wanted confirmation; he had an uneasy feeling about this.

'Let me prove it to you, Adam! For fuck's sake, no one has any faith in me.' Muttering to herself, Julie picked up her mobile. Opening her emails, she saw the email Jamie had sent out. After all, she was one of Jamie's clients. 'See? Now, tomorrow I go to Mr Noakes and ask him what it's all about. Can I have my fucking champagne now? Blimey, you would piss down my back and tell me it's raining!'

Bruce and Adam ignored Julie's mutterings and read the email.

Sure enough, there it was, informing her that the company was in financial trouble, and that their shares could be affected.

A beaming smile spread across Adam's face and he and Bruce hugged each other with excitement. 'We're fucking rich, Adam!' Bruce shouted.

'Oh, that reminds me.' Julie picked up a large brown envelope and handed it to Bruce. 'In there is your account details and your card. Your offshore account details are also in there. The money will be shared evenly, apart from with me, of course. But I think there's enough to keep you going for a while.' She winked and gave Bruce a kiss on the cheek. For once, he didn't blush, but marvelled at all the paperwork inside the envelope.

'Thank you Julie,' was all he could say. He was lost for words. Suddenly, he was a multi-millionaire!

22

HARSH REALITIES

Joining Scarlet in the club, Adam played the dutiful host while she drank champagne with the wealthy regulars. 'I'm leaving early, Adam. Something to do,' Scarlet whispered in his ear. 'I won't be long.'

Watching everyone drink and dance the night away, Adam let his mind drift to Jennifer and what she would be doing now. Was she dancing with someone? Before he could spend too much time musing, an old girlfriend of his, Marianne, linked her arm through his and kissed his cheek. 'Where have you been hiding, stranger?'

After his day, he was feeling in high spirits. He had asked Bruce to meet him at the club and he'd said he'd think about it, but he hadn't turned up yet. Adam presumed he was doing his own celebrating. He'd drunk far too much at Julie's, and now he was drinking again, alone. Suddenly he felt lonely. He had always liked Marianne; she wanted her picture in the papers and made no bones about it. Although she was a known model, she wanted to do more, possibly even venture into acting and the quickest way she could do that was by constantly being in the tabloids. Drinking champagne in Lambrianu's famous nightclub was a sure-fire way to get into the papers. She was tall with natural strawberry blonde hair that made her stand out from the crowd.

Slightly tipsy, Adam admired her long hair and stroked it. The short red, sequinned dress she wore heightened her features. 'Come on Adam, it's time we danced the night away.' Marianne led him to the dance floor and instantly her arms went around his neck in a slow embrace. He needed this ego boost; he wanted to celebrate with someone special but there was no one. Even Scarlet had done a disappearing act.

* * *

'Hi Julie.' Nervously, Scarlet walked into the lounge and gratefully accepted a drink from Lewis.

'What's the mystery Scarlet? You sounded almost desperate when you called earlier.' Julie wasn't sure what Scarlet wanted.

'I have some news and I want to tell you myself. You can say what you like but get it over with once and for all. I can stand your sarcasm here, but not in public and I don't want to fall out with you.'

Julie frowned at the seriousness of Scarlet's voice. 'Fall out? Why would we fall out after all these years? We argue, Scarlet, but we always have.'

'I'm marrying Knuckles,' Scarlet blurted out and gulped down the rest of her whisky, holding out the glass for Lewis to refill it.

'Well, I would burst out laughing but I can see you're not in the mood for banter and this is serious.'

'It is Julie. I presume you think I sound desperate or something, probably you think I'll be a laughing stock...'

Standing up, Julie came and sat beside Scarlet, indicating for Lewis to leave the room. She put her arm around Scarlet's shoulders. 'When did he ask you?'

Sweeping her hair back, Scarlet looked at Julie. 'Well actually, I asked him! There, that's desperation for you. Go on Julie, laugh. Get it over with,' snapped Scarlet.

'Personally, Scarlet, I think you're the only one that's in denial. Many people in the club think you two are already married anyway. You have children together; he follows you everywhere. The only person who thinks it's a secret is you, Scarlet. I'm sorry to say this, but it doesn't shock me. Well, it has, but not for the reasons you're thinking. I'm shocked that it's taken you so long. Knuckles must be tired of waiting.' A thought suddenly occurred to Julie, and her brows crossed. 'Does that mean we have to call him something else, now? I can't remember his real name.'

'I don't think he can either. But it's Julian. Can you imagine anyone calling him Julian? No, I'll carry on calling him Knuckles and so will everyone else.' It was the first time since arriving that Scarlet managed a smile.

'Well, I can see why he's had to fight all of his life.' Julie laughed. 'Oh God, I've just realised. He nearly has the same name as me! Oh, for fuck's sake Scarlet, have you come to tell me I'm related to Knuckles?'

They both burst out laughing.

'Is that the ring, Scarlet?' Julie held Scarlet's hand up to the light and admired it. 'Nice rock. Real too. Did he buy it?'

'Why does everyone ask me that? Adam asked the same thing when he saw it. Yes, he did buy it.' Scarlet grinned. 'So, what do you think Julie? Am I making a fool of myself?'

'I think you've already made a fool of yourself through the years Scarlet. You have his children, he lives with you and yet you tell people he only stays with you to look after the children and in case you need a driver on hand. No one is going to be shocked by this. The only person who seems to be is you! For Christ's sake, we all know you're a couple. You have been for years. When was the last time you had another man in your bed? You have been faithful to him, whether you've realised it or not, and he has to you.'

'You are right Julie, there has been no one else. I laugh and flirt and drink champagne with lords of the house and celebrities, but truth be told, they bore me. All they talk about is themselves and money. It's the glamour of it all that attracts them, not me. With Knuckles I can walk around without my make-up and my hair tied back. I wear my tracksuit bottoms and a T-shirt and when my feet hurt, I wear my old slippers. We do have separate bedrooms and he never bothers me... but I confess I have sometimes gone to him.' Scarlet blushed, avoiding Julie's eyes.

Julie smiled. 'He's got better with age, I grant you that. If it's right for you Scarlet, do it. Have no regrets when you leave this mortal coil and if that seven-foot gorilla who can't string a sentence together makes you happy then do it, get married. He's a good dad, and adores the kids. And weirdly they actually adore him, too.' Julie laughed. 'Fuck, they say love is blind.'

'I knew you wouldn't be able to resist mocking me, Julie. That's why I wanted to get it over with.'

'I will always take the piss out of you, you old chatterbox. That's just me Scarlet. I did the same to your father, although he was much more fun than Knuckles. He rose to the fight with that temper of his and he was so easy to wind up. Thanks for telling me Scarlet, I appreciate it.' Slapping her on the knee, Julie shouted for Lewis. 'Our Scarlet's to be married, which means hen night fun. I will leave that in your capable hands Lewis.' Julie turned back towards Scarlet. 'How about some good old-fashioned fish and chips with bread and butter and a gossip about the old days?'

'That sounds like a hen night in itself, Julie.' Scarlet breathed a sigh of relief. She'd dreaded telling Julie, but she felt better now. That was the worst part over with. 'I don't say this often enough, but

I love you Julie, you know that right?' Scarlet hugged Julie and kissed her on the cheek.

'And I love you, Scarlet. I remember you coming into the world. You're my family love, but I do think you should tell Knuckles you love him once in a while, too. I don't suppose anyone has ever said that to the poor bastard. Even if you say it just once in his lifetime, he will cherish it forever. Remember that.' Giving her a knowing look, Julie hugged her again.

Kicking off her shoes, Scarlet curled up on the sofa. 'I'm up for a girl's night in. Send my chauffeur away, Lewis.'

Lewis stood there with his hands on his hips and raised his eyebrows questioningly. 'And your hen night, Scarlet?' he joked.

'Okay Lewis, I know what you're getting at, though God only knows what I'm letting myself in for. You are the hen night host, and you can send someone for those chips too!'

Hearing the alarm, Adam turned, bleary-eyed, towards the clock on his bedside table. Rubbing his face with his hands and switching it off, he noticed an arm across his stomach and shocked, he turned to his side to see Marianne lying sound asleep beside him. Instantly, he remembered last night through his clouded brain. He was still woozy and hungover but flashbacks came back to him. He'd drunk far too much and ended up in bed with Marianne. Guilt washed over him, and he regretted it instantly. Cursing himself as he got out of bed, he realised that if he hurried, he would make it to the airport in time to see Jennifer off.

Quickly showering and dressing, he ran downstairs and saw one of the chauffeurs hanging around. 'Take me to Heathrow airport, and put your foot down,' he shouted as he got into the back seat.

Running through the airport doors while the chauffeur waited,

Adam scanned the boards for Jennifer's flight. He hadn't missed her. Frantically, he ran around the crowded airport looking for her. It was like looking for a needle in a haystack. Taking out his mobile, he decided to call her and ask her where she was. But as he looked up he saw her coming out of a book shop. 'Jennifer,' he called over and waved. Running towards her, he swept her off her feet and kissed her, hugging her tightly. 'I had to come,' he panted.

'I'm glad you did. To be honest, I tried calling you last night. It was late, but we all called it a night around 11 p.m. after we had finished our meal and sung a bit of karaoke in the local pub,' she laughed.

Inwardly, he cursed himself. He had judged Jennifer by his own low standards and at this moment, he felt like the lowest of the low. He hadn't heard his mobile, possibly too drunk to even notice and yet, she had called him. The bile nearly rose in his throat when he thought about last night.

'Will you let me know when you arrive safely? Send a text or something,' he asked.

'If that's what you want, Adam. I won't pester you too much over the next few weeks as I'll be up to my neck in water for most of it,' she laughed. 'I think I love you Adam... No, scrap that, I know I've fallen in love with you. But I don't feel as though there is honesty between us. Where I've made love to you, I feel you've perhaps only been having sex with me. Don't get me wrong, it was the best sex I've ever had. You've turned it into an art form!' Forcing a weak smile, she looked up at him.

'What's brought this on Jennifer? I'm here, aren't I? I'm sorry I didn't answer your call. If you're angry with me for that, I'm sorry.' Confused at her sudden outburst, he couldn't understand what she was saying.

'I'm not angry, Adam. I suppose, I'm disappointed. We've spent every day with each other over the last couple of weeks, and yet I still know nothing about you. I'm an open book to you Adam, but you clearly don't feel enough for me to be able to share anything about yourself. You know my flatmates and my work mates, but you have never introduced me to any of your friends. You are my mystery man. Honesty, it's all about honesty.' Tears brimmed in her eyes. 'I have to go.' Turning, she walked away to the check-in desk, with Adam in hot pursuit.

'Jennifer, I didn't introduce you to my friends because I wanted to spend time with you and you alone. For Christ's sake, if it means that much to you, come and meet them now. Get a later flight and meet them now!' he shouted.

'No Adam, I have to go.' Teardrops fell down her cheeks.

Adam felt choked up. 'Don't leave like this, Jen, not after our time together.' He could feel his own tears stinging his eyes but fought hard to stop them.

She leaned forward and kissed him on the lips. The she edged closer and whispered in his ear, 'Goodbye Adam. Goodbye Adam Lambrianu.'

Her words cut him like a knife. She knew who he was; maybe she had all along. He'd been a bloody fool to think she didn't. Julie had been right and now he understood her words about honesty. Shocked, he stood there and stared at her.

'You know who I am. Why didn't you say something?' he asked. Frantically, his mind tried to make sense of it all.

'No Adam, why didn't *you* say something? Do you think it would have made a difference to me? It obviously did to you. I know who you are and what you are. Admittedly I didn't at first, but my flat-mates read the same glossy magazines you're pictured in. Now I understand why you cover yourself with your motorbike helmet. Always in disguise, aren't you, Adam?'

Grabbing her hand and not wanting to let go, he hung onto her desperately. 'I've never lied to you, Jennifer. Promise me you will call me, and we can discuss this. I wanted to win you in my own right, not dazzle you with clubs and casinos. Don't leave like this, I beg you.'

'Goodbye Adam.' Turning, she walked away without a backward glance as Adam watched her disappear. He felt sick to the stomach as he walked out of the airport. He felt angry and wanted to lash out, but knew the only person to blame was himself. He should have been upfront from the start.

* * *

'I've really enjoyed myself Julie. Pouring all my anxieties and troubles onto you makes me feel stress free. Although I wish Katie had been here; she would have loved it.' Scarlet hadn't realised just how much she'd missed these girlie evenings with people she could trust and be herself with. Although their night had been simple, they had talked until the early hours. It had occurred to her in the night, when she thought about her evening, that she didn't have any female friends. Not real ones anyway.

Over the breakfast table, Scarlet ate her fill, then saw Julie's smiling face drop and grow serious. 'Talking of Katie, there is something we need to discuss.'

'You mean how to get revenge on that scumbag? I'm ready when you are. In fact, I feel like going over there and kicking his teeth in!'

'No, it's something else that has come my way. I believe Adam had a brush with death at the casino. He took a real beating, by all accounts.' Putting down her coffee cup, Julie sat back.

'Yes, I'd call it a skirmish, but it's sorted now. What do you know that you're not telling me?'

The two women looked at each other over the breakfast table. Pondering what to say next, Julie lit a cigarette and blew the smoke into the air. 'Why didn't you tell me, especially after you left three bodies in your wake? You murdered them, didn't you?'

'It was more kill or be killed Julie.' Scarlet blushed to her roots at this interrogation. Julie's once smiling happy face had suddenly grown stern and it reminded Scarlet of days stood in front of the head teacher for another lecture. 'What was there to tell? More to the point, how do you know?'

'I understand that, Scarlet, and believe me I'm not judging. I have enough blood on my own hands. But have you actually sat down and thought about that day? Why was there a sudden switch in dealers? More to the point, these new dealers knew they were onto a good thing. They were always paid on time, and it was a regular deal. Why would they spoil that? It's not good business, Scarlet. I hear you were tipped off and that was the only reason that Adam is still alive. The poor bastard who called you was stood in a bath while they sawed off his arm...'

Julie waited for her words to sink in, and by the shocked look on Scarlet's face, she could see that they were. Putting down her toast, a million questions ran through Scarlet's mind. 'How did he make the call then? Surely these people, whoever they were, must have been in the same room with him.'

'He'd already been tortured, Scarlet. And while his assassins opened a couple of beers from his own fridge and left him bleeding on the floor prolonging the inevitable, his last thought was Adam. He had heard their plans. He was a dead man already Scarlet and he knew it. Possibly, his final revenge was scuppering their plans. Who knows?' Julie threw her hands up in the air and shrugged.

Stunned, Scarlet listened to Julie's tale. 'Who gave the order for this?' Scarlet's eyes darkened with anger.

'Chris, your wonderful brother-in-law.' Julie inhaled on the cigarette. 'I still have friends in that circle Scarlet, and they tell me things.'

Scarlet's eyes widened. 'Oh my God Julie. What is he going to do next? Kill us all? He's blackmailing Katie and Diana. He wants Adam dead. Am I next, or my kids? What the fuck is wrong with that psychopath?'

'We have to act on this Scarlet, and the sooner the better. He has spiralled out of control and thinks he rules the world. I knew he would never make a good Don. There is no reasoning with him. Don Carlos was firm but fair. Chris even wants the Jewish mafia out of the circle. They were Ralph's friends and to be honest they are the ones keeping me informed. I tell you this in utter secrecy.'

'Do you believe their stories Julie, or is it just because Chris wants them out? Is it bad blood between the families?'

'They have never lied to me yet. More out of respect for Ralph and I suppose me being his wife. Or should I say his widow. The only bad apple is Don Christopher, your brother-in-law.'

Scarlet could feel her blood boiling with rage. Banging her fist on the table and spilling her coffee, she glared at Julie. 'Why have you kept this to yourself for so long? Why haven't you told me sooner?'

'Because the truth about that day has only just come to my ears. But Adam could be a dead man walking if we don't finish Chris once and for all, Scarlet.' Julie knew she had given Scarlet food for thought and would now let her leave and think about it.

Tears fell down Scarlet's face, leaving tracks. 'I have to keep Adam safe. Don't tell him, Julie. I would rather he didn't know about this, well not yet, anyway.'

'I'm not saying anything Scarlet. This is between you and me. But Adam is a grown man and he has hidden depths. He's a survivor Julie. Maybe he should know that his life is in danger; at least he would be on his guard.'

'Let me think about it. I'm not really sure what to do. This is my baby brother we're talking about. And yes, I know I go over the top with him, but I remember how a stray bullet killed my father. Adam is our father's only biological son and I can't live through the nightmare of losing him. What do we do? I can't live my life walking on eggshells.'

'I'm in the processing of sorting it out. It's taken time, but you can't just knock on Chris's door and walk in. I doubt even Katie does that. He will have henchmen protecting him, tooled up and ready for action. Don Carlos made his home a fortress. It's not when we get to him Scarlet, it's how.'

'Well, just bloody hurry up, Julie. I want that bastard's reign to end and I want the last face he sees on this earth to be mine so I can spit in his.'

'There's fire in your veins, Scarlet, but Ralph always believed patience was a virtue and if you wait long enough the opportunity arises by itself.' Julie reached her arm over the breakfast table. 'Gold and Lambrianu, fighting their battles together again, eh?'

Squeezing her hand, Scarlet nodded. 'United as always. What would we do without you Julie?'

'You'll manage. You're looking more like me every day,' she laughed.

The hoot of a car horn made them both look up from their whispered conversation. 'That will be my chauffeur, Julie. I have to go. Bloody hell, I've left Knuckles in charge so God knows what mayhem I'm going back to.' Picking up her bag, she kissed Julie on the cheek and left. The long ride home helped clear Scarlet's mind. She knew she had to think without emotion, as emotion was bad for business.

No sooner was she back in her office than Knuckles walked in. 'I'm going to change my clothes Knuckles; how many people have you threatened in my absence? Do we have any staff left?'

'Just two. Didn't threaten anyone. Just beat them up.'

Looking down at her desk, Scarlet shook her head and let out a deep sigh. 'Why?'

'Late for work.'

'Is that it? They turned up late for work and you beat them up? Why, for God's sake?'

'Next time could be important and they're not here to do their work. Just 'cos you're not here.'

Suddenly, Adam flashed through Scarlet's mind. Knuckles was right, if they had needed someone on hand quickly, there would have been no one around. Their lateness could cost Adam his life.

'Knuckles, I think Adam is in trouble, or danger, both really. Keep an eye on him for me, will you? An extra special eye.' Sitting down, she put her head in her hands. She felt as though she had the weight of the world on her shoulders.

'Police trouble?' he asked, frowning.

'No, worse than that. An old enemy who wants him out of the way.'

'Done. You go change.' Without another word, Knuckles left the office. Scarlet knew he would take care of Adam for her. She didn't want to mother Adam, but Knuckles would do it in his own sweet way. She looked up at the empty doorway where he had just been standing. She was doing the right thing, she mused to herself. Knuckles was one of the few people she trusted with this horror story and he didn't ask questions.

She smiled to herself. Yes, she would marry him and be proud to do so. Looking at the photo of her father on the wall, she grinned. 'I know you think I'm crazy Papa,' she said aloud. 'But he cares about the family and protects them. Just as you did.' For a brief moment, Scarlet thought the photo of her father smiled at her and she shook her head to wake herself. It must be a trick of the light, she thought to herself, or she was tired from her late night with Julie. Either way, she felt calm inside as though she had his blessing.

23

JUSTICE

Days passed and still Adam hadn't heard from Jennifer. He'd sent numerous messages and could see they'd been read, but she still hadn't answered. He felt helpless. If only he could have the chance to explain, he thought to himself. Night after night, he'd lain in his bed wondering what she was doing and if she hated him. He hadn't let the cleaner send his shirt to the laundry; he'd wanted to keep it because Jennifer had worn it and it smelt of her.

He felt in torment but couldn't understand why. Why should he even care, he mused to himself. He'd walked away from many women without a second thought.

'I am sick of you turning up for work like a bear with a sore head. You don't do anything while you're here anyway. What's wrong? Woman troubles?' Scarlet snapped. 'For God's sake Adam get over it, you always have before. What's this one got, fur lined knickers?'

'It's got fuck all to do with you! Just leave me alone. I'm doing my bit. I've been at the casino all night laundering money. I even went to your salons and sorted the deliveries out there. Money is rolling in Scarlet so what are you moaning about?' Adam spat out.

Taken aback, Scarlet sat and took the brunt of his anger. Looking at him properly, she could see the change in him. He looked like shit; his hair wasn't combed, and he had hair on his chin, which was unusual because his vanity wouldn't let him cover that handsome face of his. She'd been too busy over the last few days to notice, but now she looked closely, she could see something was seriously wrong.

Lowering her voice as though she was talking to a child, Scarlet took off her glasses and laid them on the desk. 'Where is she Adam? Why can't you pop around and see her or send flowers? What's happened, love?'

Adam put his head in his hands. 'Because I've disappointed her! She hates me and as for flowers, she is somewhere deep-sea diving in the Caribbean or Mediterranean. Christ, she could be in the Thames for all I know.' Adam threw his hands up in the air in despair and sat opposite Scarlet. 'I don't know what to do, Scat.'

Hating seeing him in pain like this, and she could see it was pain, she threw her head back against her chair. 'Is this the woman who's at a university...?' At Adam's confused look, Scarlet smiled. 'Don't worry, Julie rambles on a lot when she's tipsy. But if it is, and you're not a hundred per cent where she is, I'm sure her university would tell you. I bet they're in some form of contact with her.'

'Julie has a big mouth,' Adam snapped, but it was as though a light switch had just been turned on. 'But you're right, they would, wouldn't they? They would know exactly where she was.'

'Take a plane, take the yacht, God knows it could do with an outing. Find her and tell her what your heart feels.'

The sparkle seemed to come back to Adam's eyes. Standing up, he walked over to Scarlet. 'Thanks Scat. I'm sorry for shouting at you. You're the last person I would want to hurt.' As they embraced, Scarlet felt better. Although the main thought that wandered through her mind was to get him on the yacht as far away to safety as possible. No one could reach him there... Julie was right: patience was a virtue.

'Oh, I'm just a sounding board. You know I never listen to anything you say,' she laughed.

As Adam walked out of the office, he bumped into Knuckles, who held his good arm out to stop him. 'Need a best man,' Knuckles muttered, averting his eyes.

Not thinking straight, Adam frowned. 'I'm sure you will when the time comes, so what about it?' Intrigued, Adam waited, although he wasn't paying attention. He had his own agenda. Looking even closer, he thought he saw Knuckles blush slightly.

Moving from one foot to the other, Knuckles bit his bottom lip uncomfortably. Adam could see he was out of his comfort zone. 'You,' he said. 'What about you?' he asked nervously.

The penny finally dropped for Adam. 'You want me to be your best man at the wedding Knuckles?' Seeing Knuckles nod his head, he walked up to his huge bulk and shook his hand enthusiastically. 'That would be an honour Knuckles. I would love to, thanks for asking.' He beamed. Adam watched as Knuckles walked on. He wasn't one for sentiment, but Adam knew him well enough to know he was pleased with Adam's answer.

Walking into work with a skip in his step, Jamie greeted everyone he passed in the office. 'Morning everyone,' he said.

'Jamie! Jamie, get your arse in here!' Mr Noakes bellowed from his office. Seeing Kim avert her eyes and carry on looking at her computer, Jamie sensed something was terribly wrong, and it wasn't because he was late again.

Knocking on Mr Noakes' door, which was already open, Jamie

saw two men stood with Mr Noakes. 'You wanted me sir?' His throat went dry and he moistened his lips with his tongue.

'This is him!' Mr Noakes pointed, his face red with anger. 'Arrest him. I'm ruined, bloody ruined.'

Panicking, Jamie wanted to run, but his legs felt heavy. Words escaped him. 'You're mistaken, Mr Noakes. I haven't done anything!' he shouted in his own defence. Then he saw one of the men in the room nod his head to someone behind him and when he turned, he saw two police officers. Panic rose and he felt sick. Running for it, he barged past the two policemen, who gave chase and apprehended him before he could reach the exit. Shaking with fear, he stood there as they read him his rights, not quite taking it in. Tears rolled down his cheeks and he fell to his knees. 'Please, Mr Noakes, I haven't done anything. Please!' Holding his hands together in prayer, he begged and pleaded as the policemen put handcuffs on him. Bile rose in his throat. It frothed up to his lips and spewed out. The two policemen stood back a little as he emptied the contents of his stomach onto the office floor.

The two detectives from Mr Noakes' office walked slowly up to him. 'Jamie Williams, you are charged with embezzlement, theft and fraud. What's in the bag?' they questioned. Jamie's heart sank as the detective walked over to his desk. Opening it, he saw the laptop and brought it into the office. 'Mr Noakes, do you recognise this? I see it has your logo on the front.'

'It's one of my office laptops. We use them sometimes in meetings and so forth. Why is that out of the office? Those laptops are full of client information and data. They are not for personal use!' This find caused another outburst from Mr Noakes.

Quaking with fear and pleading for mercy, Jamie looked between everyone wild eyed. 'It was Julie Gold. She made me do it. She forced me!' he screamed. 'She's the one you need to arrest!' The policemen put their arms under his and helped him stand up.

'What makes you think it was me? I'm an innocent man!' Jamie was digging himself an even bigger hole. The facts were apparent. Jamie had the office laptop with him and had walked in full of bravado over the last few weeks, flashing his cash and boasting about his fortune.

'I knew you would blame someone. You've been caught red-handed. Let's see what they find when they search the new fancy flat that you've bought with my money! It was Mrs Gold that alerted me about all of this. She is your client, and she was very upset. She, as well as a few others, want to know about this email I'm supposed to have sent out. Everyone is threatening to sue me! I've even had the newspapers on the telephone. She's lost over a million pounds and people think I've stolen all their money. You've forged my signature and sent numerous emails out to our customers saying the business is failing, while clearing out their accounts. I hope you hang for it, you bastard!' Mr Noakes spewed venom, until the police intervened and asked him to stop.

Stunned at this revelation, Jamie stood like a statue when he realised Julie Gold had betrayed him. His eyes darted around the room and he saw his colleagues craning their necks to watch the whole performance. He wanted the ground to swallow him up, as his face burnt with shame. He knew he was doomed. Cursing himself, he realised he hadn't checked those accounts for days. He had been too busy booking holidays and living it up. Work had come second place to his spending.

Everyone averted their gaze as he was marched through the office in handcuffs to the awaiting police car.

24

FAMILY UNITY

'I've had a letter from Katie. It's coded so Chris wouldn't be able to decipher it. Don't look at me like that, Adam,' Scarlet scoffed. 'We're twins and we have our own code. Let's go up to your apartment; we can talk properly there.'

Once away from eyes and ears, Scarlet showed Adam the letter. There were lines and letters that Scarlet had circled with a red pen. He frowned at it. It meant nothing to him and looking up at Scarlet, he passed it back. 'Sorry Scarlet, maybe I'm being a bit slow here, but how can I read it when you have written all over it?'

'Look at the heading. Ode to sis. That's it. I think that is what Julie has been waiting for.'

Perplexed, Adam sat on the sofa. Scarlet was running paces ahead of him and he didn't understand what she was talking about. All this cloak and dagger was beginning to annoy him. 'Just start from the beginning and spit it out, will you. I have no fucking idea what this letter means let alone all your red doodling.'

Taking a large breath, Scarlet let out a sigh. 'Normally, when we send postcards or letters, it says "letter to sis". We both know that when it says, "ode to sis", every fourth line has letters at the beginning so we can decipher the real reason for writing. We used to do it at school or leave notes at home so Mum and Dad couldn't read them, if we needed a lie to cover our tracks. Well, here it is. Ode to sis. Chris wouldn't think twice about it because he has seen it loads of times and thinks it's just a bonkers heading.' Scarlet smiled. 'That is why my pen marks are all over it. I can see what she is really writing about.'

Adam raised his eyebrows at this revelation and gave Scarlet an odd stare. 'Go on.'

'Now read the letters I have ringed.' Scarlet handed the letter over again to Adam and sat there patiently while he wrote down the letters Scarlet had circled. Then he looked up at her. 'Okay, I'm no wiser. What's the big deal? It spells out "Hen weekend in Italy. Chris happy about it. Let's do this." So you're planning your hen night in Italy? I'm surprised it's not the club, but still, it's nice of Chris and Katie to agree to host...'

'For fuck's sake you're stupid at times,' Scarlet snapped and whipped the letter out of his hands. 'Read between the lines, Adam. When we usually go to Italy mobhanded, like we have in the past, when has Chris ever been happy about it? Never. This isn't really about my hen do. Julie needed a good reason for us all to go to Italy united and kill that bastard once and for all. Well, this is it, our golden opportunity.'

Nodding his head and taking in what she was saying, Adam half grasped the conversation, but decided now was the time to pour cold water on Scarlet's plan. 'I see what you're saying, but won't Chris find it a bit weird that you're taking your brother to your hen party?'

'We could work on that, say you're just coming for the holiday... or I could buy you a dress!' Scarlet laughed. 'But this is our opportunity to get inside Don Carlos's house. Us girls partying and getting pissed up, he wouldn't even pay us any attention. I used to think he wanted to be involved in our family gatherings, but now we both know that wasn't the case. He wanted to know what Katie was talking about so he could control her and the kids. He really has been a devious bastard. He's pulled the wool over all of our eyes Adam, and it stops here and now. Well, the ball is in Julie's court now. She said she had most of her plan in place, well, this might just be the excuse she has been waiting for. Come on, grab your jacket, we're going over there.'

'Now?' Adam couldn't believe Scarlet's urgency. 'I had plans for today, can't you go alone?'

Glaring at him, Scarlet pouted. Realising there was no room for argument, Adam picked up his jacket.

'So, what plans did you have for today Adam?' Scarlet snapped while they drove along to Julie's.

'Nothing really, I was just going to find out when that woman I told you about was coming home. It must be soon; I just don't know when. I did what you said and contacted the university and they confirmed where she was.'

'You're going to have to put her on ice a bit longer Adam. Girl-friends come and go but family lasts forever. I'm sorry. I appreciate you like this woman, and for God's sake Adam use her name, she's not James's Bond!'

'Jennifer, her name is Jennifer,' Adam almost whispered under his breath.

Scarlet strained to hear him, but nodded. 'Right, well Jennifer will have to wait, just as you have while she's been away.' Scarlet looked at his downhearted expression and thought now was the best time to tell him the truth about Chris and his plans. 'The thing is, Adam, there is something I haven't told you about Chris. He wants you dead. He was the one that organised for those dealers to kill you. You have a target on your back. And if Chris acts quickly and gets it right this time, Jennifer will have nothing to come home to, except your funeral! He's a dangerous, twisted man, Adam, fuelled by jealousy, envy and bitterness,' Scarlet spat out.

Amazed, Adam looked at her. 'Why didn't you tell me sooner? I can't believe you kept this from me, Scarlet. I'm a grown-up, you know. Sometimes I think you forget that.' Their eyes met as they both glared at each other, but Scarlet dismissed it.

'It wasn't the right time, but it is now. Besides, Knuckles has been keeping a special eye on you.'

Reaching forward to the driver's seat, Adam patted Knuckles on the shoulder. 'Thanks Knuckles. You've always had my back.'

Knuckles met Adam's eyes in the rear-view mirror and nodded.

'Will Knuckles be coming with us to your hen do in Italy?' Adam asked.

'I might get away with buying you a dress Adam, but where the hell am I going to get him one from?' Scarlet laughed.

A smile spread across Adam's face. 'I see what you mean.' They both burst out laughing.

* * *

Julie read the letter and listened to Scarlet's weird explanation of her and Katie's code and nodded. 'I agree, Scarlet, this opportunity has fallen into our lap. But you're both missing the obvious.'

Scarlet and Adam cast a furtive glance towards each other and waited. Scarlet thought she'd covered most of it, but obviously Julie had another idea. They both waited as Julie paused for effect.

'I have a house in Italy. I don't go there much these days, but the boys do and the staff are still there. Chris has probably even forgotten about it. Adam can go there. That way he's safely out of the way and yet around to finish Chris off and take his place as Don Lambrianu when the time comes.'

'I don't know about being Don Lambrianu, Julie. I'm okay as I am. That is a big responsibility and I don't know if I want it,' Adam confessed. 'Anyway, I would have to live in Italy, wouldn't I? I don't really want to move there.'

'You will do as you're fucking told!' Julie shouted. 'No one said about moving locations. Carlos only stayed in Italy when the need arose. Most of the time he lived at the Hilton in London. This is for your father, your grandfather and grandmother and all the Lambrianus before them. This is your rightful place, and I am going to make damn sure you get it. He's robbed you, all of us, and Italy is in mourning for a real leader, not this power-crazed tyrant. You will have the Jewish mafia behind you and the Italian mafia and everyone else in between. He has no loyalty from the villagers, only fear. You would have their loyalty, because they would know you as a fair man, like Don Carlos. Nobody steals off us Adam. We do the stealing!'

Both Scarlet and Adam bowed their heads and looked at the floor. It had been a long time since they had heard Julie lose her temper and shout at them. It was clear she meant business and they both acknowledged it without argument.

Doing her best to break the tension, Scarlet looked up. 'Do you have a plan, Julie? Anything forming in your head, or do you need more time?'

'Some time. I need to get my inside men sorted so that you are all safe. I know Don Carlos's house like the back of my hand. Possibly even things Chris doesn't know about it. Carlos kept his secrets close to his chest, and some I only know through Ralph who always made sure there was an escape plan for me, if I should need it.'

'How would I get in though Julie?' Adam stammered. 'I mean, without being seen. There are guards surrounding that fortress. Christ, it's like a prison!'

'Outside, near the main road, is a large iron square. A water main.' Julie's mind wandered off, deep in thought. Her eyes rolled to the ceiling as memories returned. She thought about the dark, black tunnel Carlos and Ralph had once used to escape their enemies and get back into the house safely, without anyone's knowledge of them leaving. Looking back at Adam and Scarlet, she dismissed her memories, and carried on. 'It's as rusty as fuck, but Carlos had it made into a tunnel that goes up into the house. He could get in or out without being seen, even with all of those cameras. Don't get me wrong,' she laughed and wagged a finger at both of them, 'it's a shithole. Rusty, dirty and possibly full of water and rats, but it served its purpose on many occasions. That's how you get in, Adam.' Looking towards Scarlet, she smiled. 'I suppose your fiancé will be going too. I take it he's in the kitchen eating his way through the contents of the fridge at the moment?'

'Where else?' Scarlet smiled. 'But I'd like him to come. He knows his stuff, whatever anyone thinks.'

'He does indeed, I grant you that.' Julie nodded. 'I'll inform Diana, and you will reply to Katie and tell her we're on for the weekend coming. I will get my inside boys to get tooled up over there. Book your flight tickets, and Adam and Knuckles...' Julie was tempted to call him Julian for the joke of it, but decided not to. 'You two come by yacht. Chris will check the flights and when he sees you haven't boarded a plane with the others, he will assume you're taking care of things here and that's when he'll send his goons to strike. If nothing else it would be easier and cleaner to kill you on home turf while he is hosting a party for his wife's family in Italy. He has the perfect alibi. I know it sounds ghoulish, but get your affairs in order, it's for the best,' Julie added.

Scarlet looked towards Adam, and seeing him nod, she looked back at Julie. 'We're in this for the long-haul Julie. Whatever happens, God help us.'

Each of them sat in silence for a moment and thought about the forthcoming operation. The realisation that at least one of them could die in their plan to murder Chris sent cold shudders through Scarlet's spine. She thought about her children, and decided to spend the next couple of days with them before her flight.

Adam's heart pounded; this was a big undertaking and anything could go wrong. What if the tunnel had been filled up over the years? He could suffocate or be killed at the hands of Chris's henchmen. What would happen to Katie and the kids if they failed? Chris would take his revenge out on her, that was for sure. And would he ever see his lovely Jennifer again? He suddenly regretted not being honest with her about who he was so he could share this with her, but maybe keeping her in the dark was for the best if he didn't make it out alive? There was suddenly a lot of ifs and buts, and they all knew they only had the one chance at this, so they had better get it right.

They were all afraid. Who wouldn't be? They were planning to kill the mafia boss. Blood would be spilt in either direction. Clearing her throat, Scarlet broke the silence. 'I think before we all leave, we should organise a big family dinner. All of us. After all, it may be the last time we all sit around the table together in the family home. Let's make the last memories we may share, happy ones.'

A sombre mood filled the room as each of them contemplated their own mortality in silence. This was the cold light of day and their journey was just beginning. This was possibly the biggest undertaking they would ever have to endure and they all felt a cold hollow feeling inside of them. Scarlet reached her hands out to Adam and Julie and between them they formed a triangle as they held hands, each of them wondering what their fate would be.

ACKNOWLEDGEMENTS

Many thanks to my patient editor, Emily Ruston, for turning this manuscript into a book and thank you to Boldwood Books for publishing it. Many thanks to all the Lambrianu fans out there for enjoying the series as much as I've enjoyed writing it.

ABOUT THE AUTHOR

Gillian Godden is a Northern-born medical secretary for NHS England. She spent thirty years of her life in the East End of London, hearing stories about the local striptease pubs. Now in Yorkshire, she is an avid reader who lives with her dog, Susie.

Sign up to Gillian Godden's mailing list here for news, competitions and updates on future books.

Follow Gillian on social media:

 x.com/GGodden

 instagram.com/goddengillian

 facebook.com/gilliangoddenauthor

ALSO BY GILLIAN GODDEN

Gold Digger

Fools' Gold

The Lambrianus

Dangerous Games

Nasty Business

Francesca

Dirty Dealings

Bad Boy

The Diamond Series

Diamond Geezer

Rough Diamonds

Queen of Diamonds

Forever Diamond

PEAKY READERS

GANG LOYALTIES. DARK SECRETS.
BLOODY REVENGE.

A READER COMMUNITY FOR
GANGLAND CRIME THRILLER FANS!

DISCOVER PAGE-TURNING NOVELS
FROM YOUR FAVOURITE AUTHORS
AND MEET NEW FRIENDS.

JOIN OUR BOOK CLUB
FACEBOOK GROUP

BIT.LY/PEAKYREADERSFB

SIGN UP TO OUR
NEWSLETTER

BIT.LY/PEAKYREADERSNEWS

Boldwood

Boldwood Books is an award-winning fiction publishing company seeking out the best stories from around the world.

Find out more at www.boldwoodbooks.com

Join our reader community for brilliant books, competitions and offers!

Follow us
@BoldwoodBooks
@TheBoldBookClub

Sign up to our weekly deals newsletter

https://bit.ly/BoldwoodBNewsletter